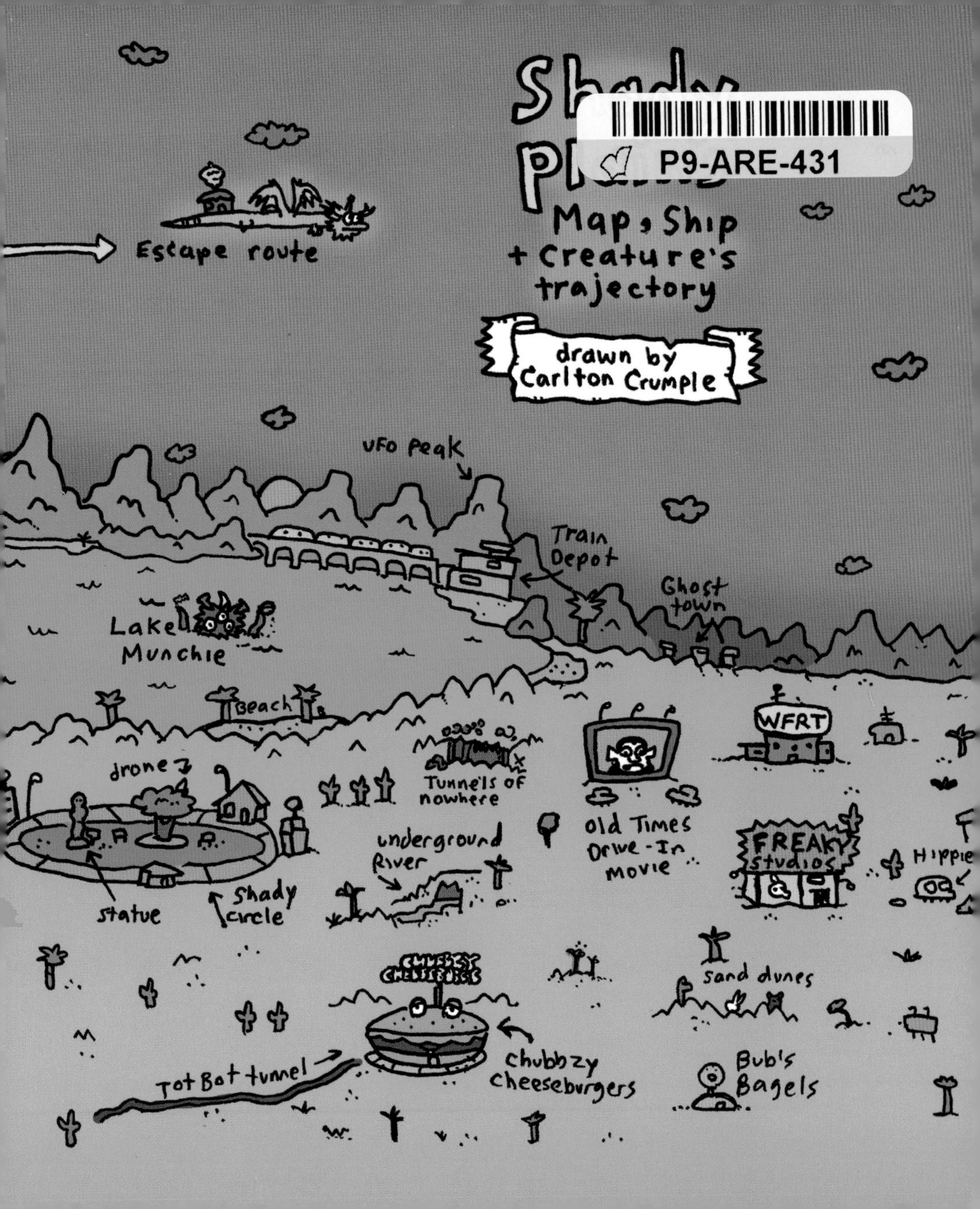
Map, Ship
+ Creature's
trajectory
drawn by
Carlton Crumple
Escape route
UFO Peak
Train
Depot
Ghost
town
Lake
Munchie
Beach
drone
Tunnels of
nowhere
WFRT
Old Times
Drive-In
movie
FREAKY
Studios
Hippie
underground
River
statue
Shady
circle
sand dunes
Chubbzy
Cheeseburgers
Tot Bot tunnel
Bub's
Bagels

Read all the books in the
Carlton Crumple Creature Catcher series:

#1 Catch the Munchies!
#2 Tater Invaders!

REPTOIDS FROM SPACE!

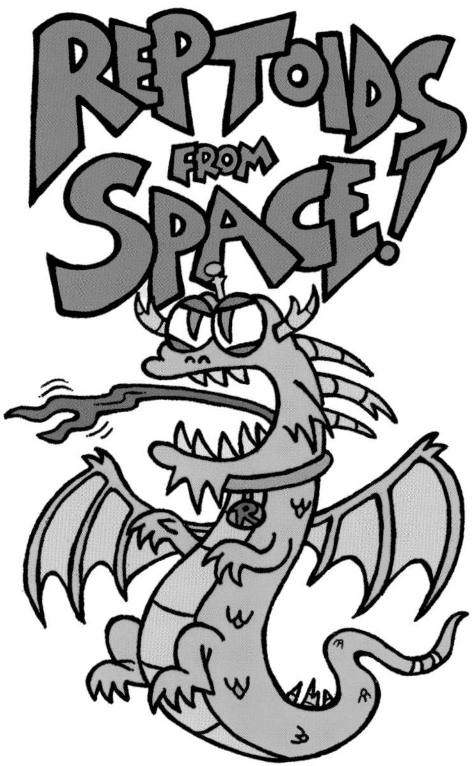

Written and Illustrated by David Fremont

Color by Jimbo Matison

PIXEL+INK

For Dexter Kane Justice James

PIXEL✚INK

Text and illustrations copyright© 2021 by David Fremont
All rights reserved
Pixel+Ink is a division of TGM Development Corp.
Printed and bound at Toppan Leefung, DongGuan City, China, in 2021
Color by Jimbo Matison
Book design by Sammy Yuen
www.pixelandinkbooks.com
Library of Congress Control Number: 2021930052
Hardcover ISBN: 978-1-64595-008-0
eBook ISBN: 978-1-64595-009-7
First Edition
1 3 5 7 9 10 8 6 4 2

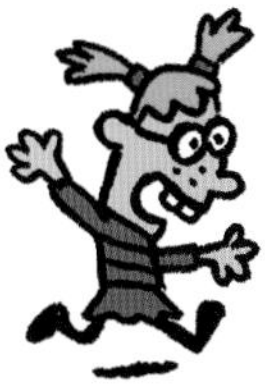

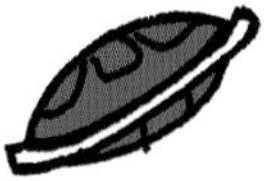

CHAPTER 1

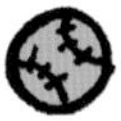

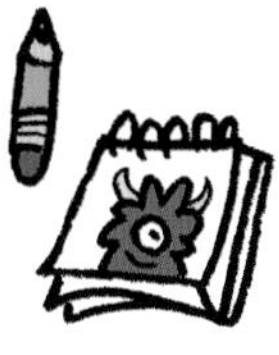

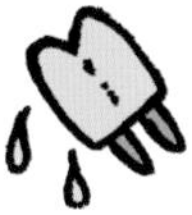

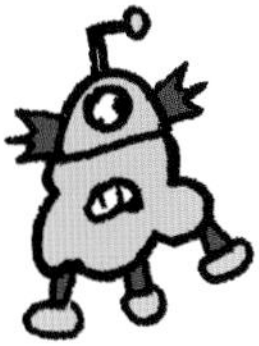

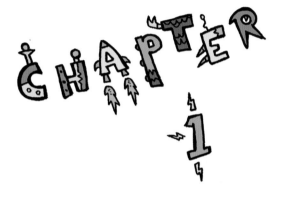

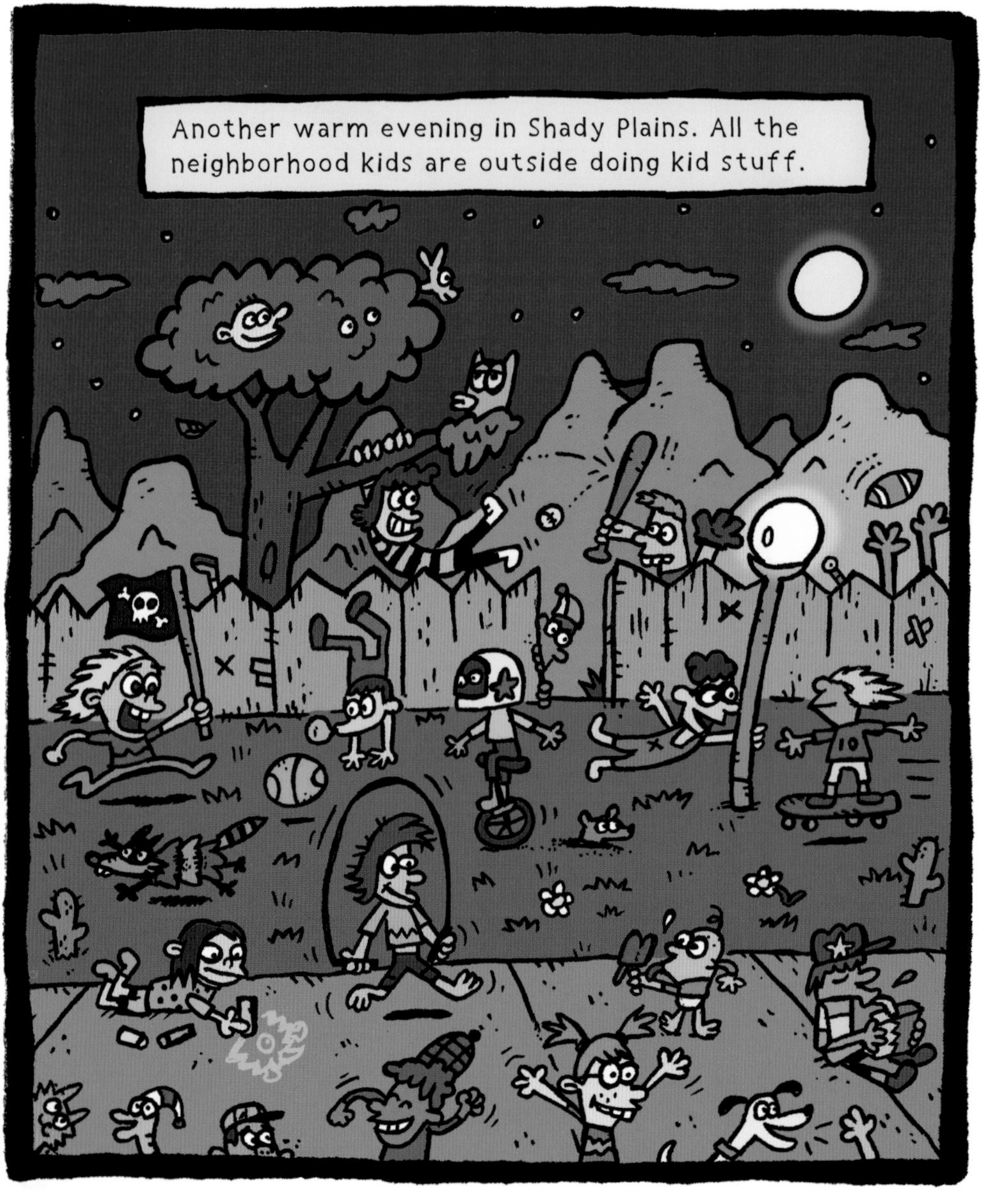
Another warm evening in Shady Plains. All the neighborhood kids are outside doing kid stuff.
10

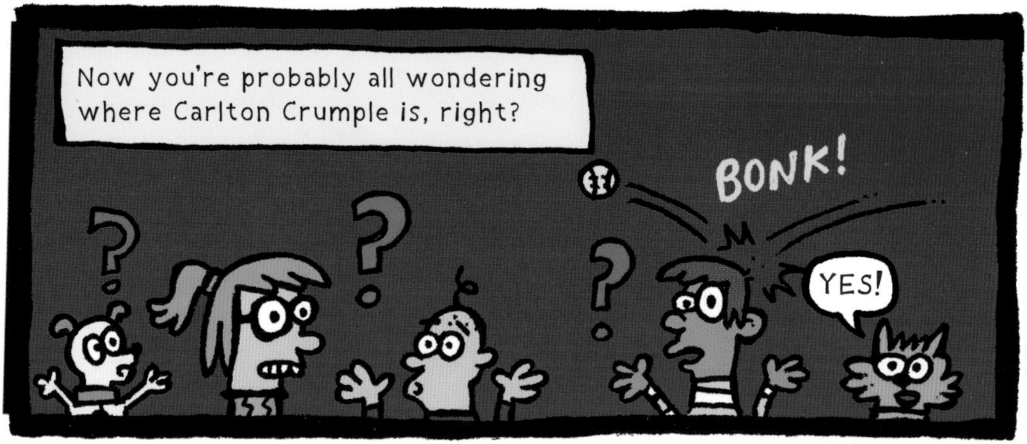
Now you're probably all wondering where Carlton Crumple is, right?
BONK!
YES!

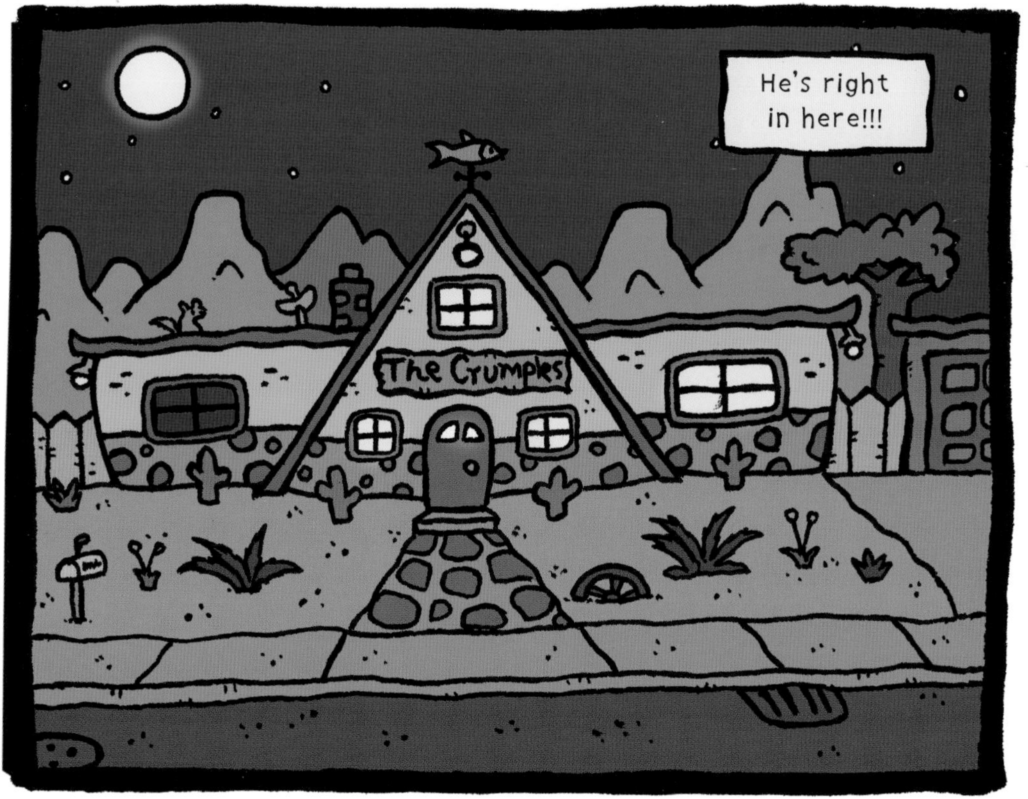
He's right in here!!!
The Crumples

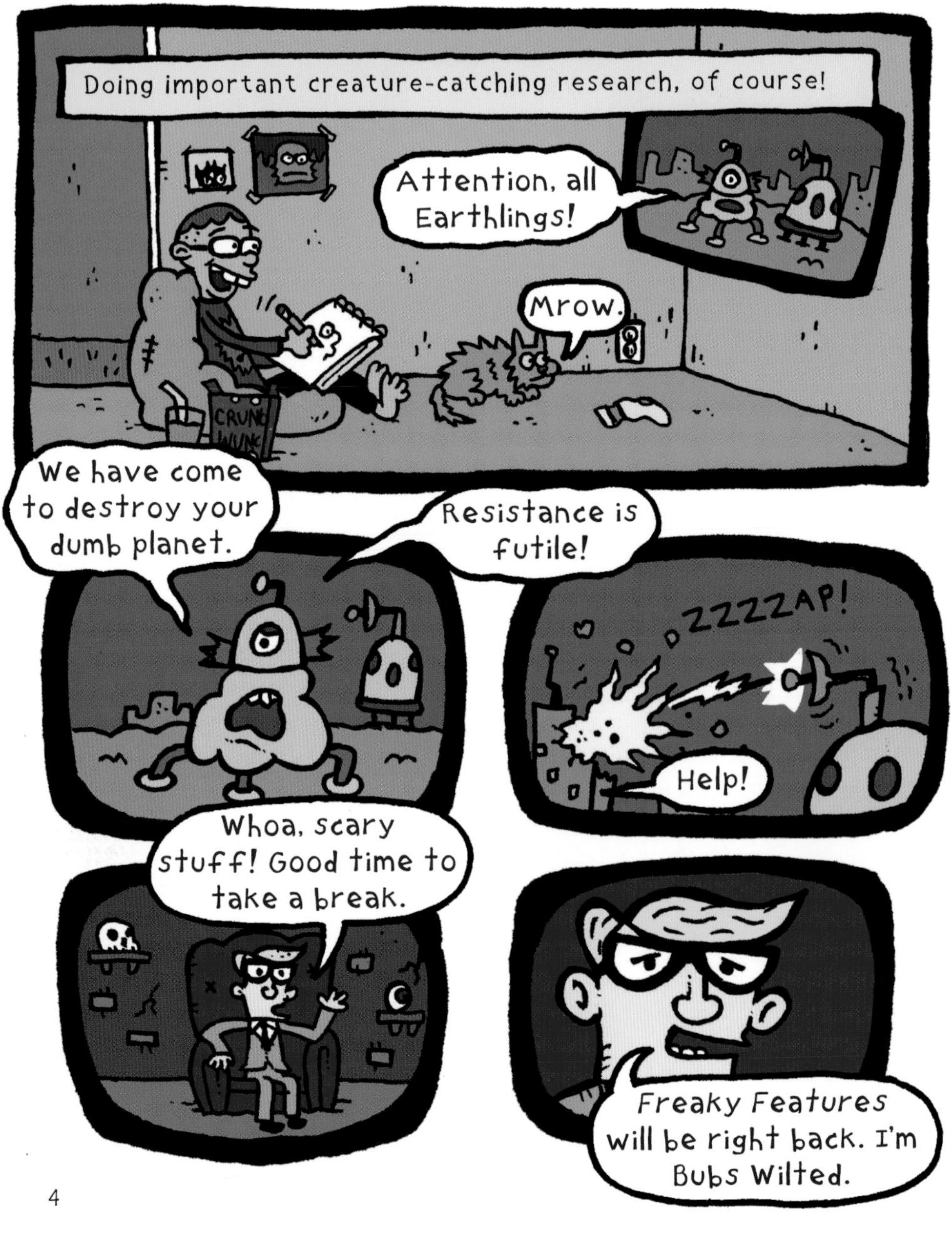
Doing important creature-catching research, of course!
Attention, all Earthlings!
Mrow.
CRUNCH MUNCH
We have come to destroy your dumb planet.
Resistance is futile!
ZZZZAP!
Help!
Whoa, scary stuff! Good time to take a break.
Freaky Features will be right back. I'm Bubs Wilted.

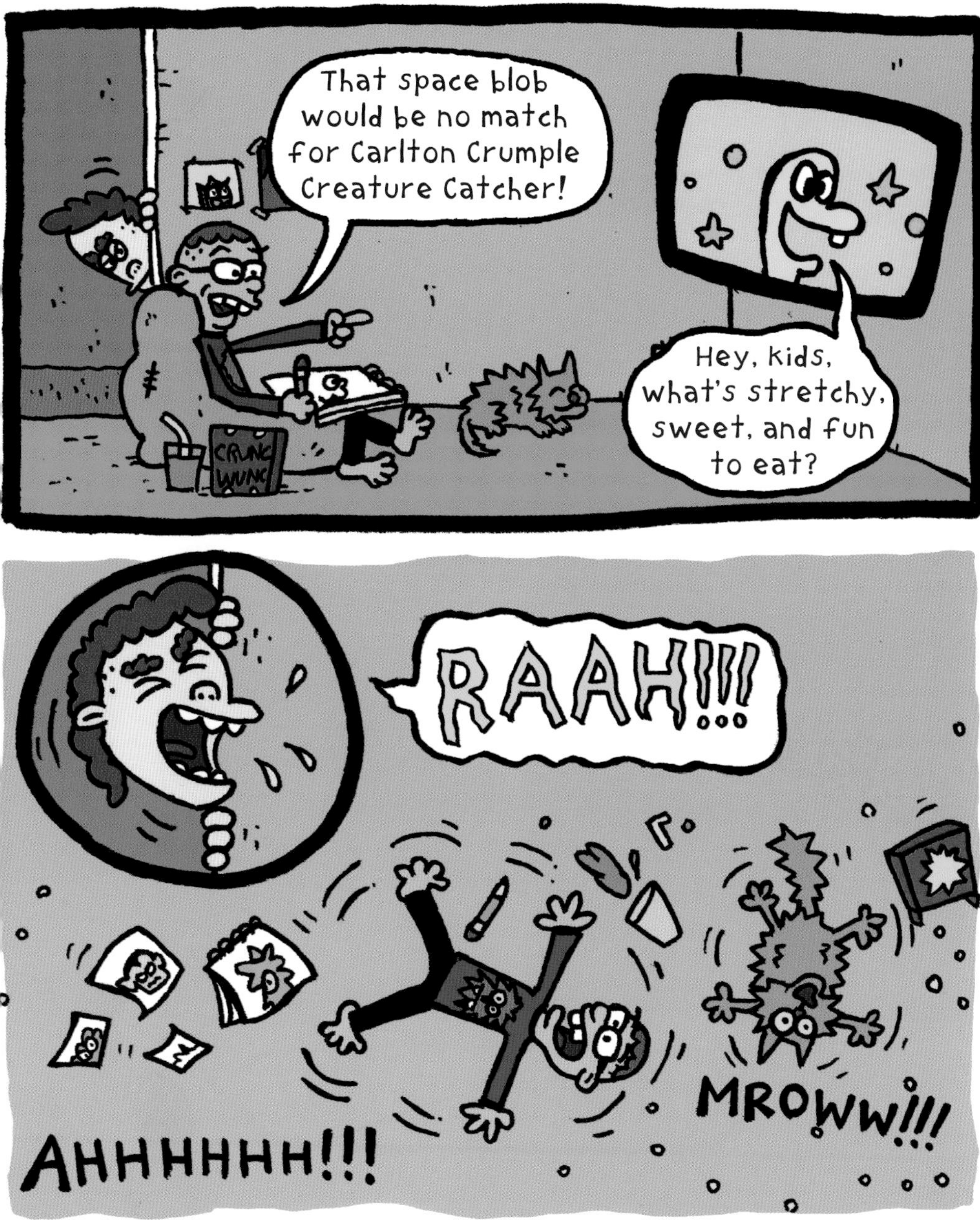
That space blob would be no match for Carlton Crumple Creature Catcher!
Hey, kids, what's stretchy, sweet, and fun to eat?
CRUNC WUNC
RAAH!!!
AHHHHHH!!!
MROWW!!!

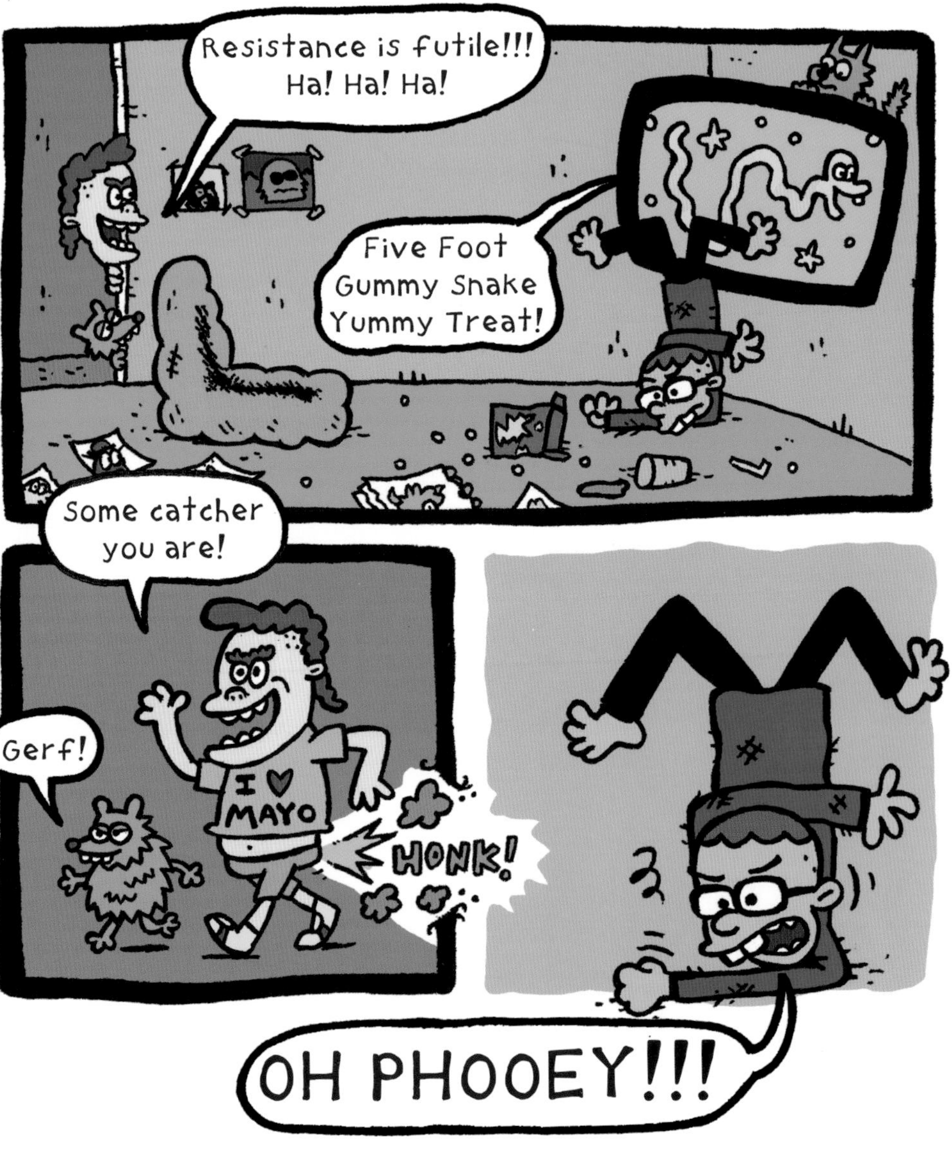
Resistance is futile!!! Ha! Ha! Ha!
Five Foot Gummy Snake Yummy Treat!
Some catcher you are!
Gerf!
I ♥ MAYO
HONK!
OH PHOOEY!!!

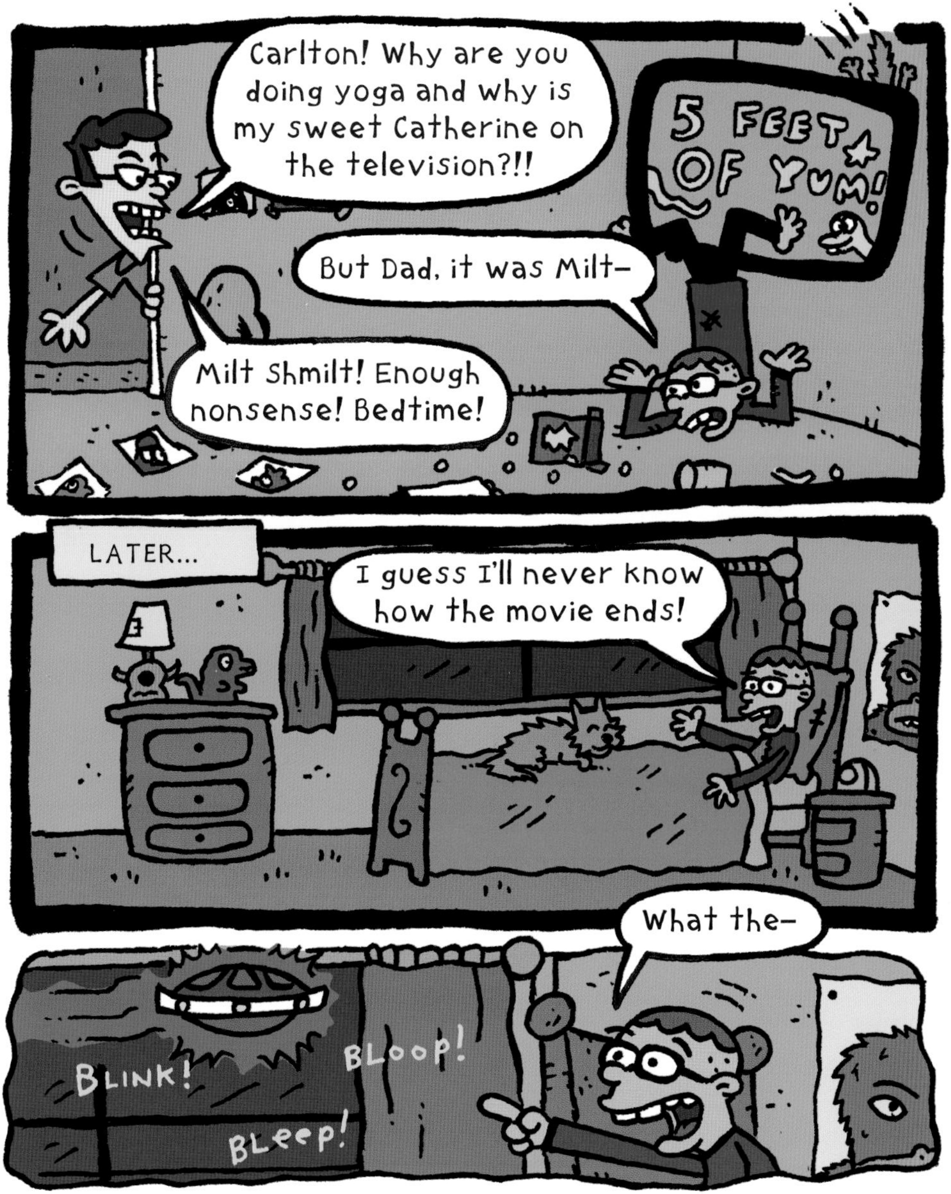

Carlton! Why are you doing yoga and why is my sweet Catherine on the television?!!
5 FEET OF YUM!
But Dad, it was Milt–
Milt Shmilt! Enough nonsense! Bedtime!
LATER...
I guess I'll never know how the movie ends!
What the–
BLINK!
BLOOP!
BLEEP!

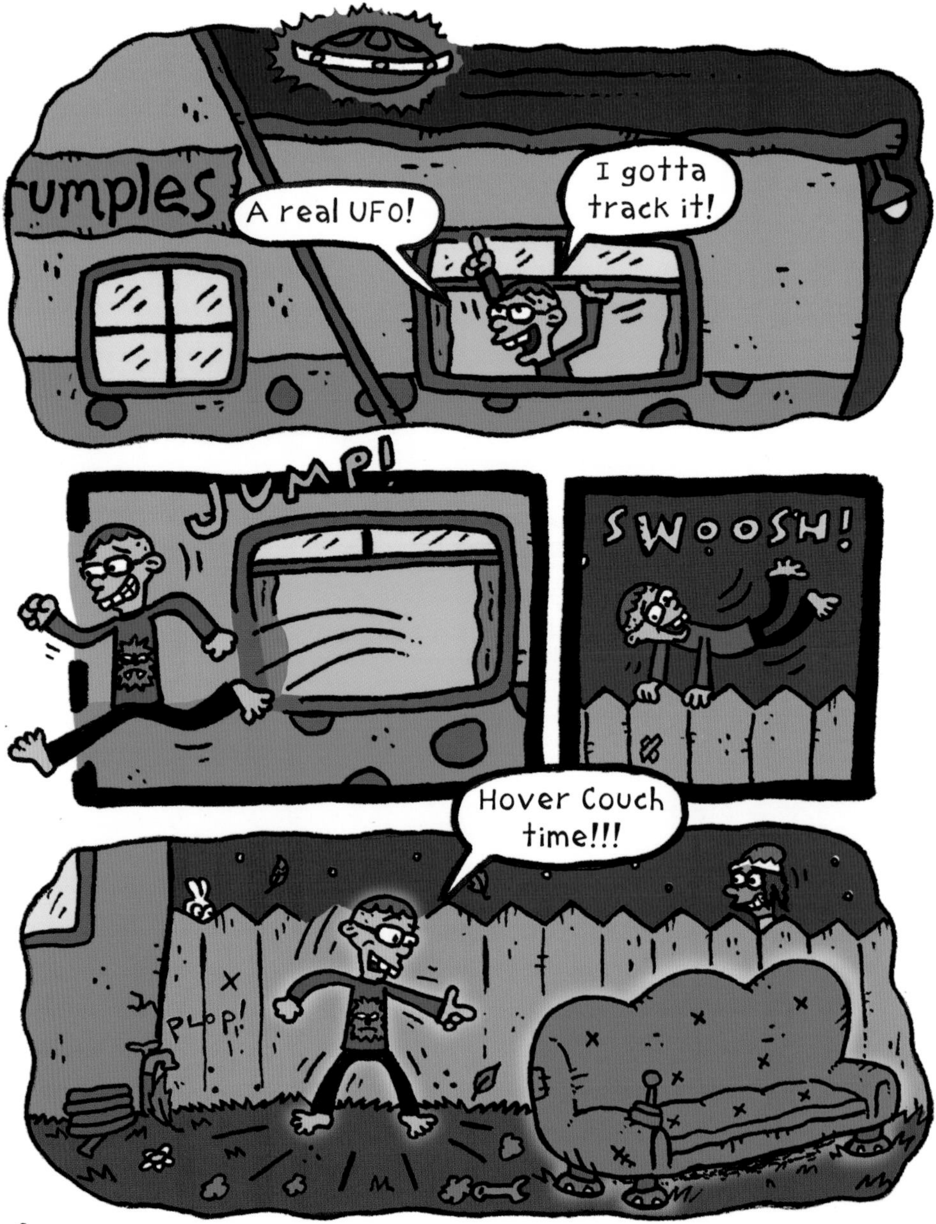

umples
A real UFO!
I gotta track it!
JUMP!
SWOOSH!
Hover Couch time!!!
PLOP!

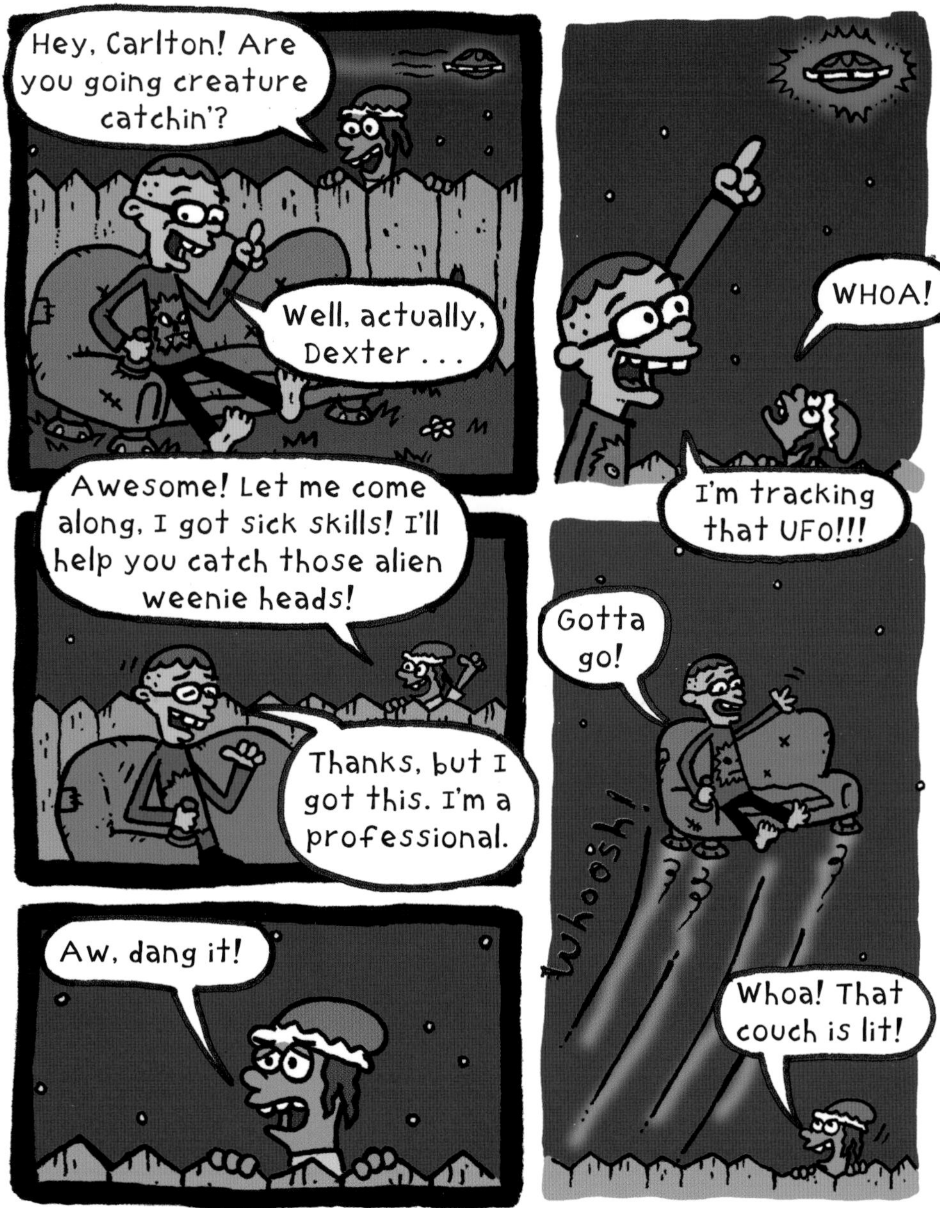
Hey, Carlton! Are you going creature catchin'?
Well, actually, Dexter . . .
WHOA!
I'm tracking that UFO!!!
Awesome! Let me come along, I got sick skills! I'll help you catch those alien weenie heads!
Thanks, but I got this. I'm a professional.
Aw, dang it!
Gotta go!
whoosh!
Whoa! That couch is lit!

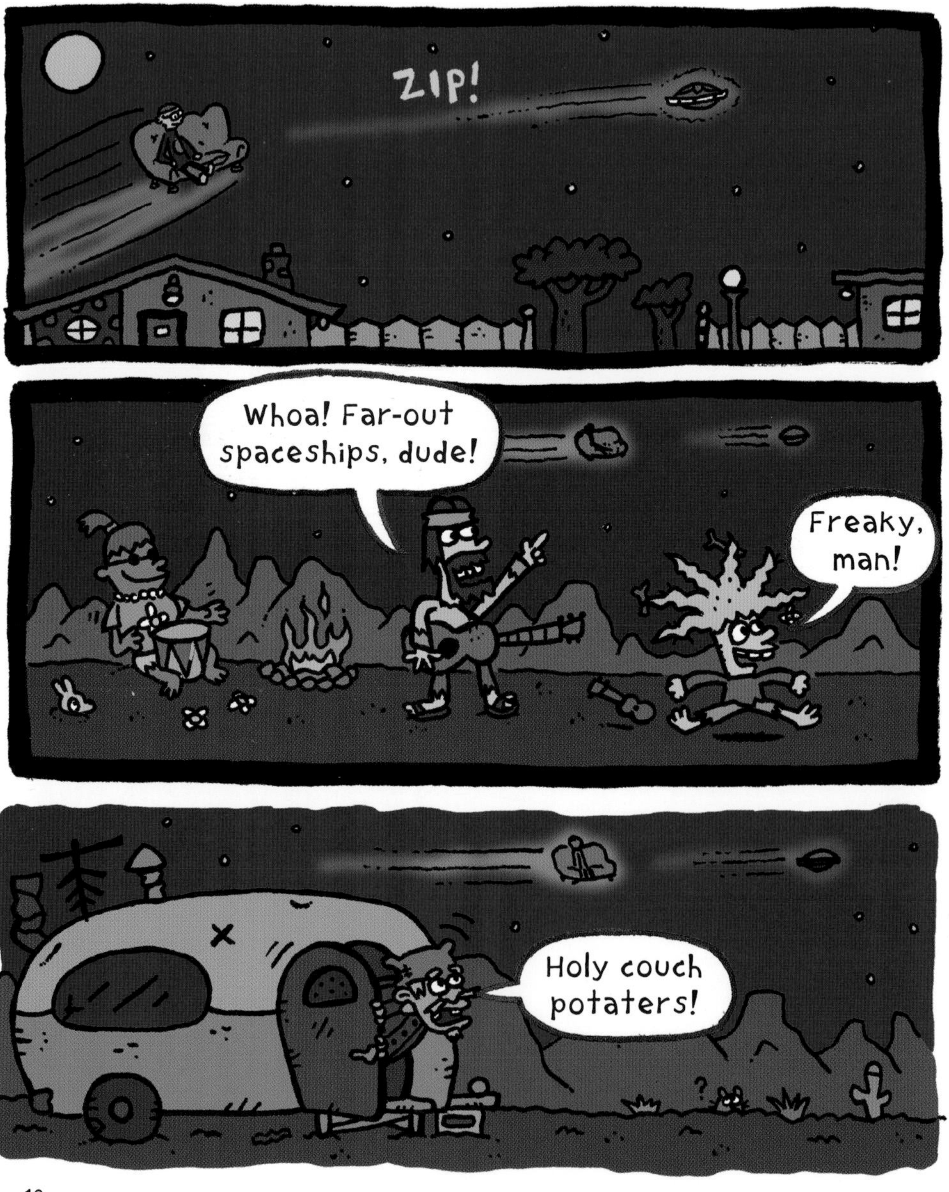
ZIP!
Whoa! Far-out spaceships, dude!
Freaky, man!
Holy couch potaters!

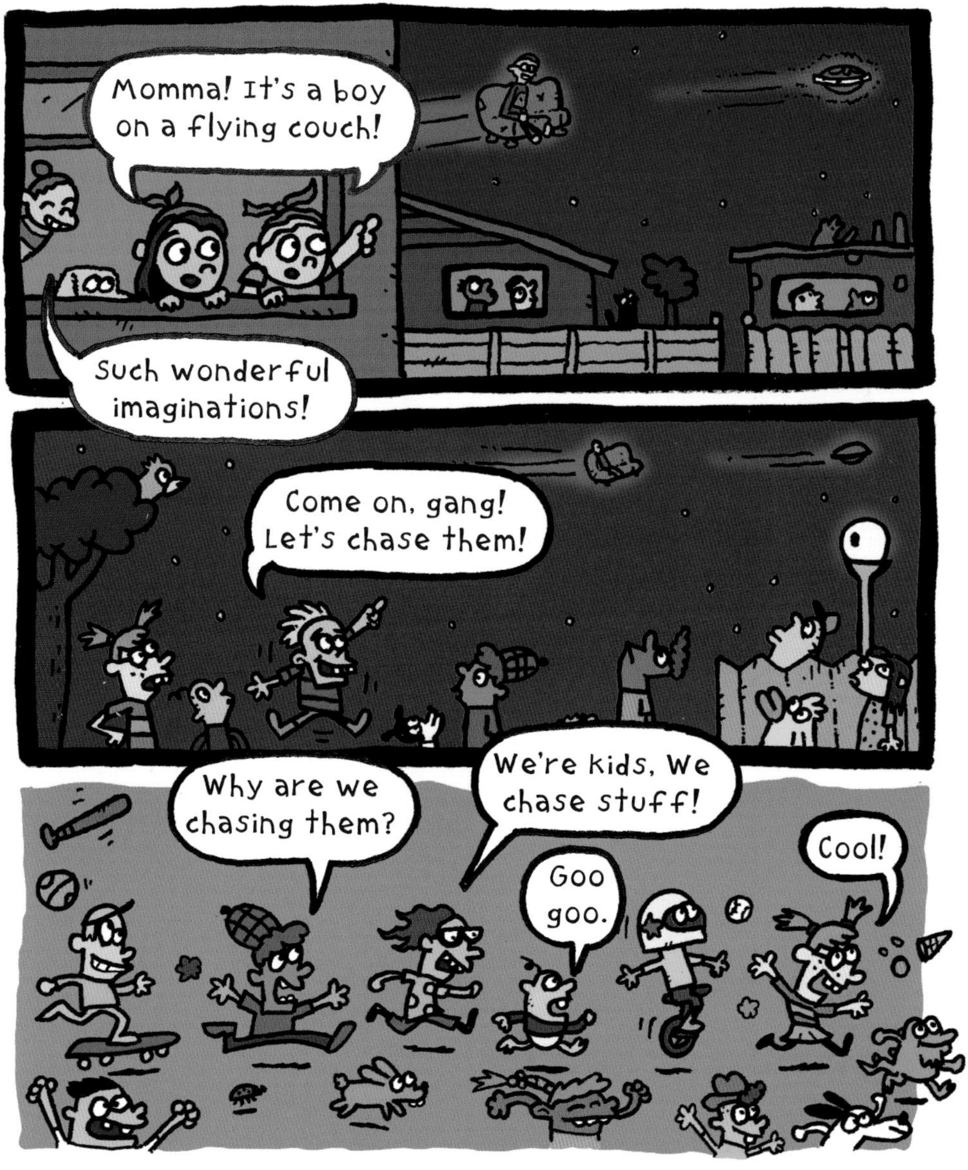
Momma! It's a boy on a flying couch!
Such wonderful imaginations!
Come on, gang! Let's chase them!
Why are we chasing them?
We're kids. We chase stuff!
Goo goo.
Cool!

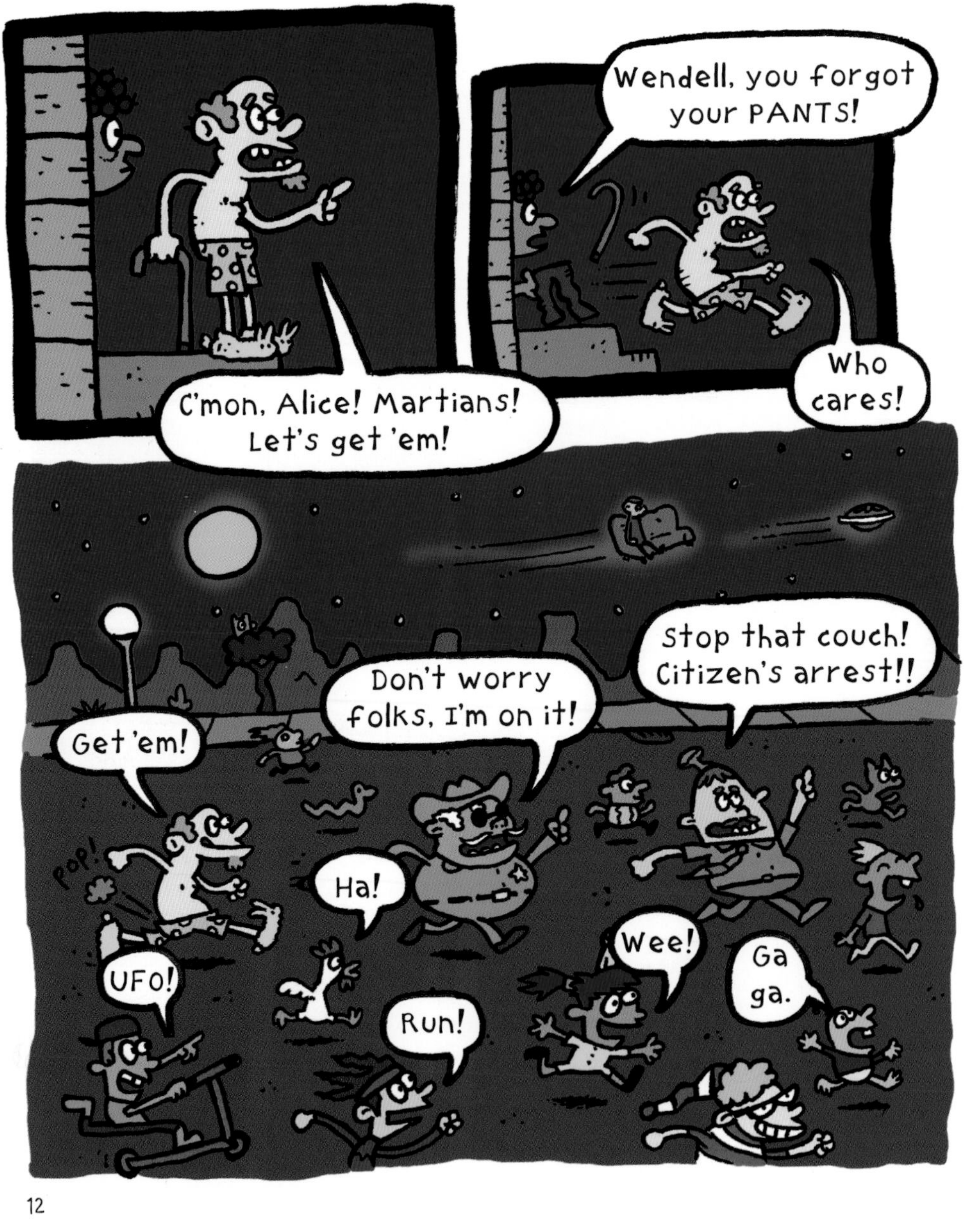
C'mon, Alice! Martians! Let's get 'em!
Wendell, you forgot your PANTS!
Who cares!
Get 'em!
Don't worry folks, I'm on it!
Stop that couch! Citizen's arrest!!
POP!
Ha!
UFO!
Wee!
Ga ga.
Run!

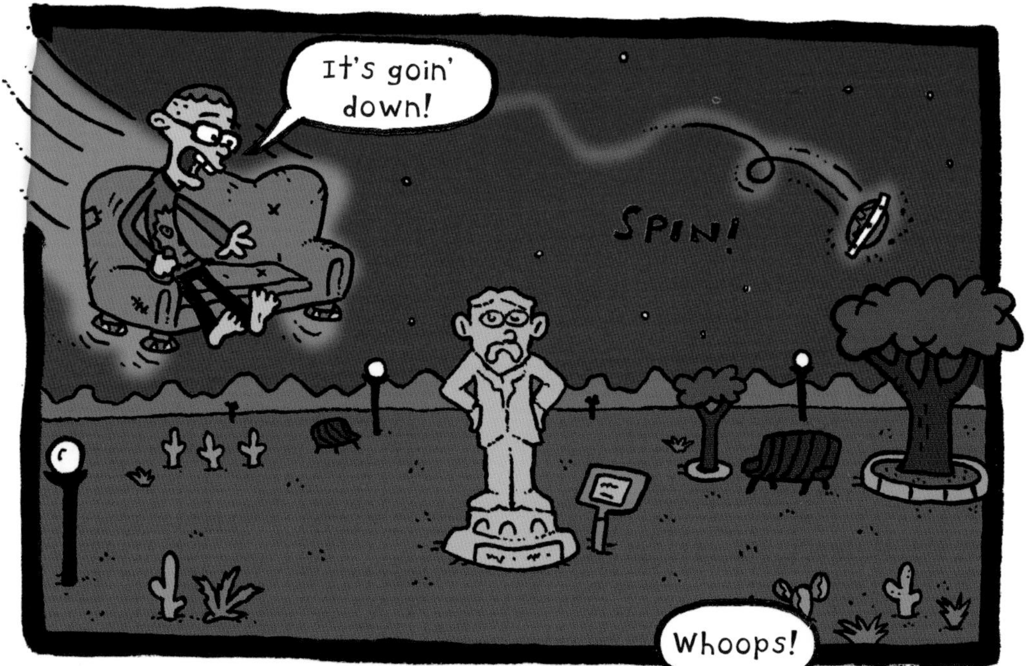
It's goin' down!
SPIN!

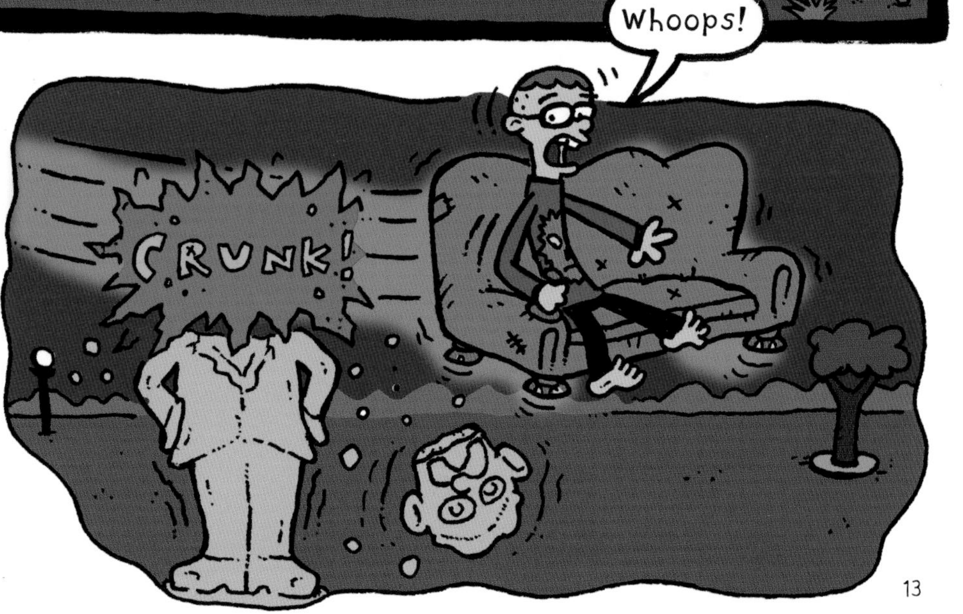
Whoops!
CRUNK!

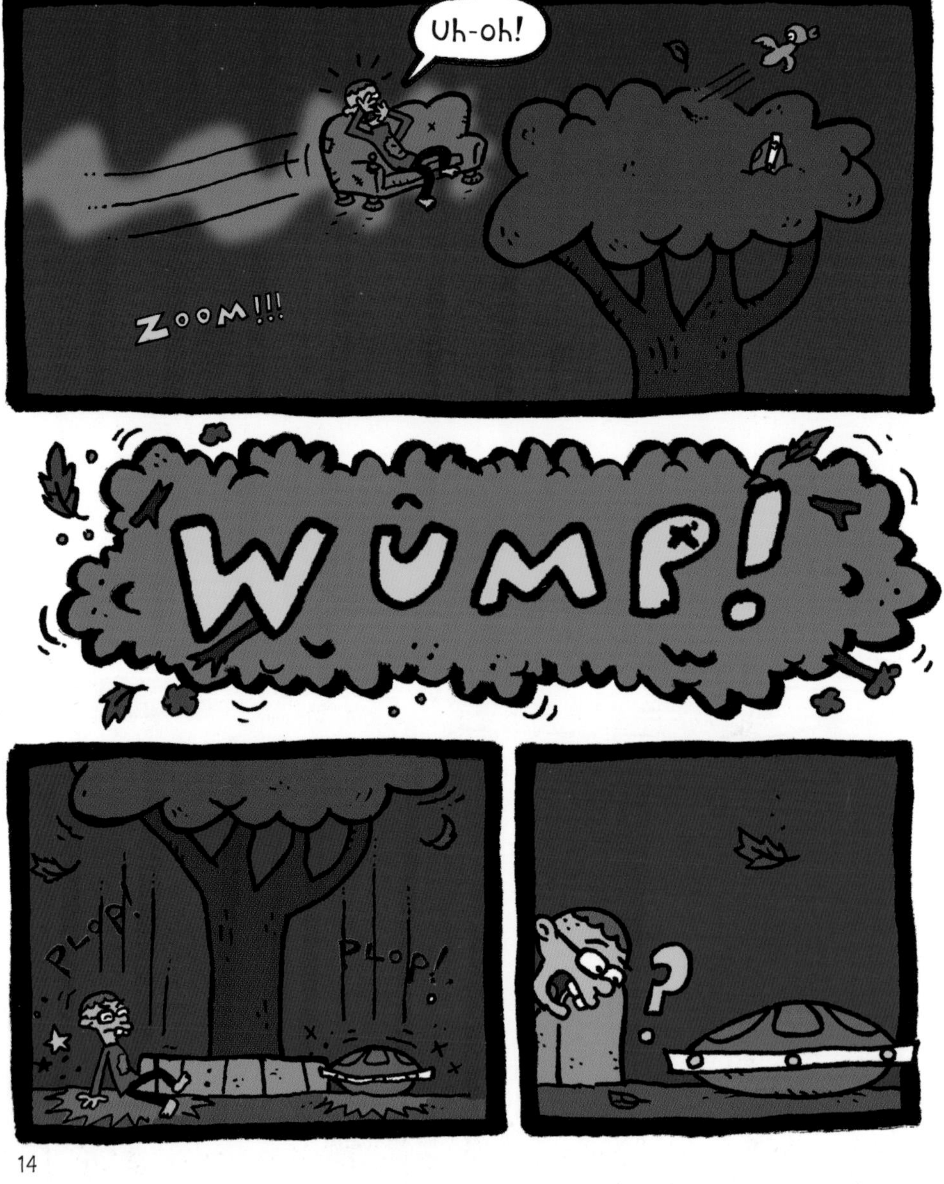
Uh-oh!
ZOOM!!!
WUMP!
PLOP!
PLOP!
?

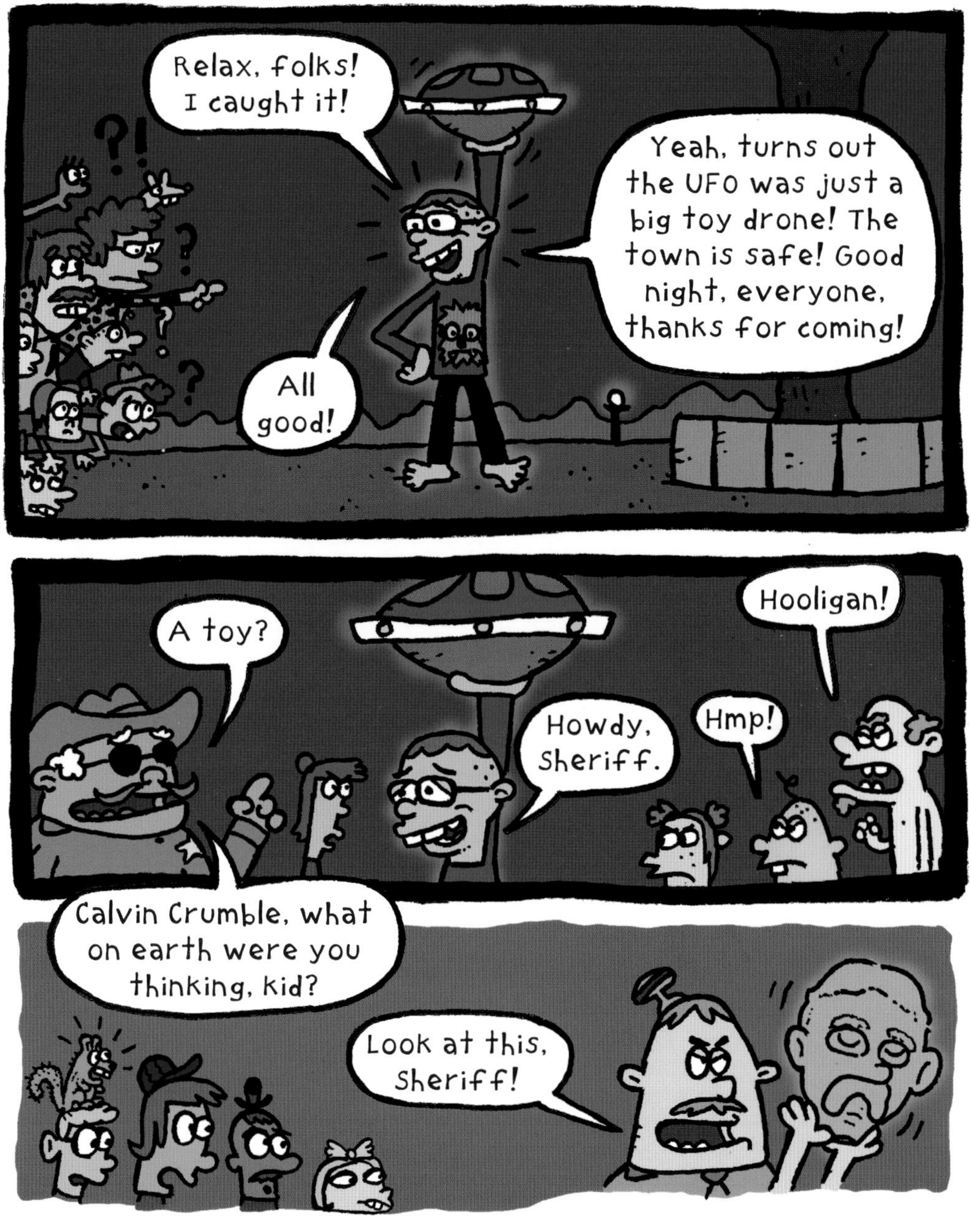
Relax, folks! I caught it!
?!
?
?
?
Yeah, turns out the UFO was just a big toy drone! The town is safe! Good night, everyone, thanks for coming!
All good!
A toy?
Hooligan!
Howdy, Sheriff.
Hmp!
Calvin Crumble, what on earth were you thinking, kid?
Look at this, Sheriff!

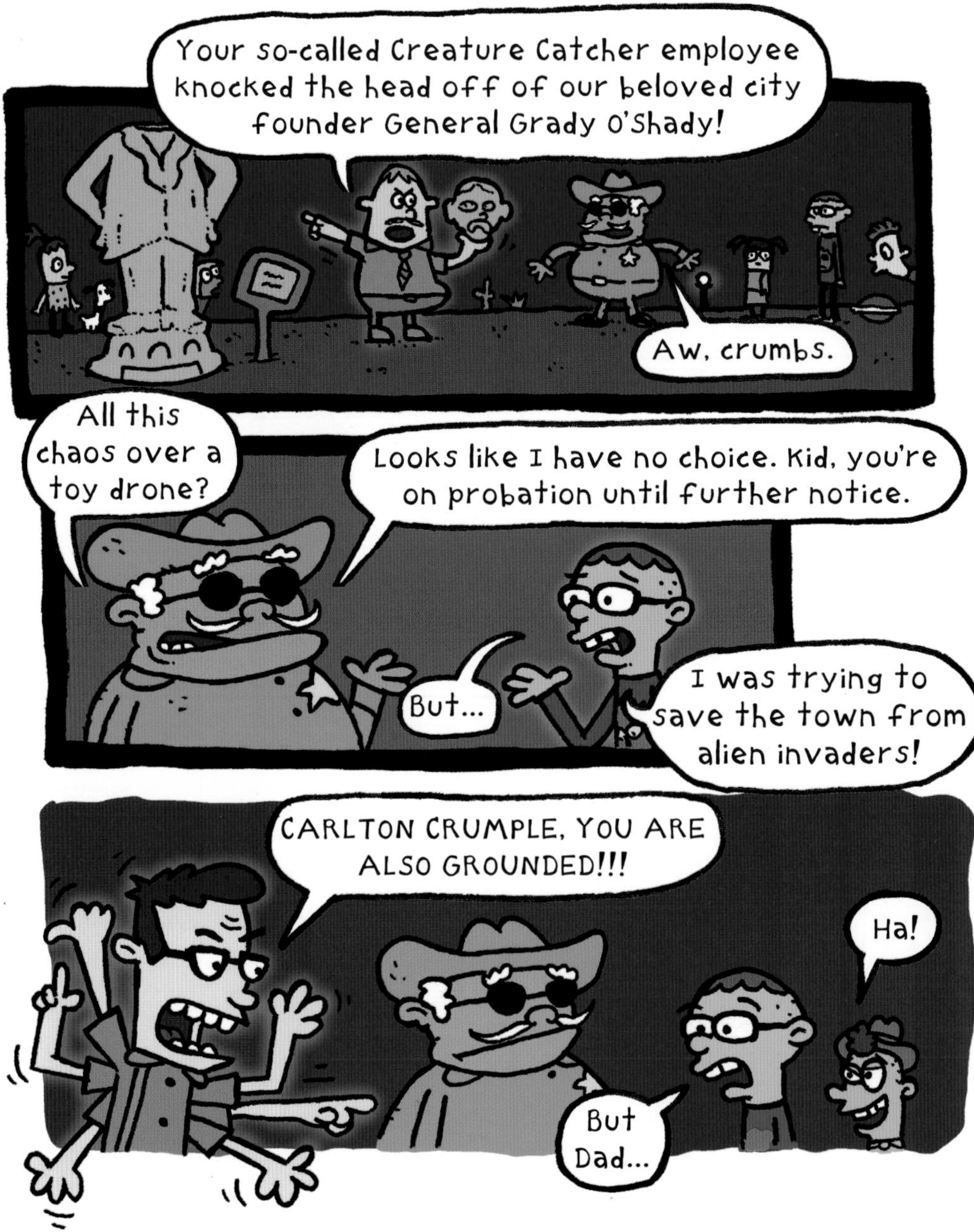
Your so-called Creature Catcher employee knocked the head off of our beloved city founder General Grady O'Shady!
Aw, crumbs.
All this chaos over a toy drone?
Looks like I have no choice. Kid, you're on probation until further notice.
But...
I was trying to save the town from alien invaders!
CARLTON CRUMPLE, YOU ARE ALSO GROUNDED!!!
Ha!
But Dad...

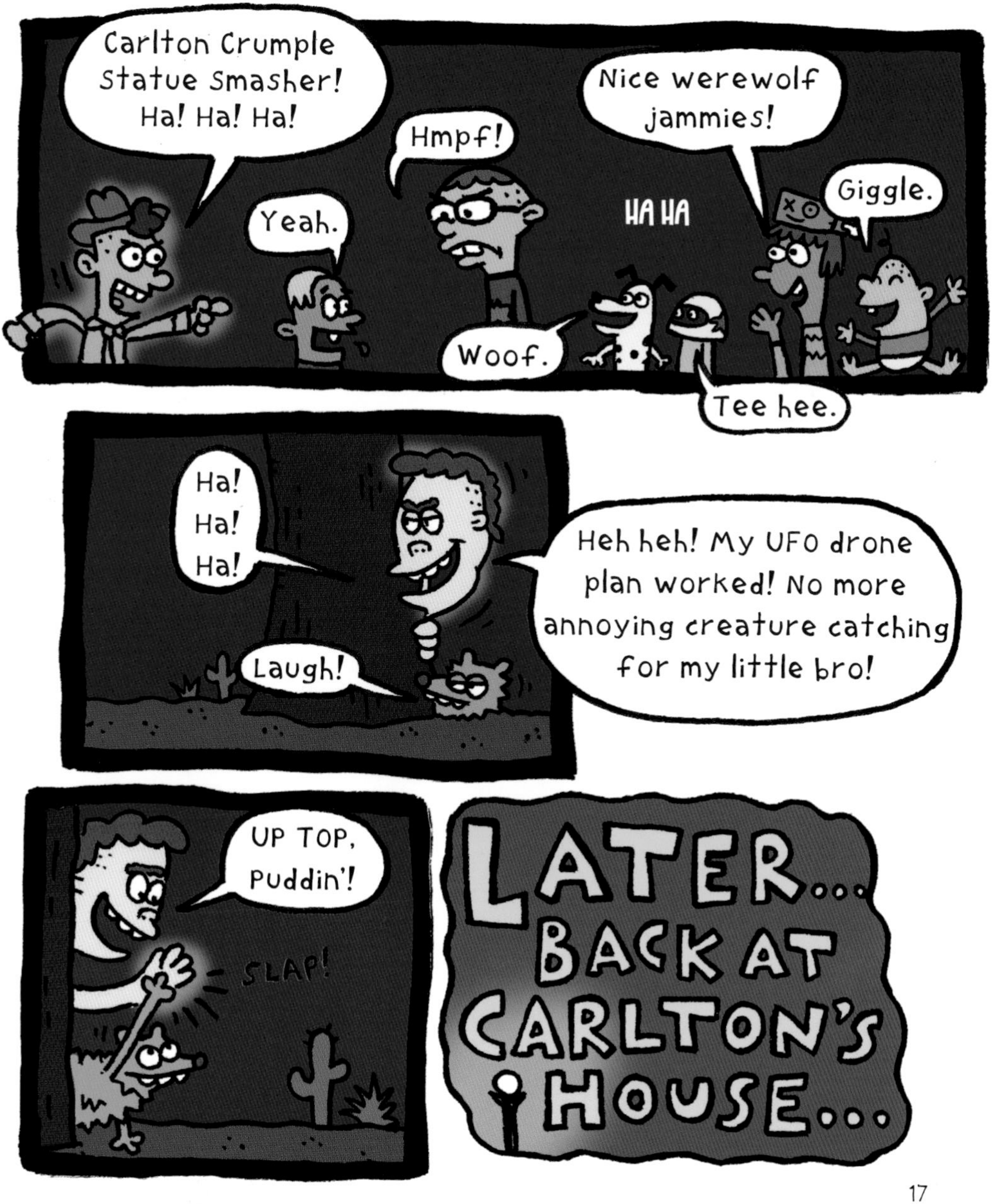
Carlton Crumple Statue Smasher! Ha! Ha! Ha!
Yeah.
Hmpf!
HA HA
Nice werewolf jammies!
Giggle.
Woof.
Tee hee.
Ha! Ha! Ha!
Heh heh! My UFO drone plan worked! No more annoying creature catching for my little bro!
Laugh!
UP TOP, Puddin'!
SLAP!
LATER... BACK AT CARLTON'S HOUSE...

CHAPTER 2

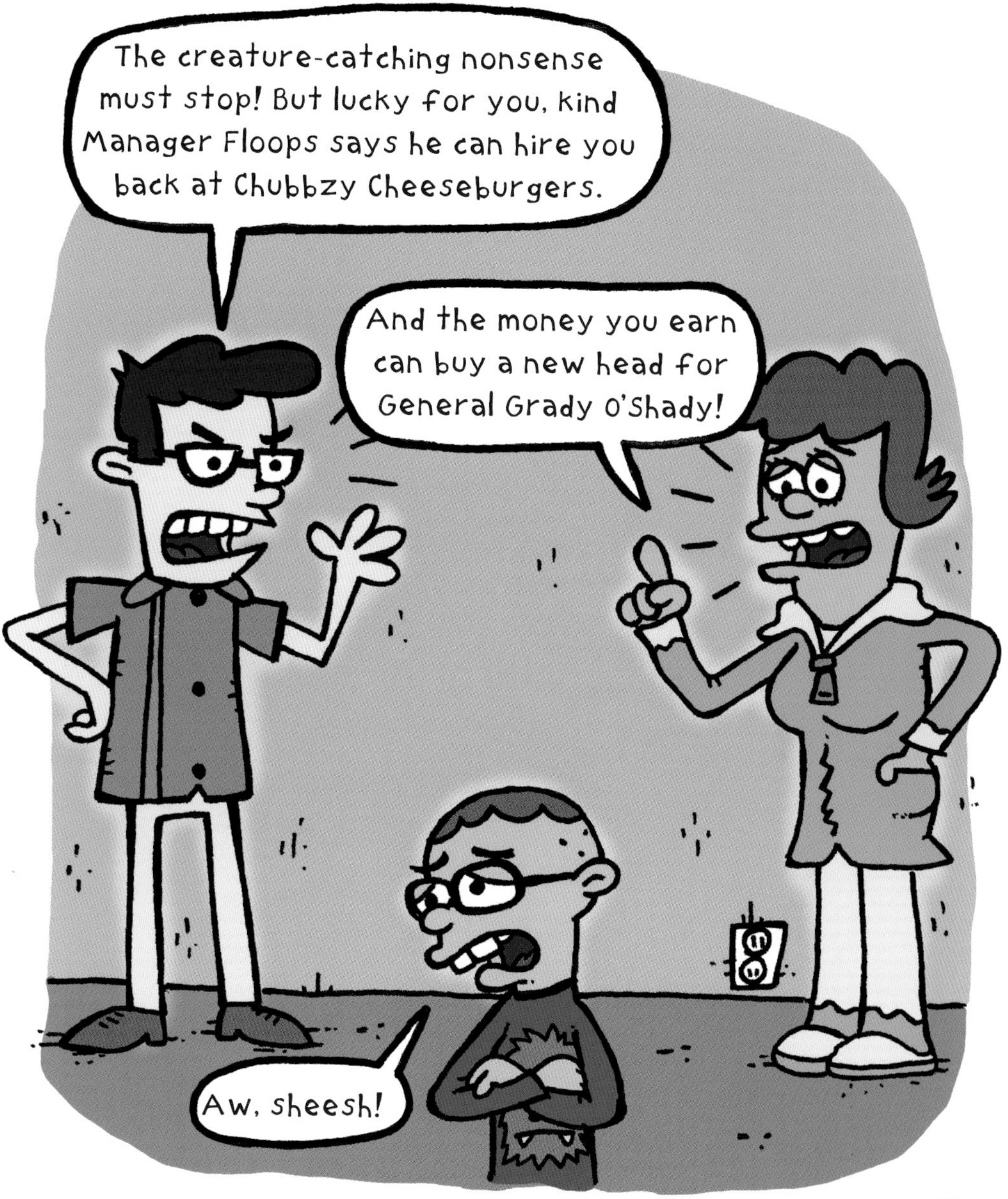
The creature-catching nonsense must stop! But lucky for you, kind Manager Floops says he can hire you back at Chubbzy Cheeseburgers.
And the money you earn can buy a new head for General Grady O'Shady!
Aw, sheesh!

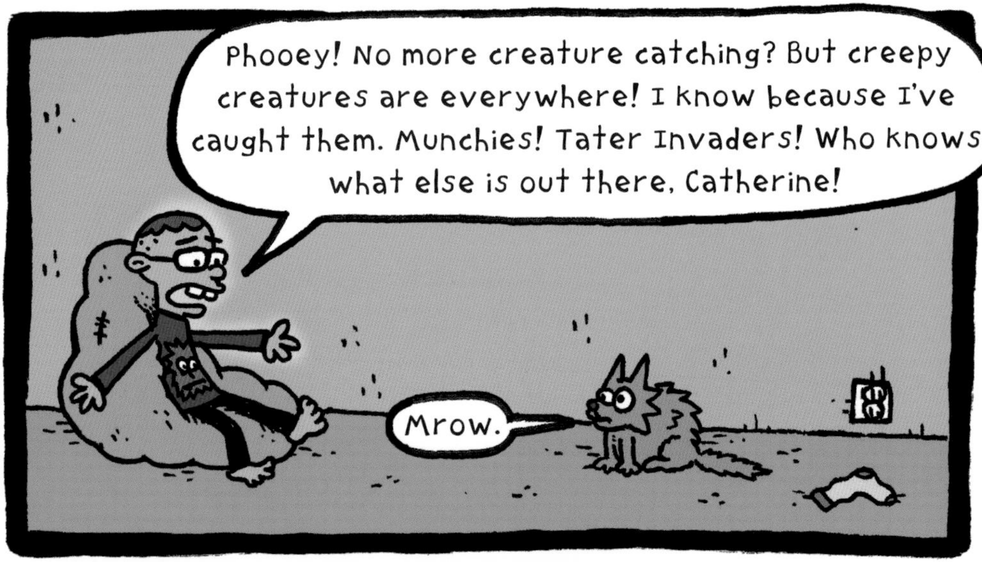
Phooey! No more creature catching? But creepy creatures are everywhere! I know because I've caught them. Munchies! Tater Invaders! Who knows what else is out there, Catherine!
Mrow.

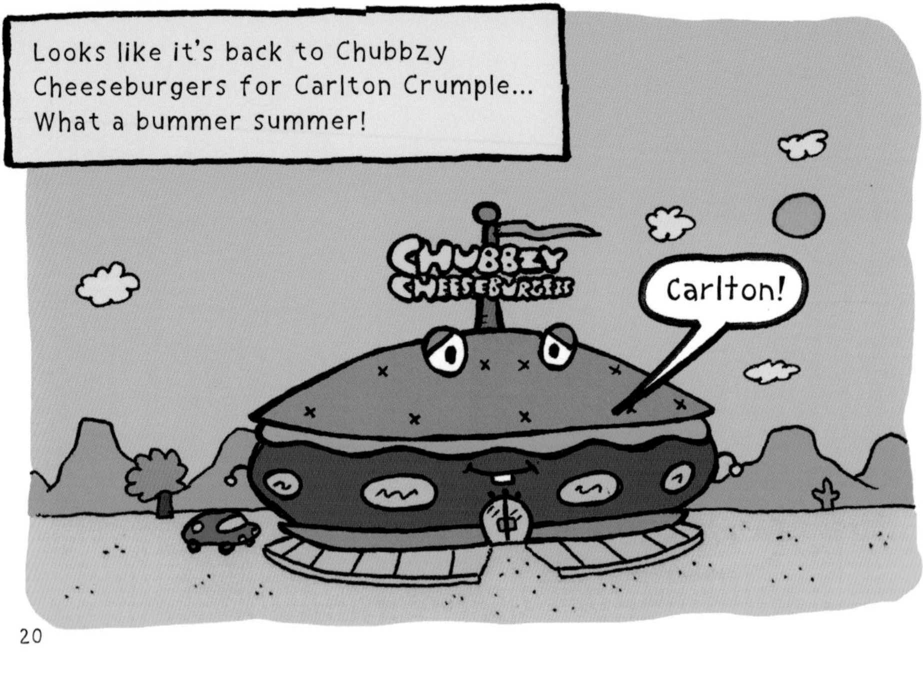
Looks like it's back to Chubbzy Cheeseburgers for Carlton Crumple... What a bummer summer!
CHUBBZY CHEESEBURGERS
Carlton!

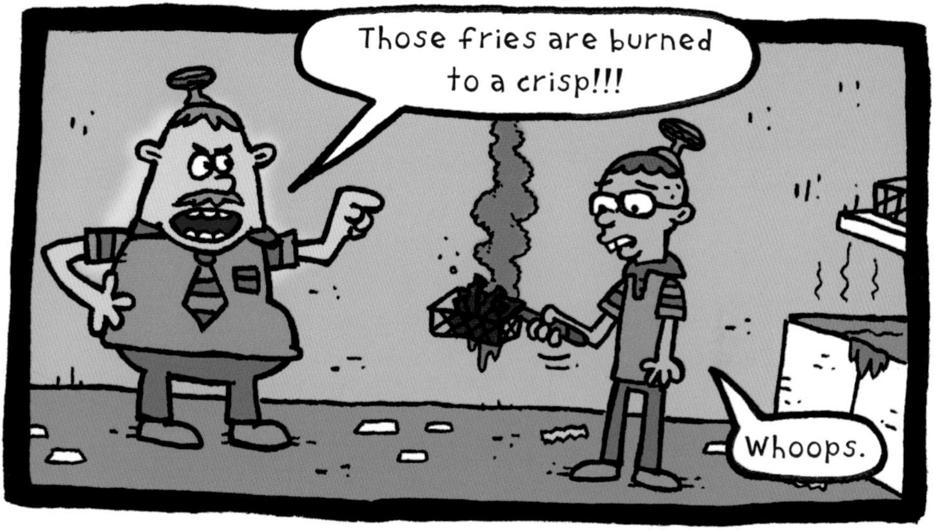
Those fries are burned to a crisp!!!
Whoops.

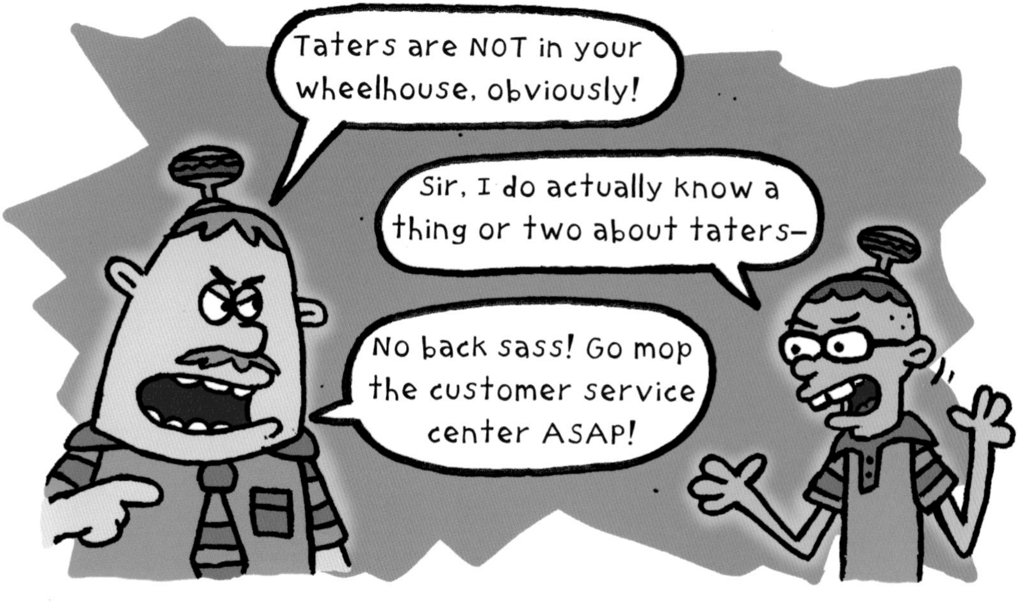
Taters are NOT in your wheelhouse, obviously!
Sir, I do actually know a thing or two about taters–
No back sass! Go mop the customer service center ASAP!

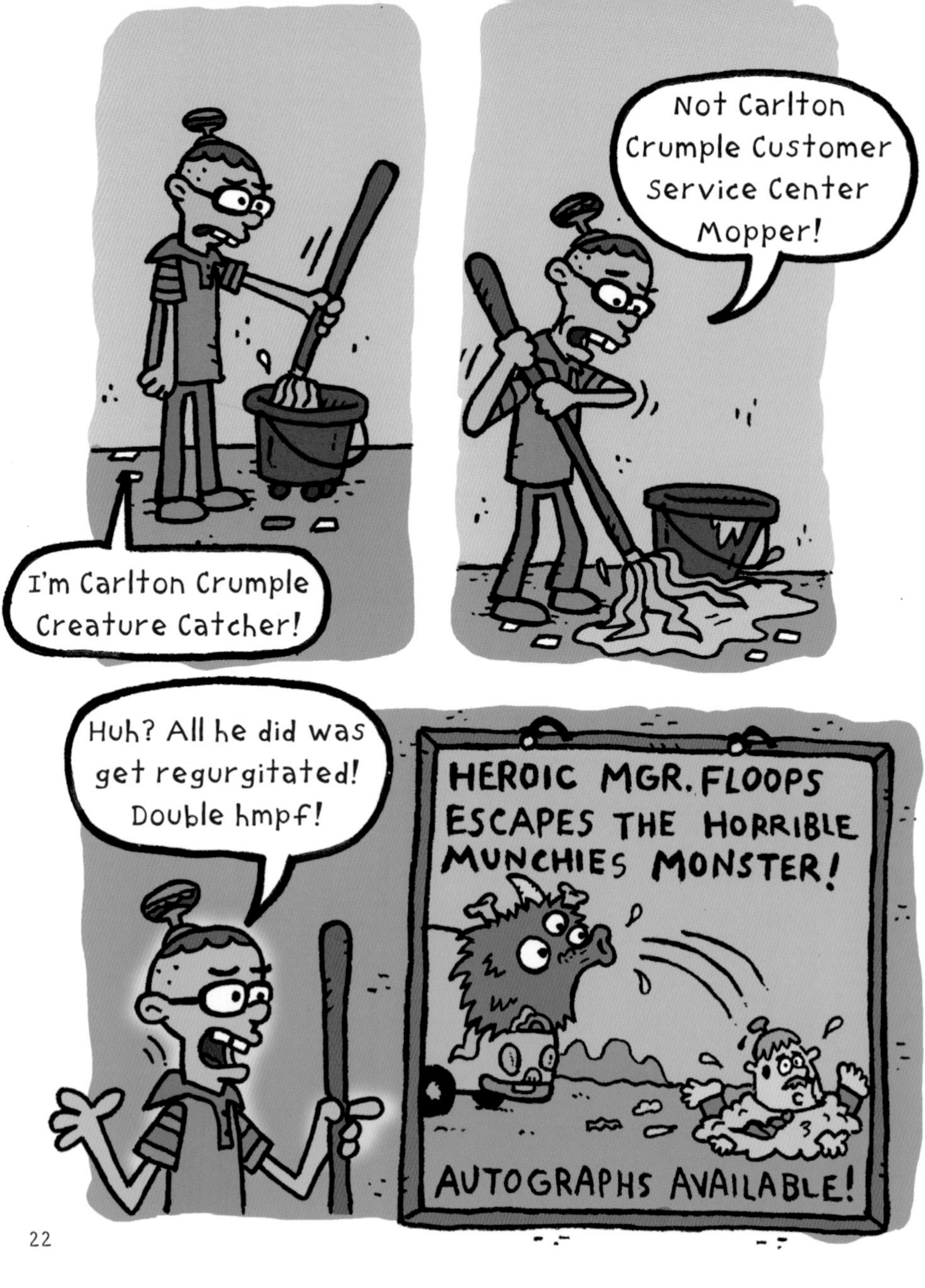
I'm Carlton Crumple Creature Catcher!
Not Carlton Crumple Customer Service Center Mopper!
Huh? All he did was get regurgitated! Double hmpf!
HEROIC MGR. FLOOPS ESCAPES THE HORRIBLE MUNCHIES MONSTER!
AUTOGRAPHS AVAILABLE!

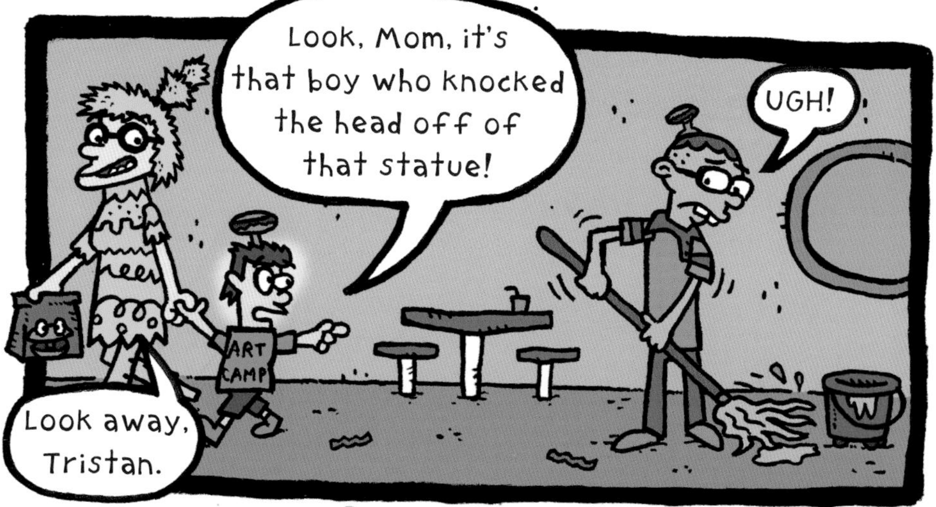
Look, Mom, it's that boy who knocked the head off of that statue!
UGH!
Look away, Tristan.
ART CAMP

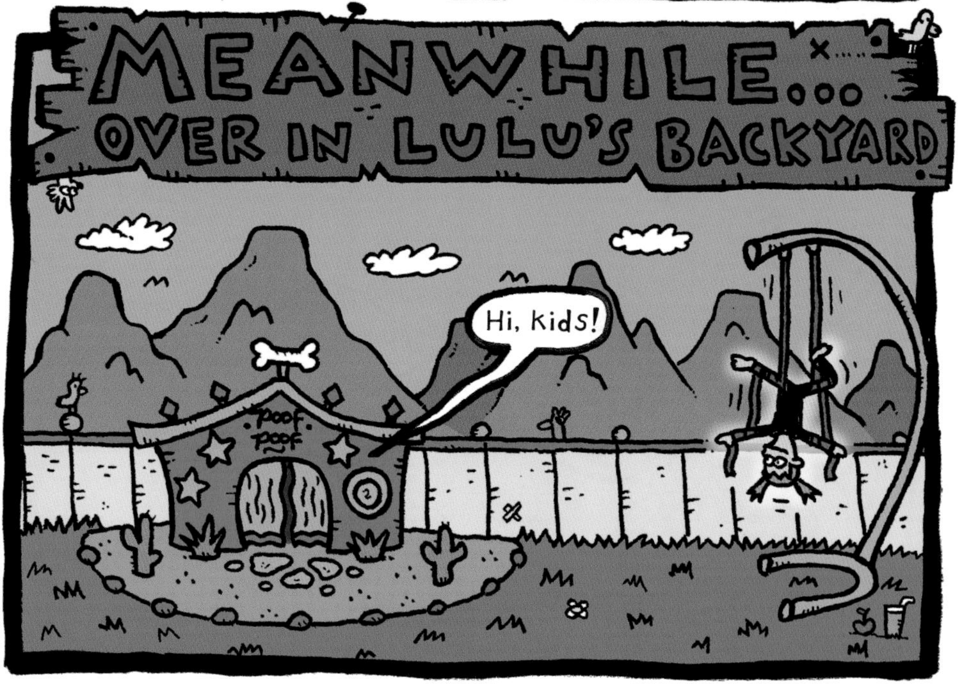
MEANWHILE...
OVER IN LULU'S BACKYARD
Hi, kids!
poof poof

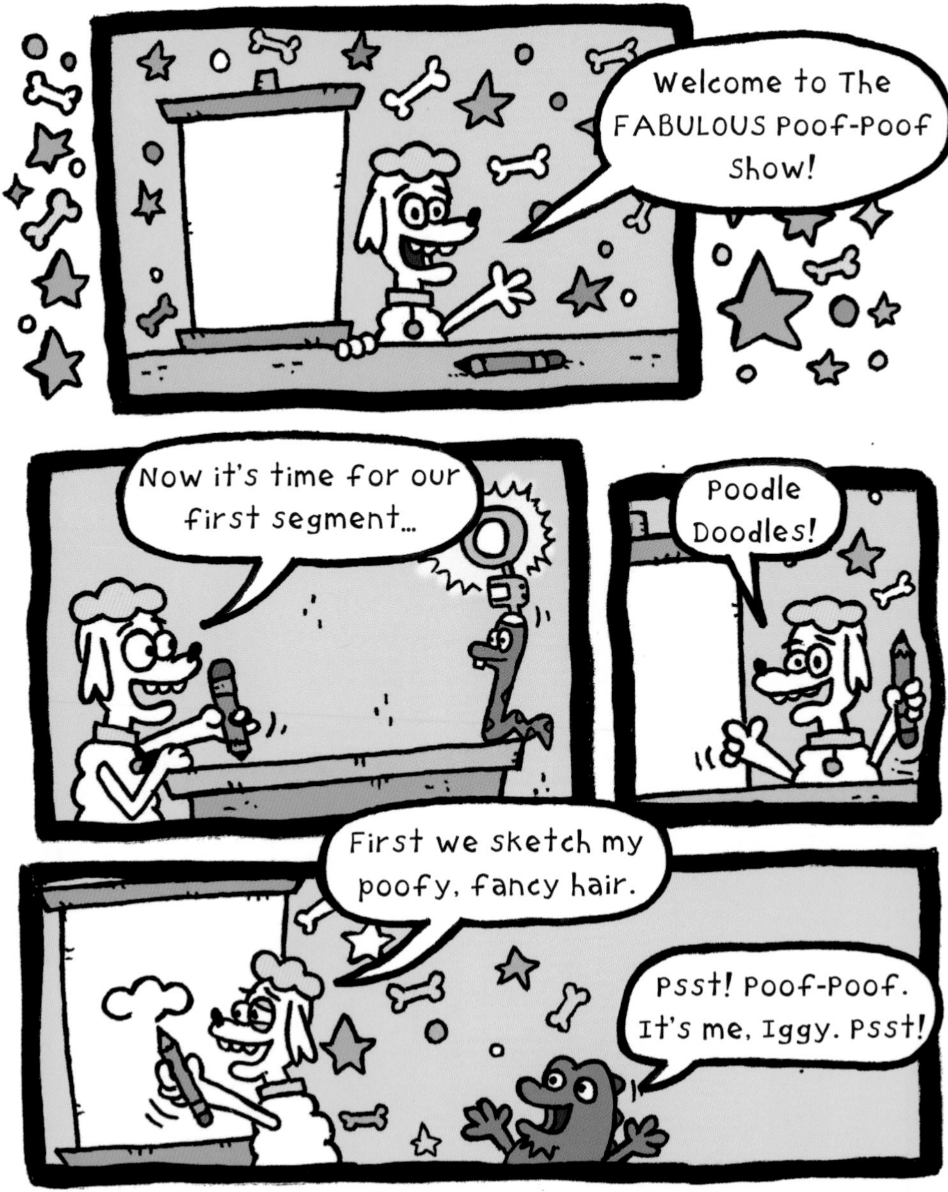
Welcome to The FABULOUS Poof-Poof Show!
Now it's time for our first segment...
Poodle Doodles!
First we sketch my poofy, fancy hair.
Psst! Poof-Poof. It's me, Iggy. Psst!

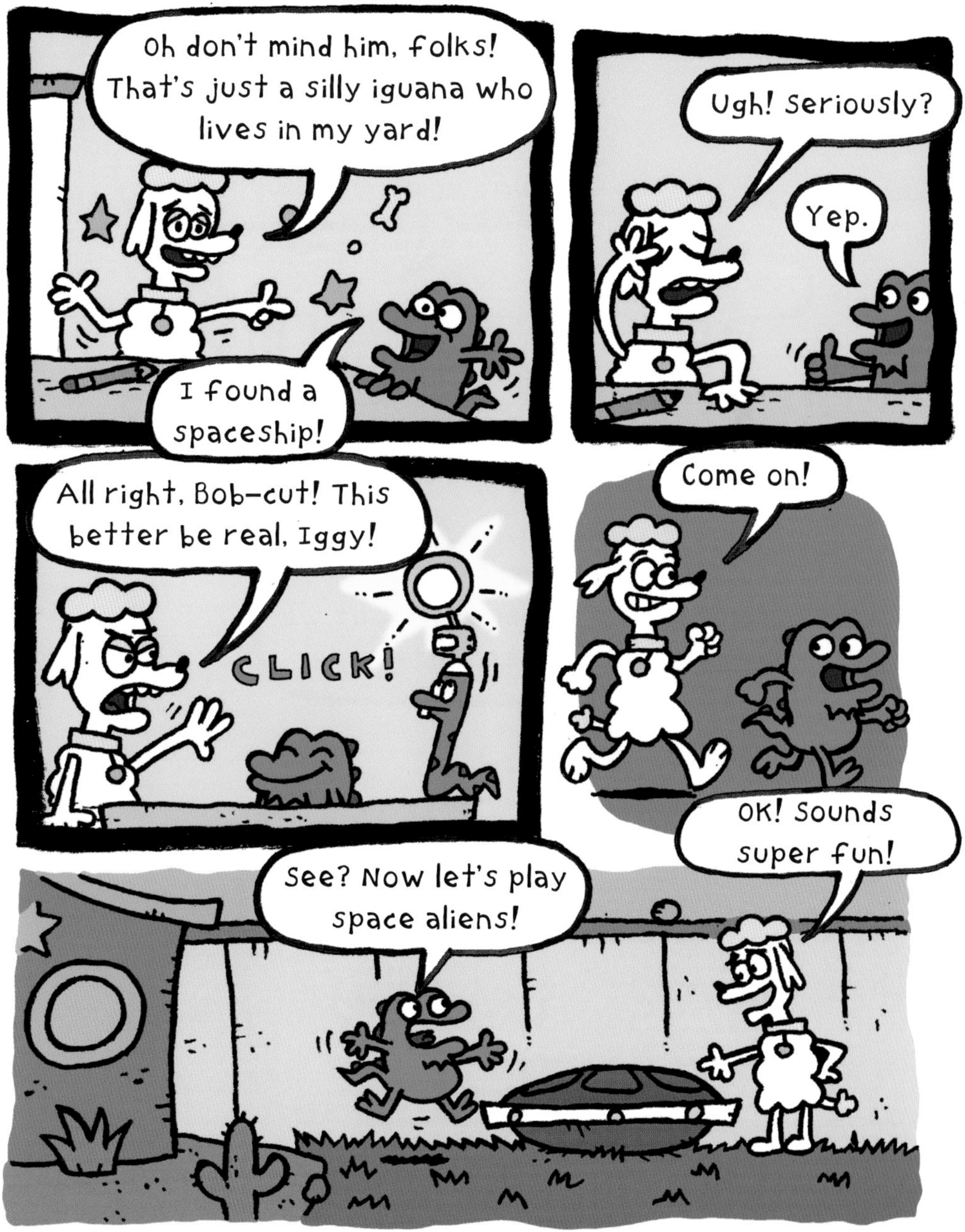
Oh don't mind him, folks! That's just a silly iguana who lives in my yard!
I found a spaceship!
Ugh! Seriously?
Yep.
All right, Bob-cut! This better be real, Iggy!
CLICK!
Come on!
See? Now let's play space aliens!
OK! Sounds super fun!

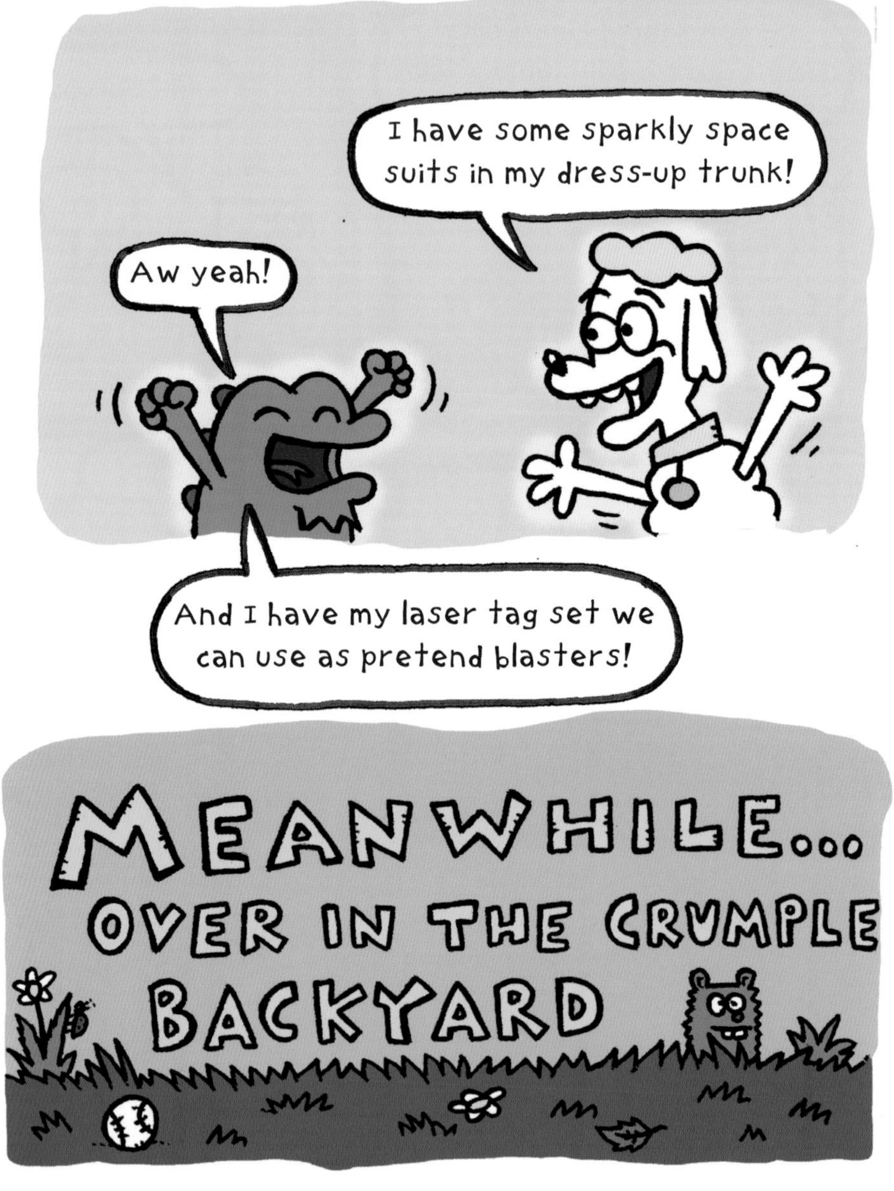

Aw yeah!
I have some sparkly space suits in my dress-up trunk!
And I have my laser tag set we can use as pretend blasters!
MEANWHILE...
OVER IN THE CRUMPLE BACKYARD

CHAPTER 3

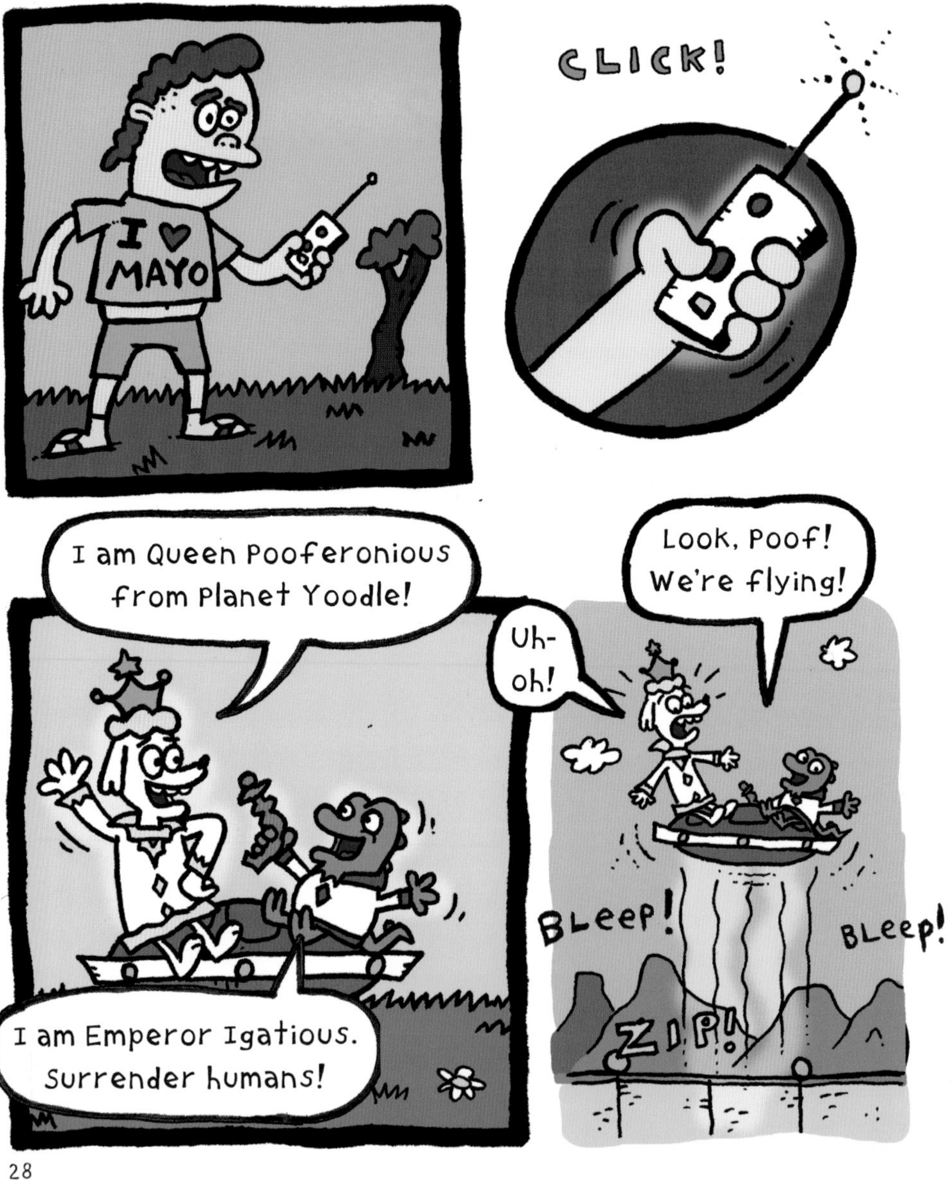
I ♥ MAYO
CLICK!
I am Queen Pooferonious from Planet Yoodle!
I am Emperor Igatious. Surrender humans!
Look, Poof! We're flying!
Uh-oh!
BLEEP!
BLEEP!
ZIP!

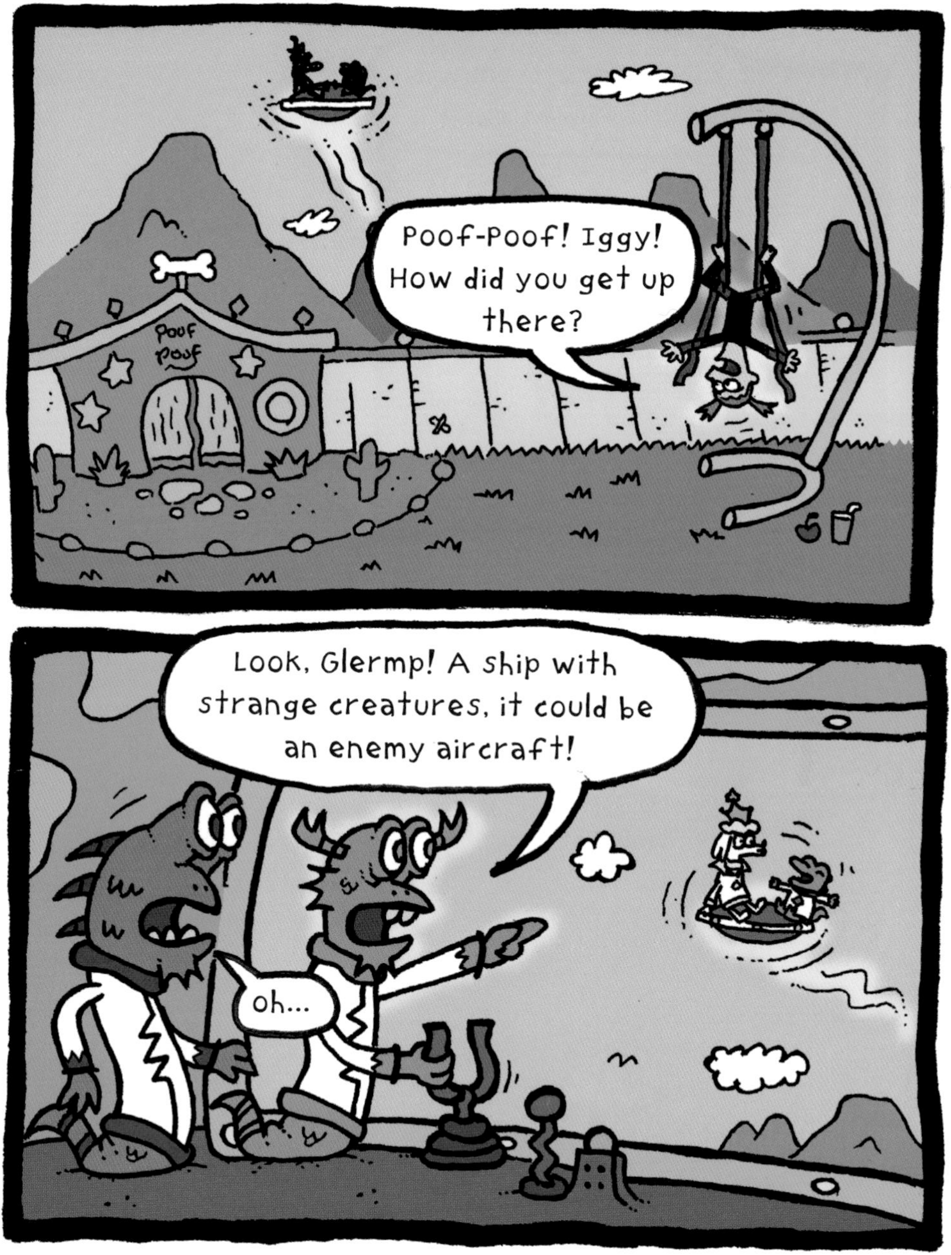
Poof Poof
Poof-Poof! Iggy! How did you get up there?
Look, Glermp! A ship with strange creatures, it could be an enemy aircraft!
Oh...

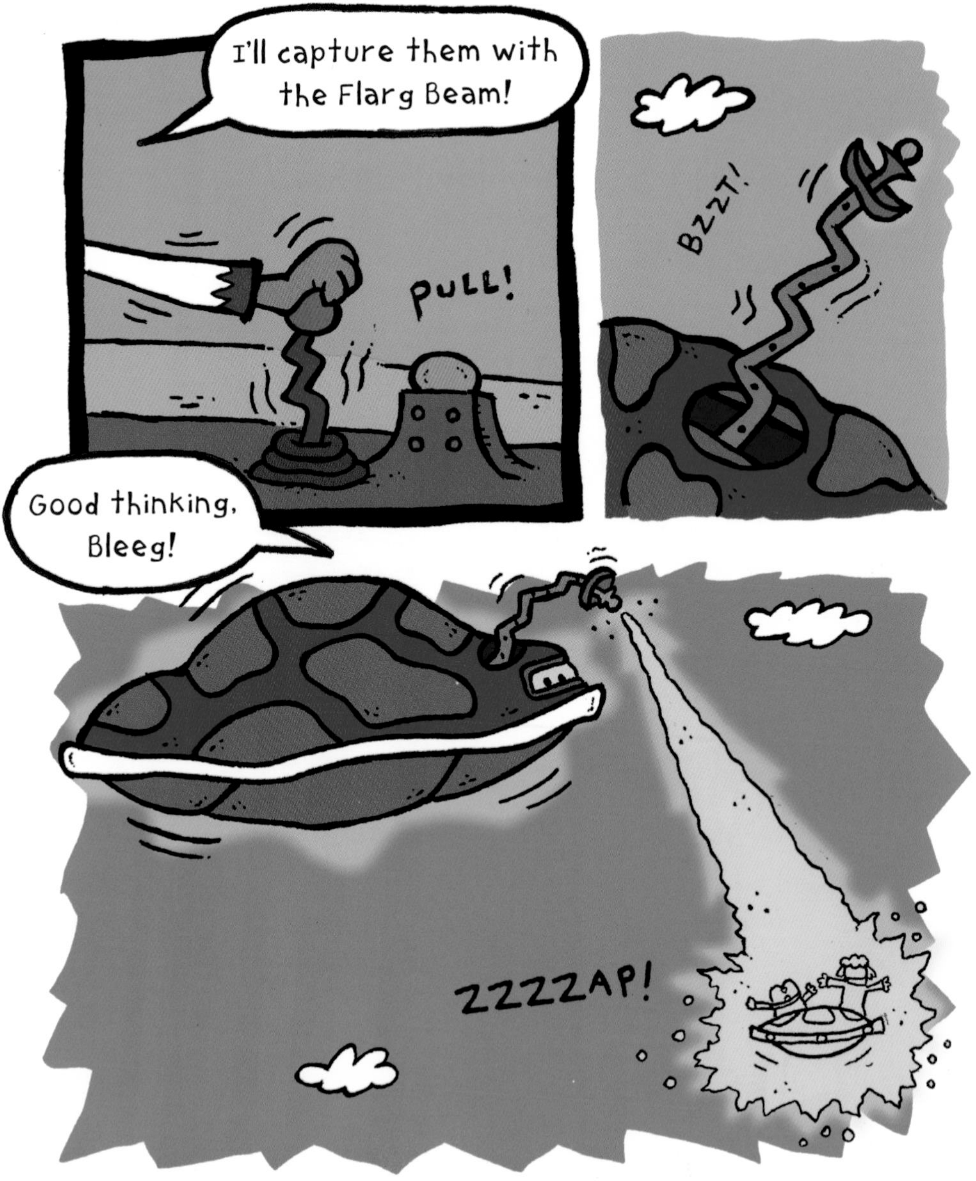
I'll capture them with the Flarg Beam!
PULL!
BZZT!
Good thinking, Bleeg!
ZZZZAP!

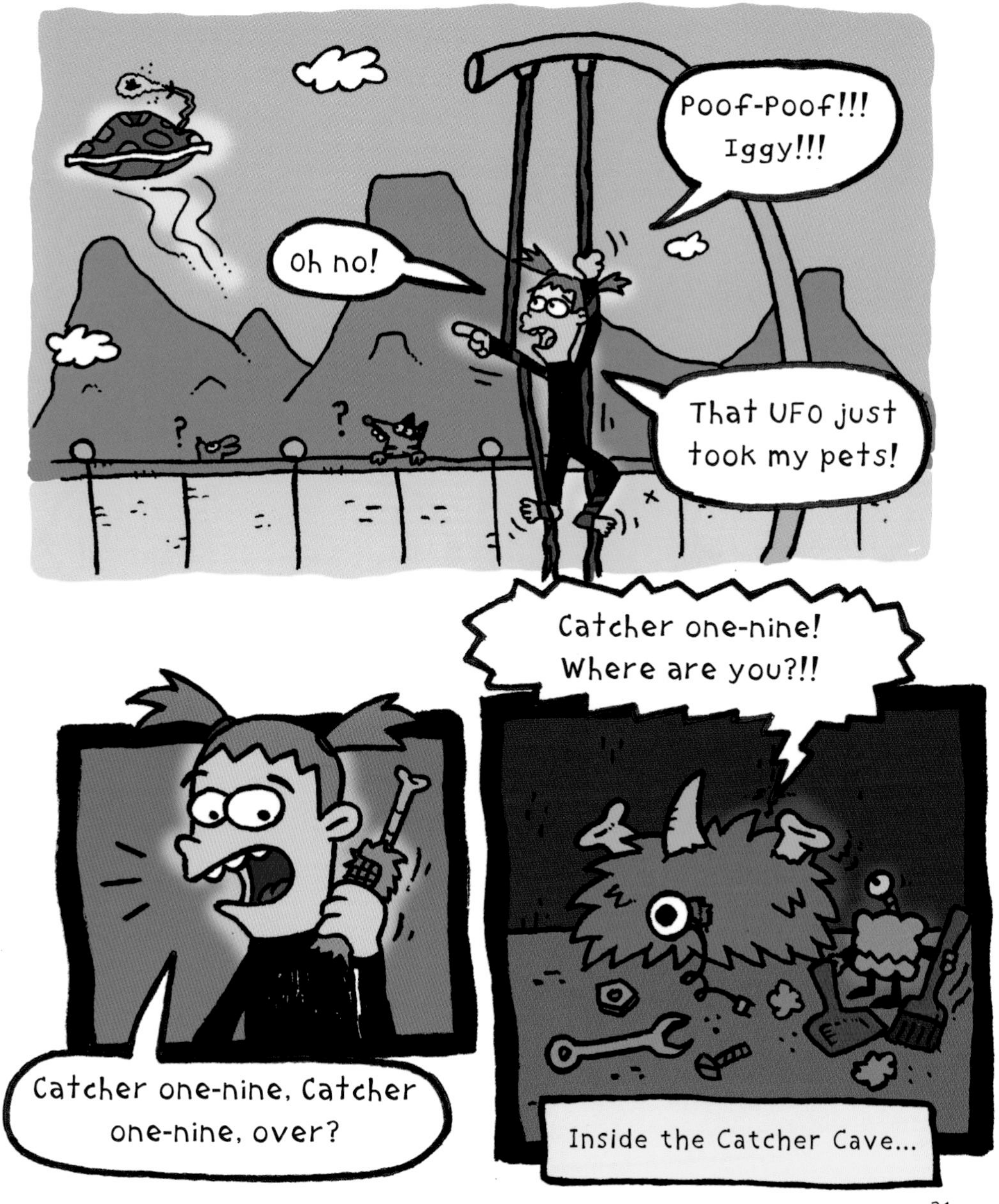
Poof-Poof!!! Iggy!!!
Oh no!
That UFO just took my pets!
Catcher one-nine, Catcher one-nine, over?
Inside the Catcher Cave...
Catcher one-nine! Where are you?!!

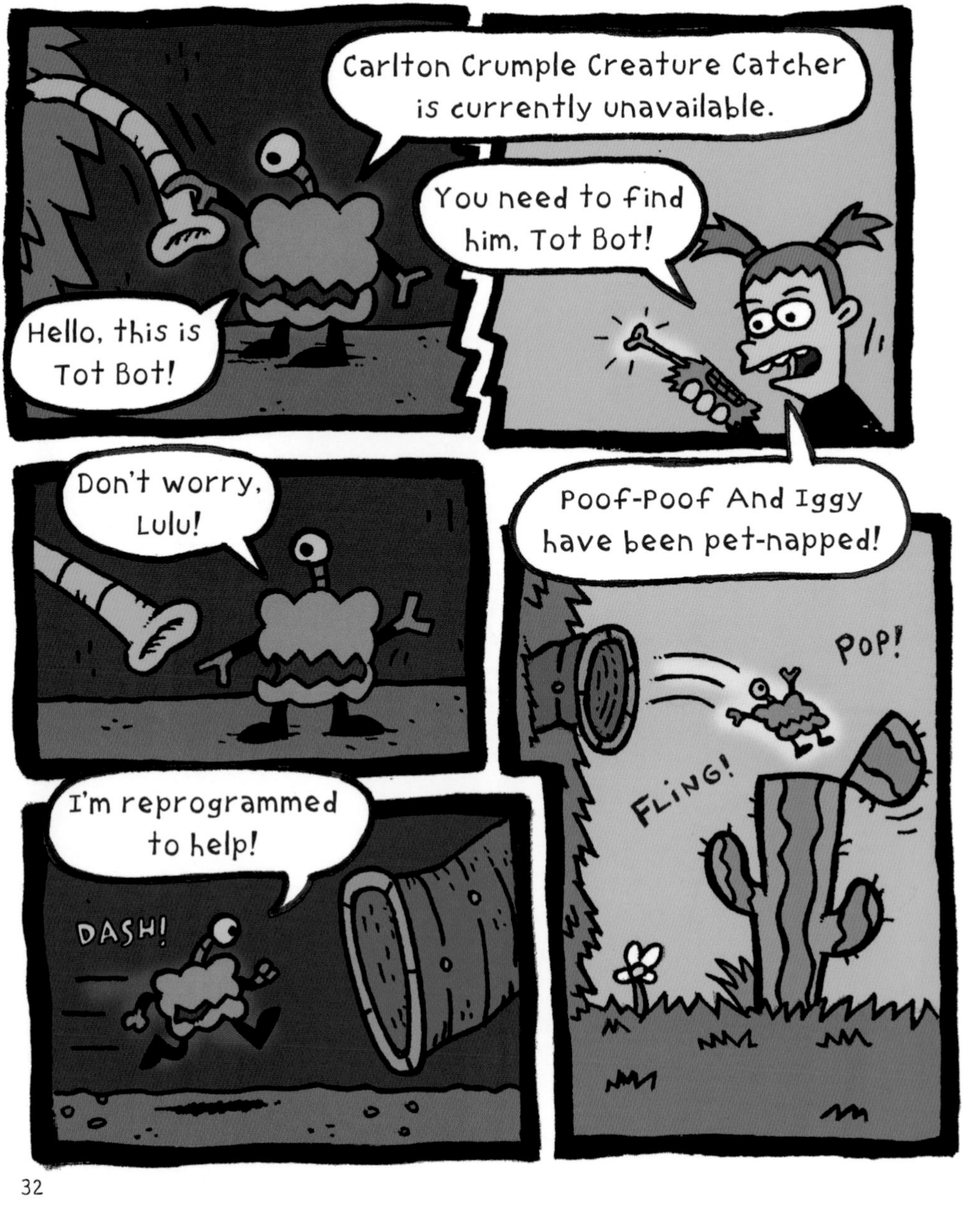
Carlton Crumple Creature Catcher is currently unavailable.
Hello, this is Tot Bot!
You need to find him, Tot Bot!
Poof-Poof And Iggy have been pet-napped!
Don't worry, Lulu!
I'm reprogrammed to help!
DASH!
POP!
FLING!

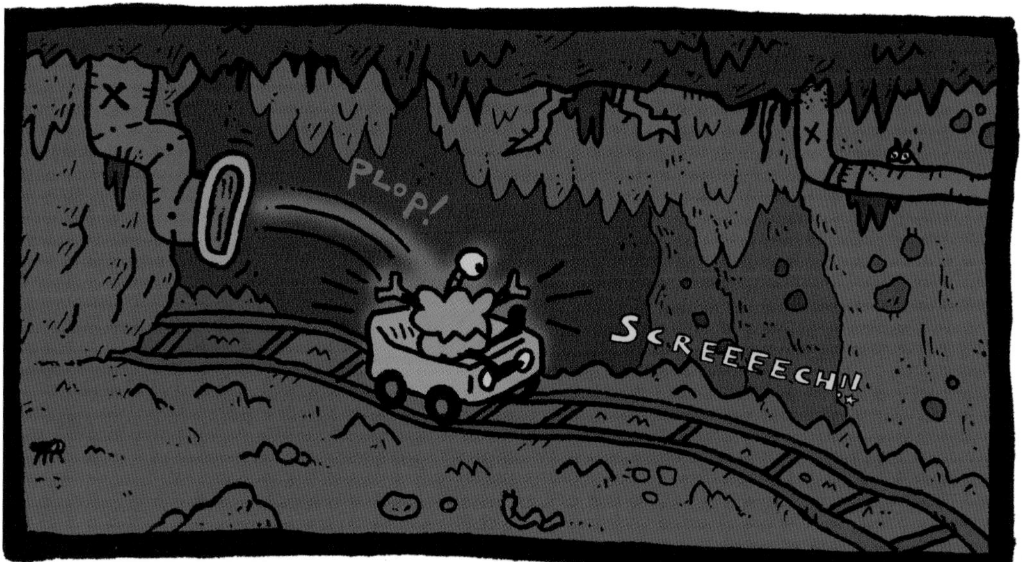
PLOP!
SCREEEEECH!!

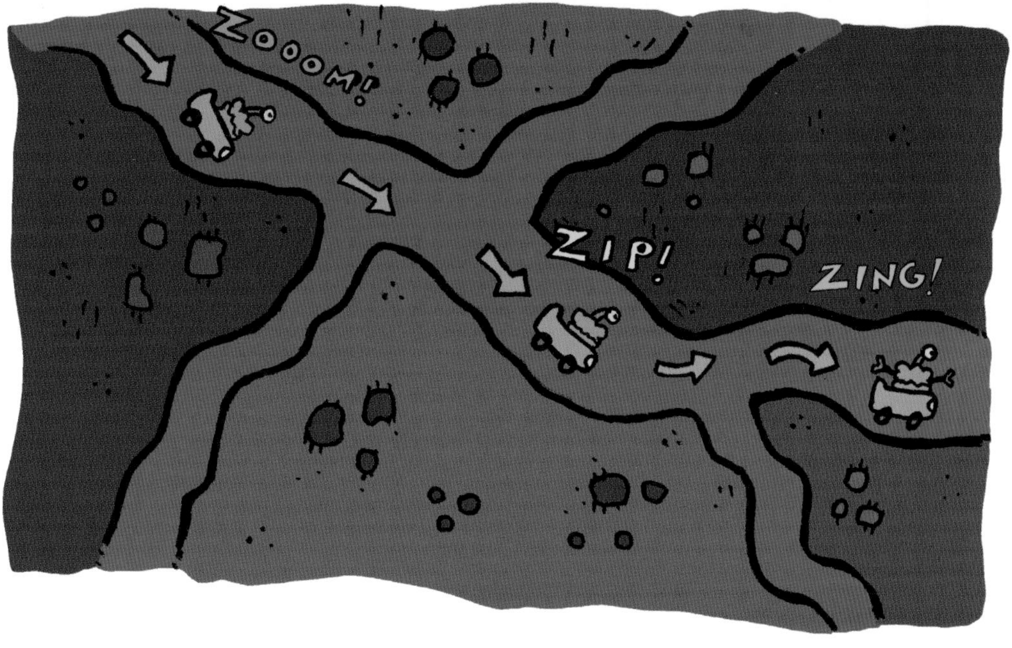
ZOOOOM!
ZIP!
ZING!

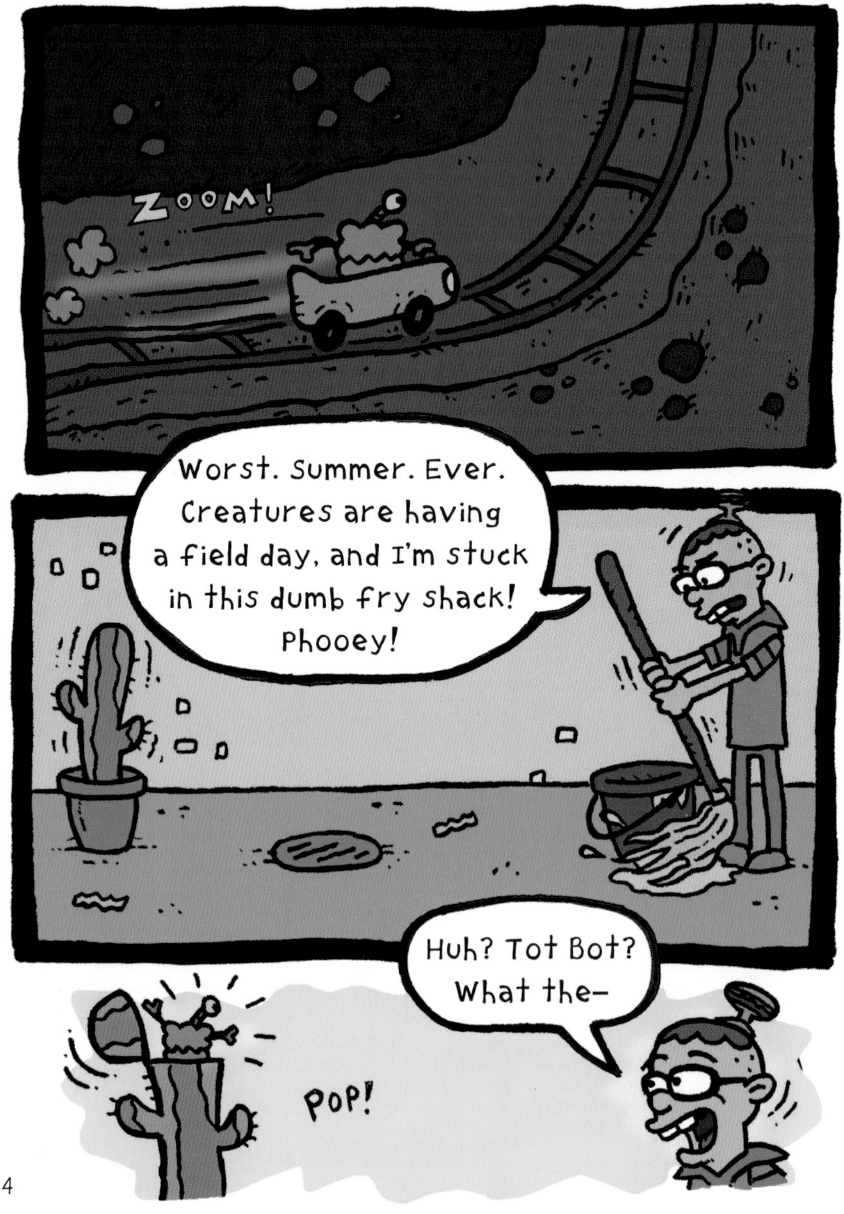
ZOOM!
Worst. Summer. Ever. Creatures are having a field day, and I'm stuck in this dumb fry shack! Phooey!
Huh? Tot Bot? What the-
POP!

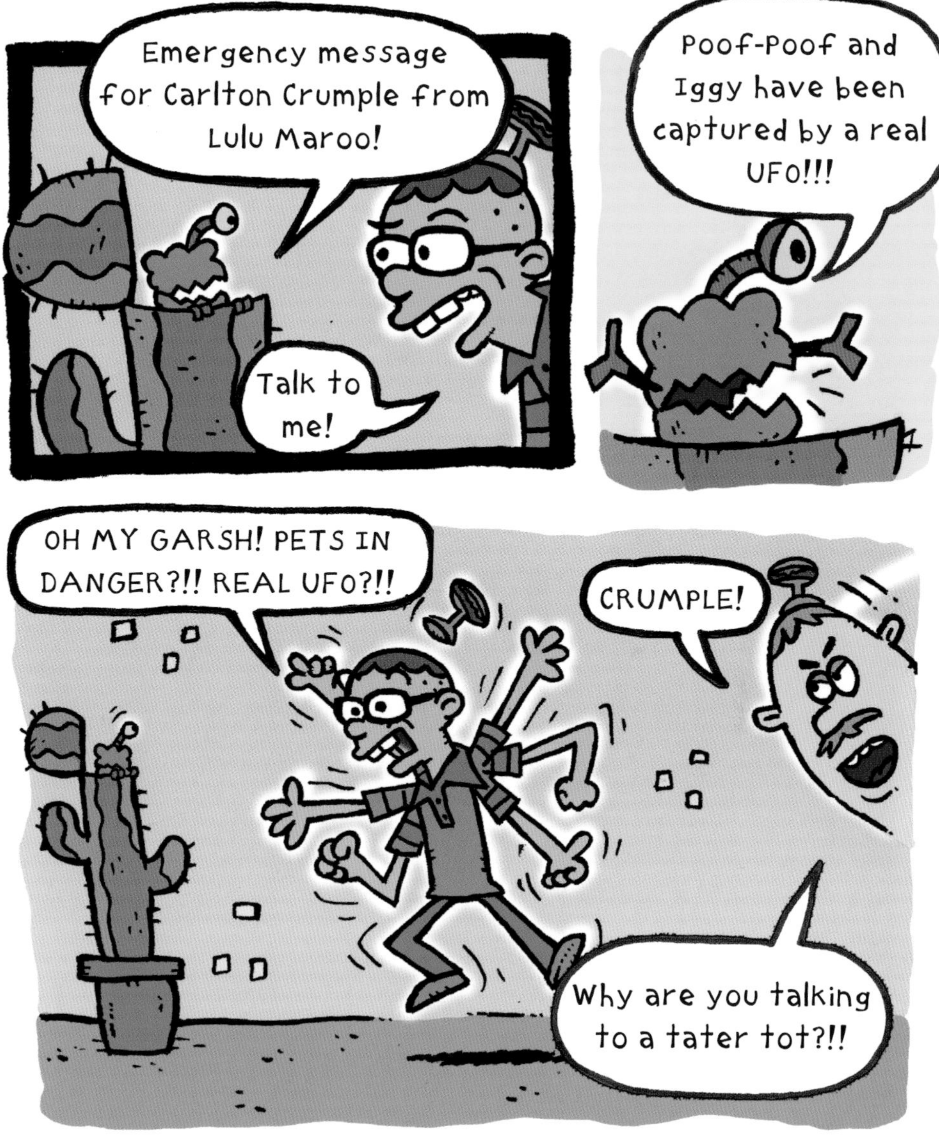
Emergency message for Carlton Crumple from Lulu Maroo!
Talk to me!
Poof-Poof and Iggy have been captured by a real UFO!!!
OH MY GARSH! PETS IN DANGER?!! REAL UFO?!!
CRUMPLE!
Why are you talking to a tater tot?!!

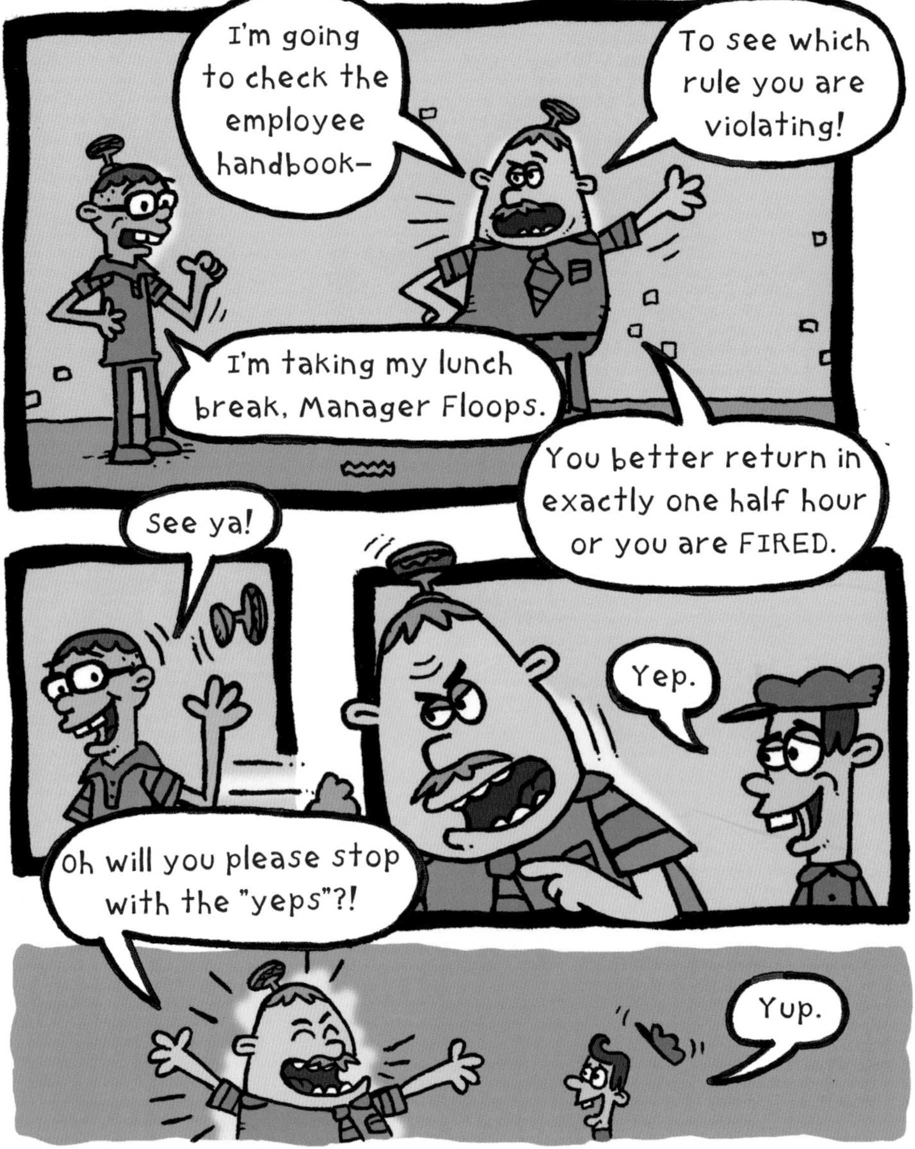
I'm going to check the employee handbook–
To see which rule you are violating!
I'm taking my lunch break, Manager Floops.
You better return in exactly one half hour or you are FIRED.
See ya!
Yep.
Oh will you please stop with the "yeps"?!
Yup.

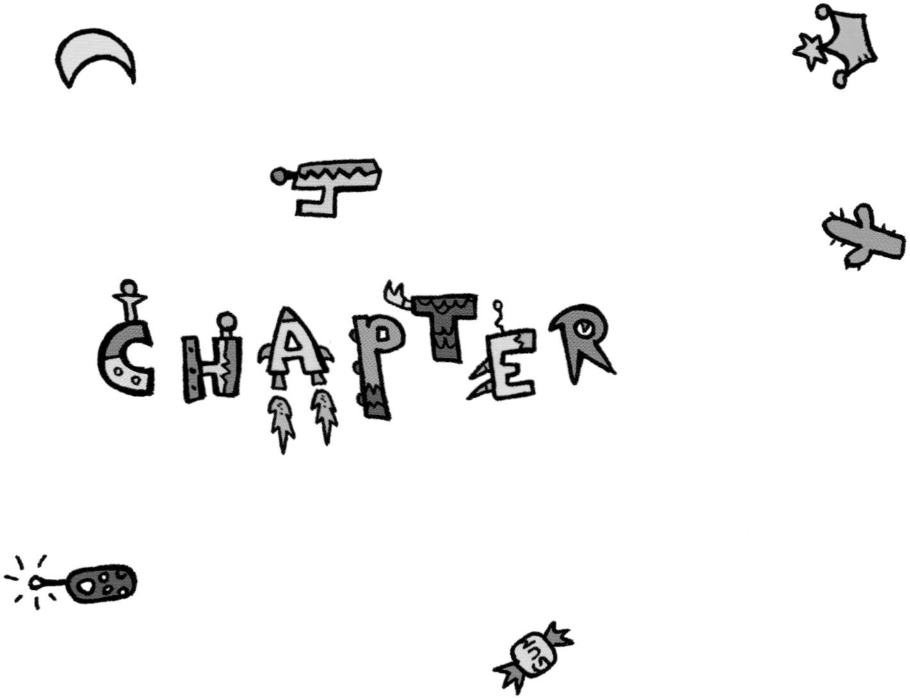
CHAPTER
4
GUM

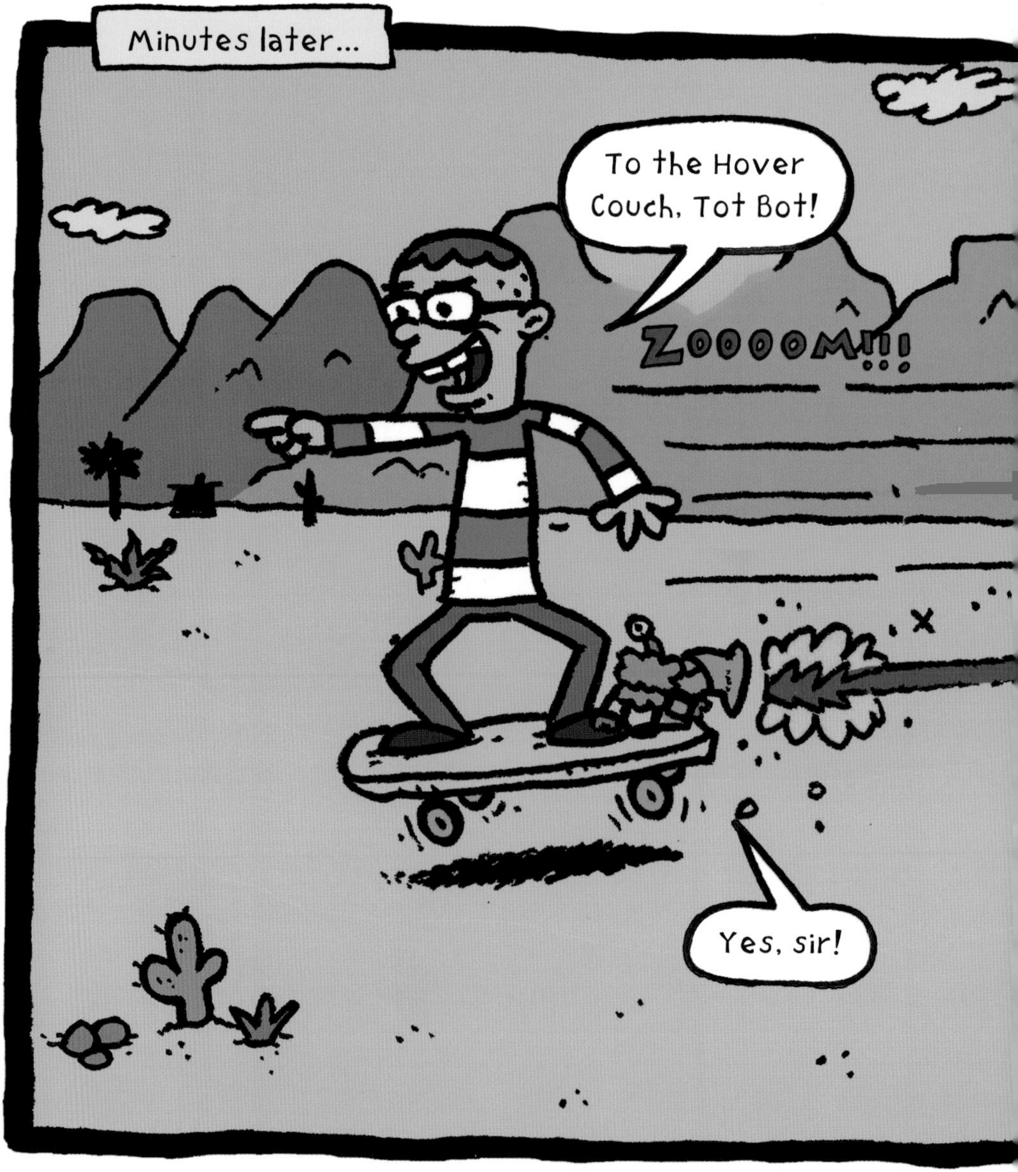
Minutes later...
To the Hover Couch, Tot Bot!
ZOOOOOM!!!
Yes, sir!

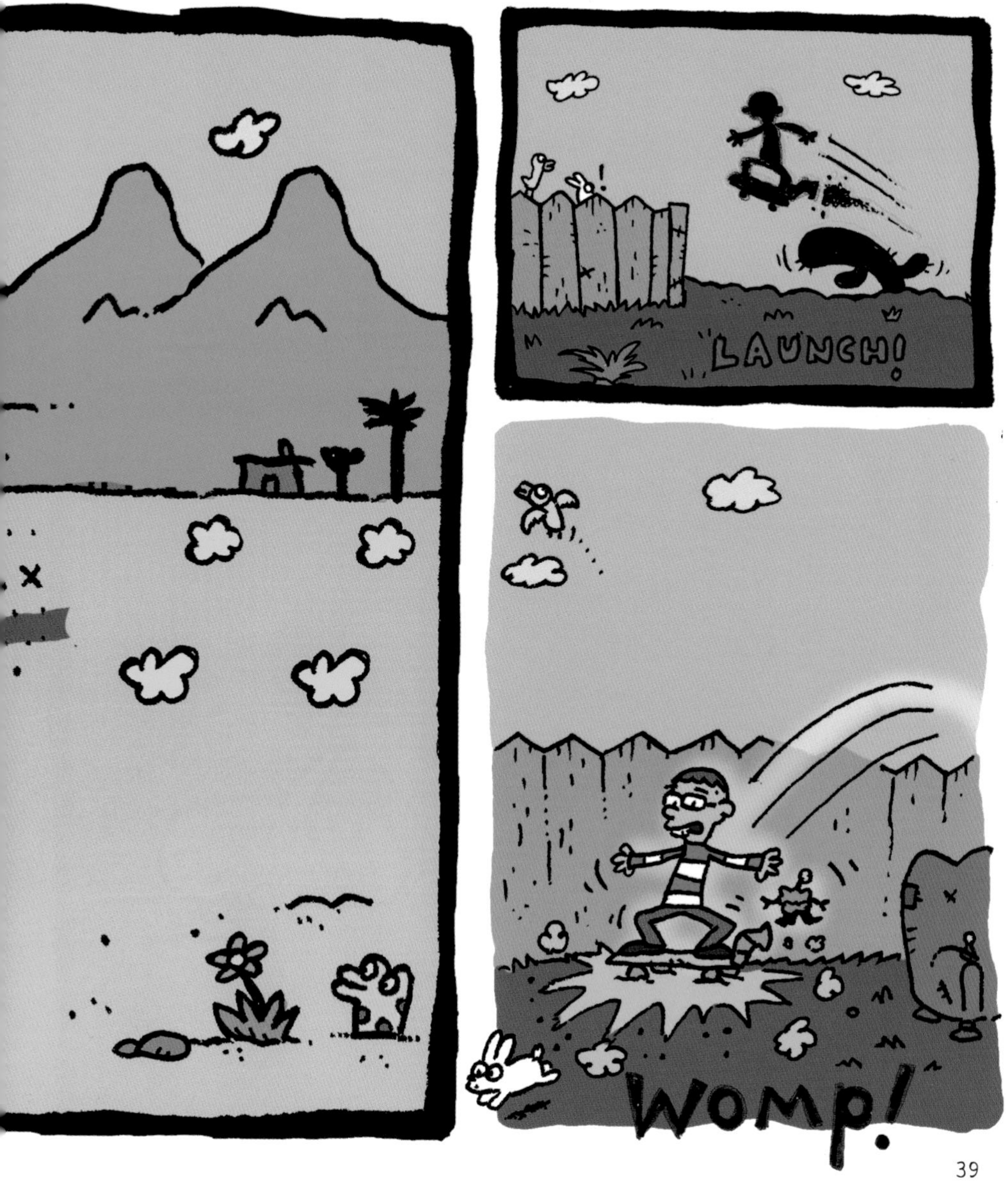
LAUNCH!
WOMP!

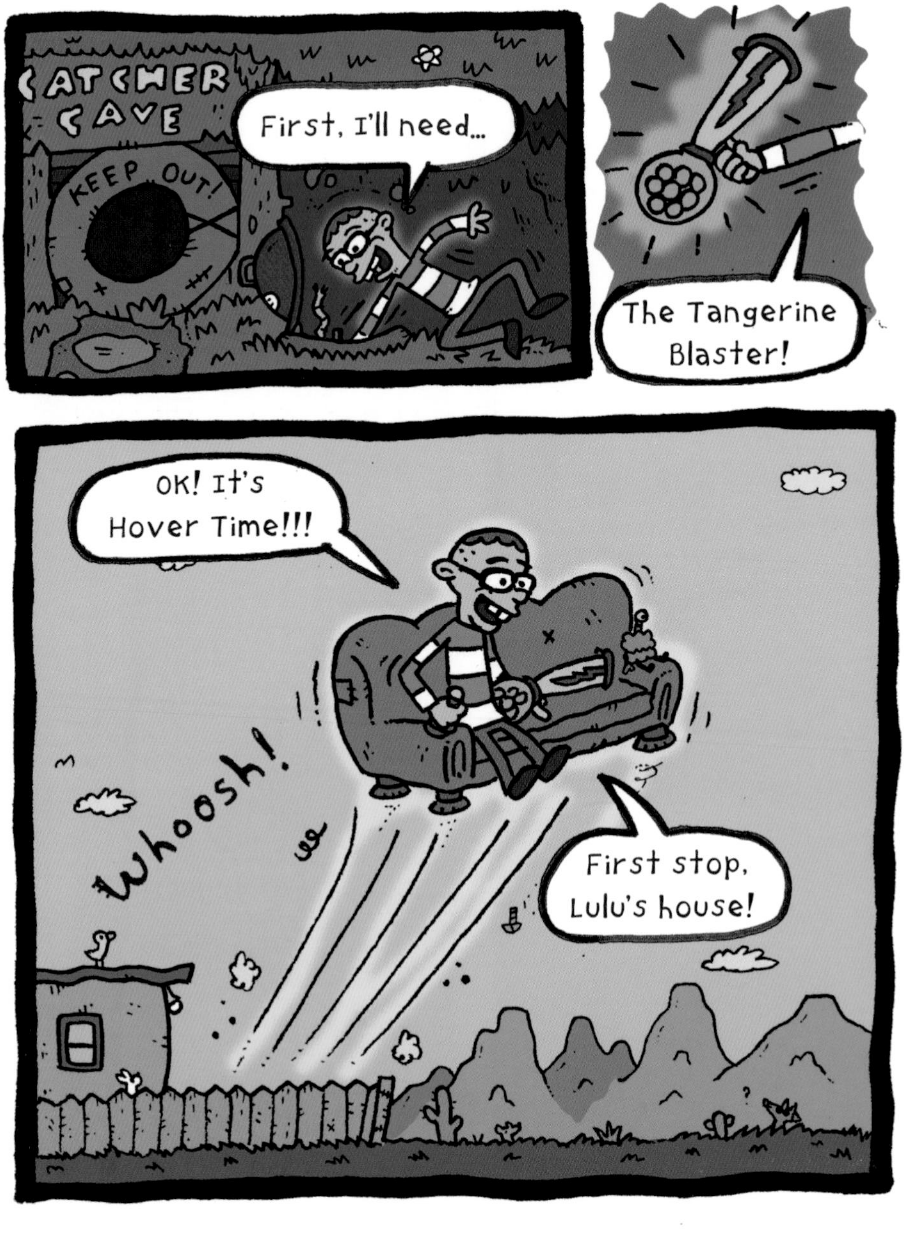
CATCHER CAVE
KEEP OUT!
First, I'll need...
The Tangerine Blaster!
OK! It's Hover Time!!!
Whoosh!
First stop, Lulu's house!

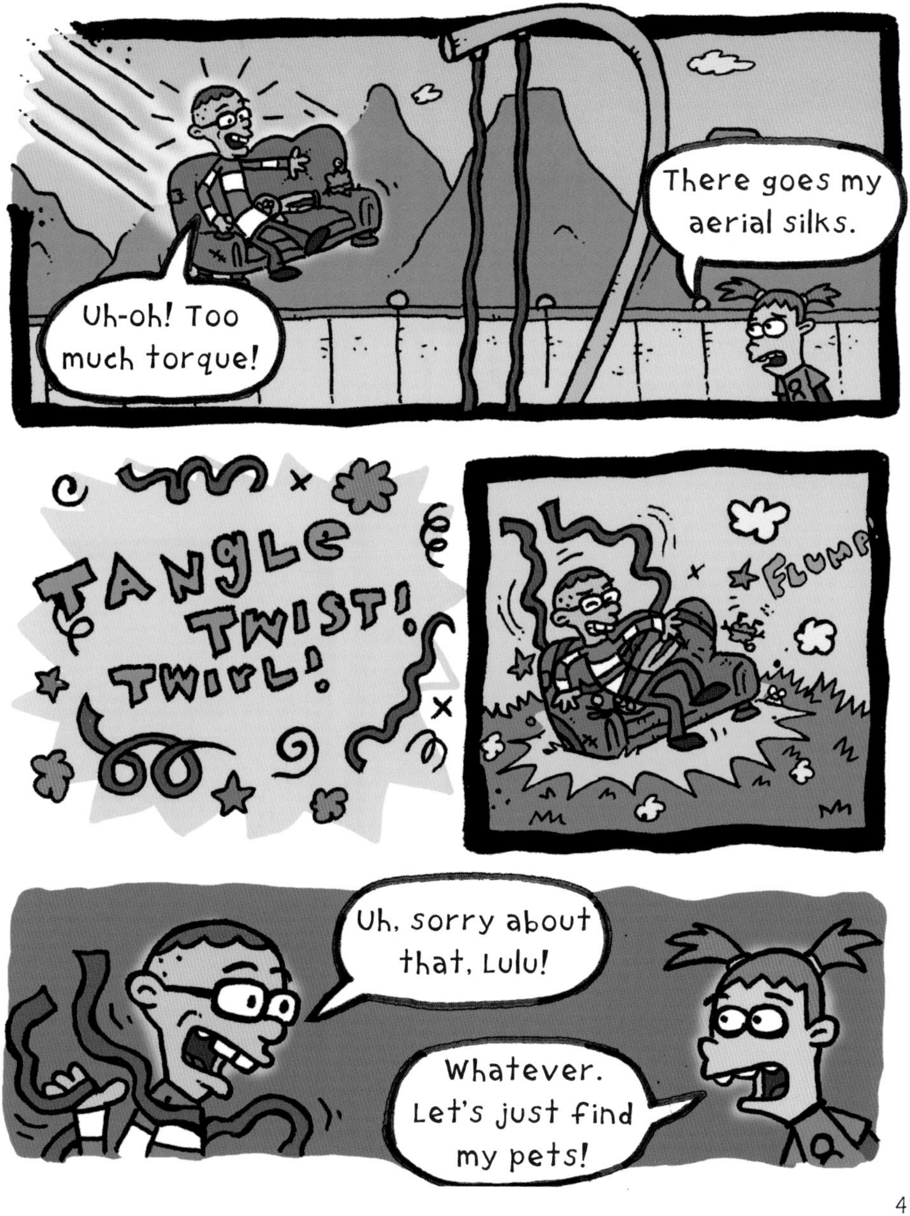
Uh-oh! Too much torque!
There goes my aerial silks.
TANGLE TWIST! TWIRL!
FLUMP!
Uh, sorry about that, Lulu!
Whatever. Let's just find my pets!

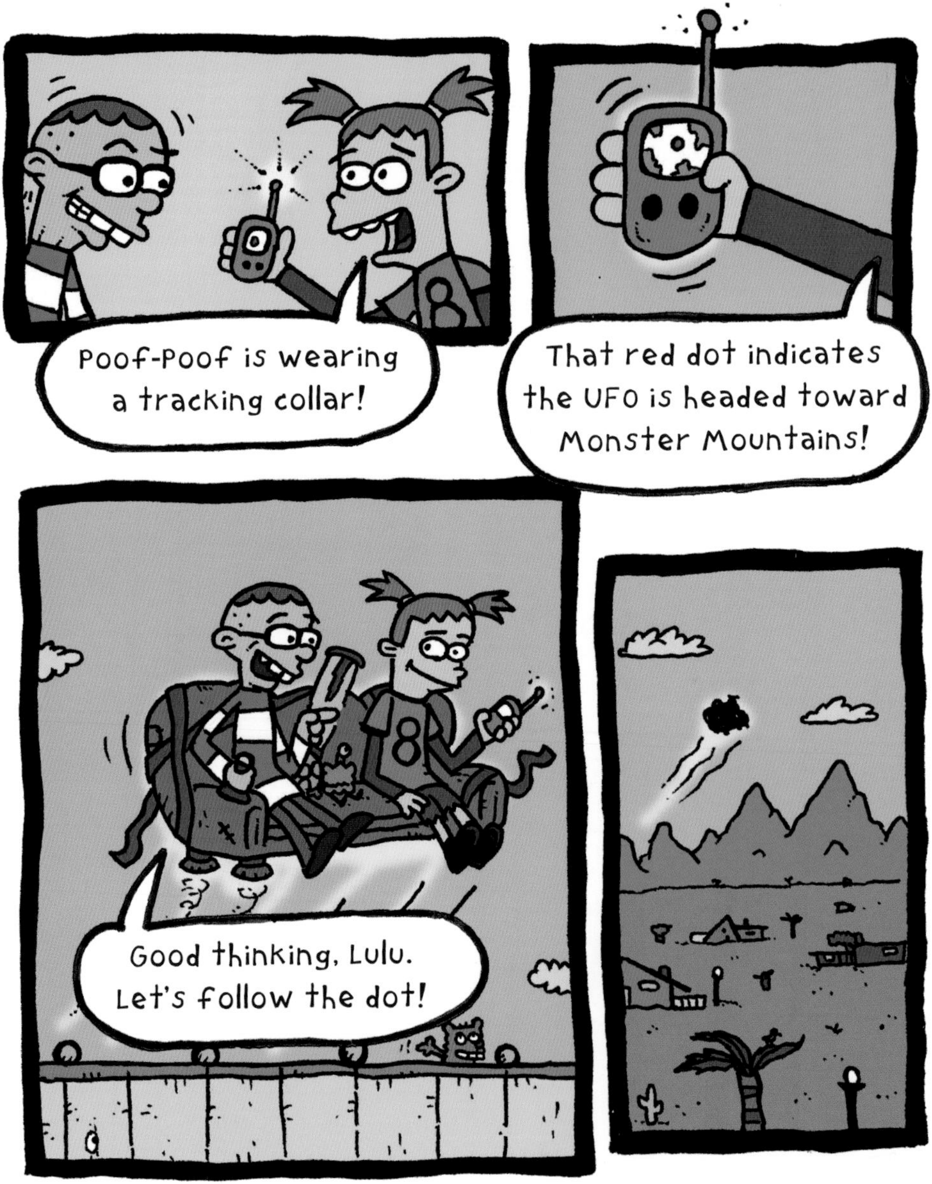
Poof-Poof is wearing a tracking collar!
That red dot indicates the UFO is headed toward Monster Mountains!
Good thinking, Lulu. Let's follow the dot!

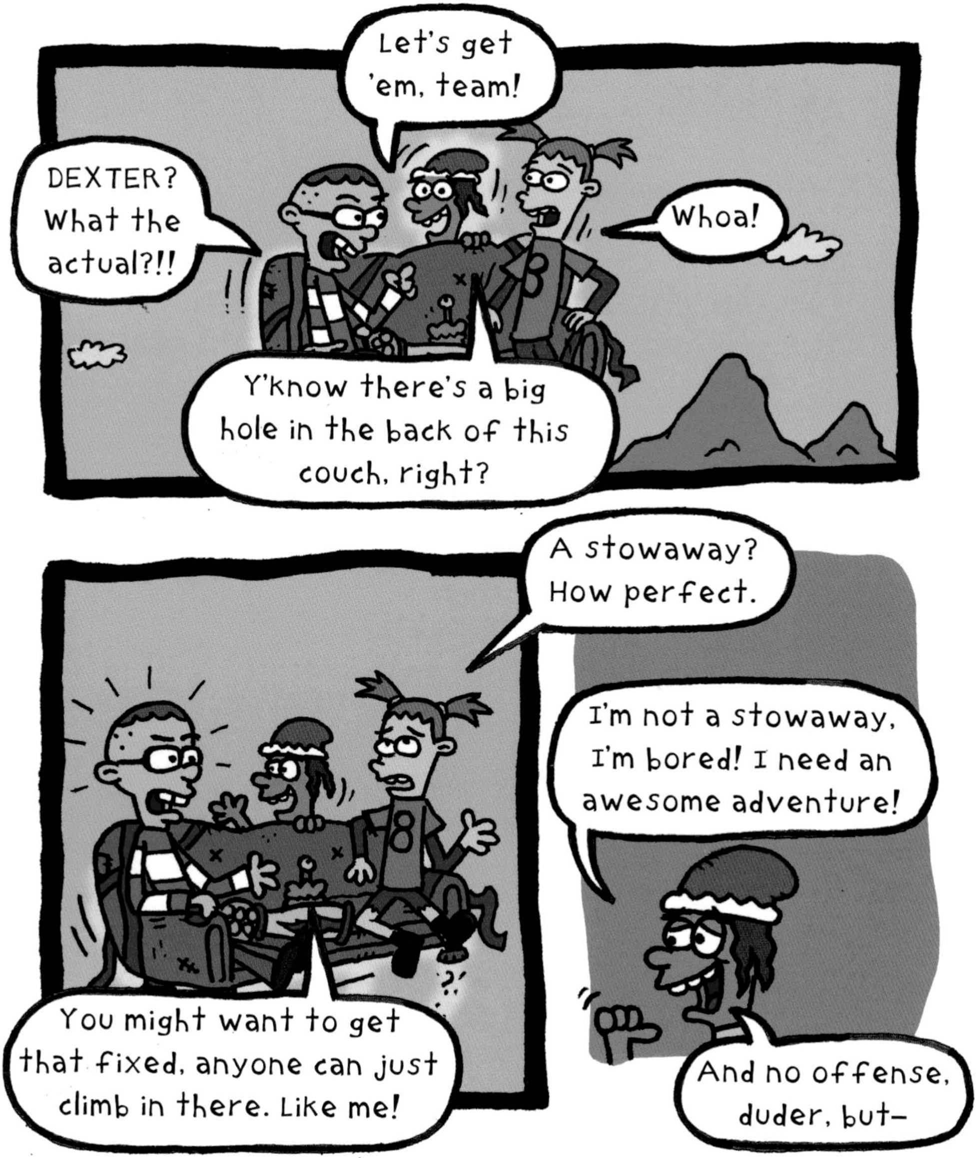
Let's get 'em, team!
DEXTER? What the actual?!!
Whoa!
Y'know there's a big hole in the back of this couch, right?
A stowaway? How perfect.
You might want to get that fixed, anyone can just climb in there. Like me!
I'm not a stowaway, I'm bored! I need an awesome adventure!
And no offense, duder, but–

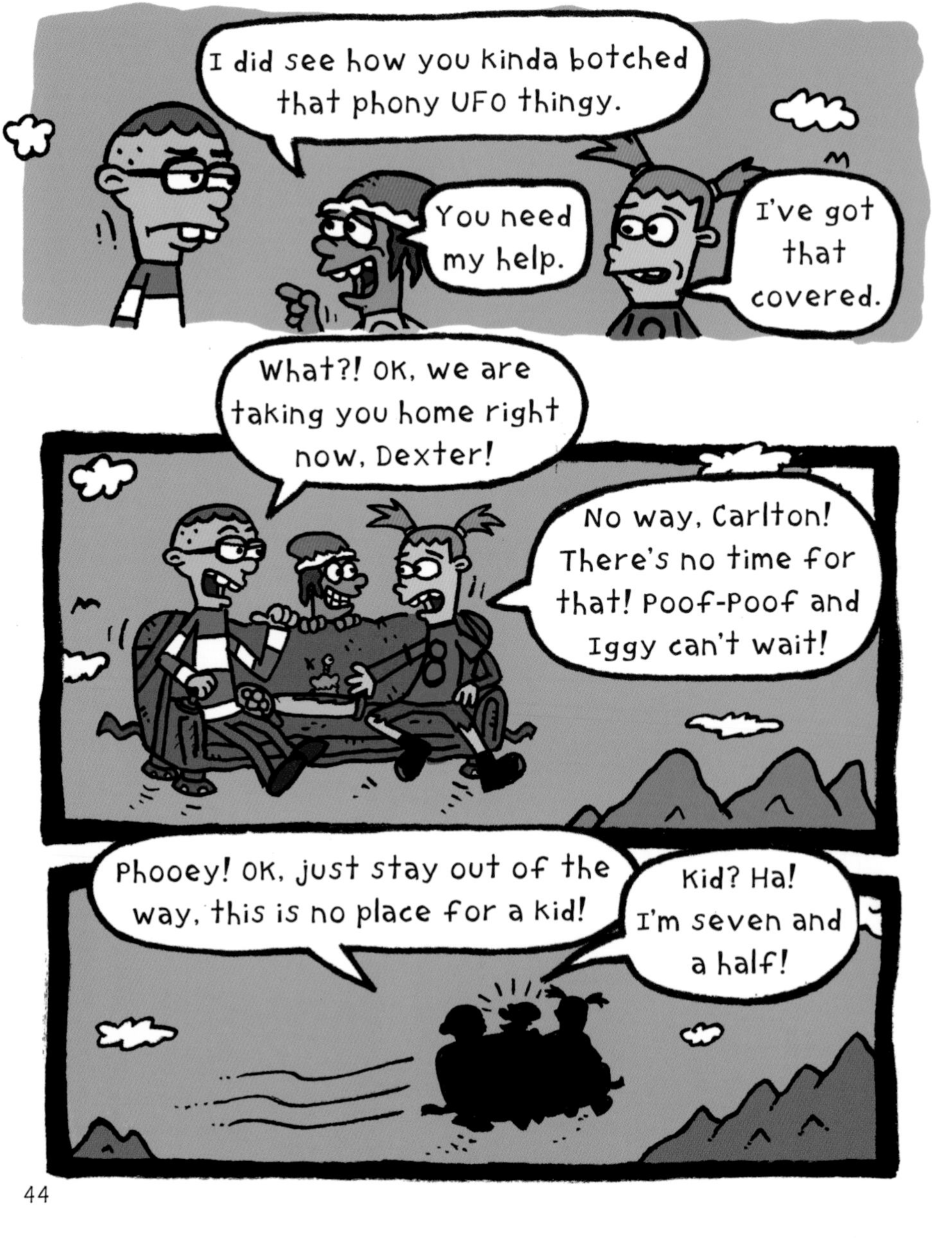
I did see how you kinda botched that phony UFO thingy.
You need my help.
I've got that covered.
What?! OK, we are taking you home right now, Dexter!
No way, Carlton! There's no time for that! Poof-Poof and Iggy can't wait!
Phooey! OK, just stay out of the way, this is no place for a kid!
Kid? Ha! I'm seven and a half!

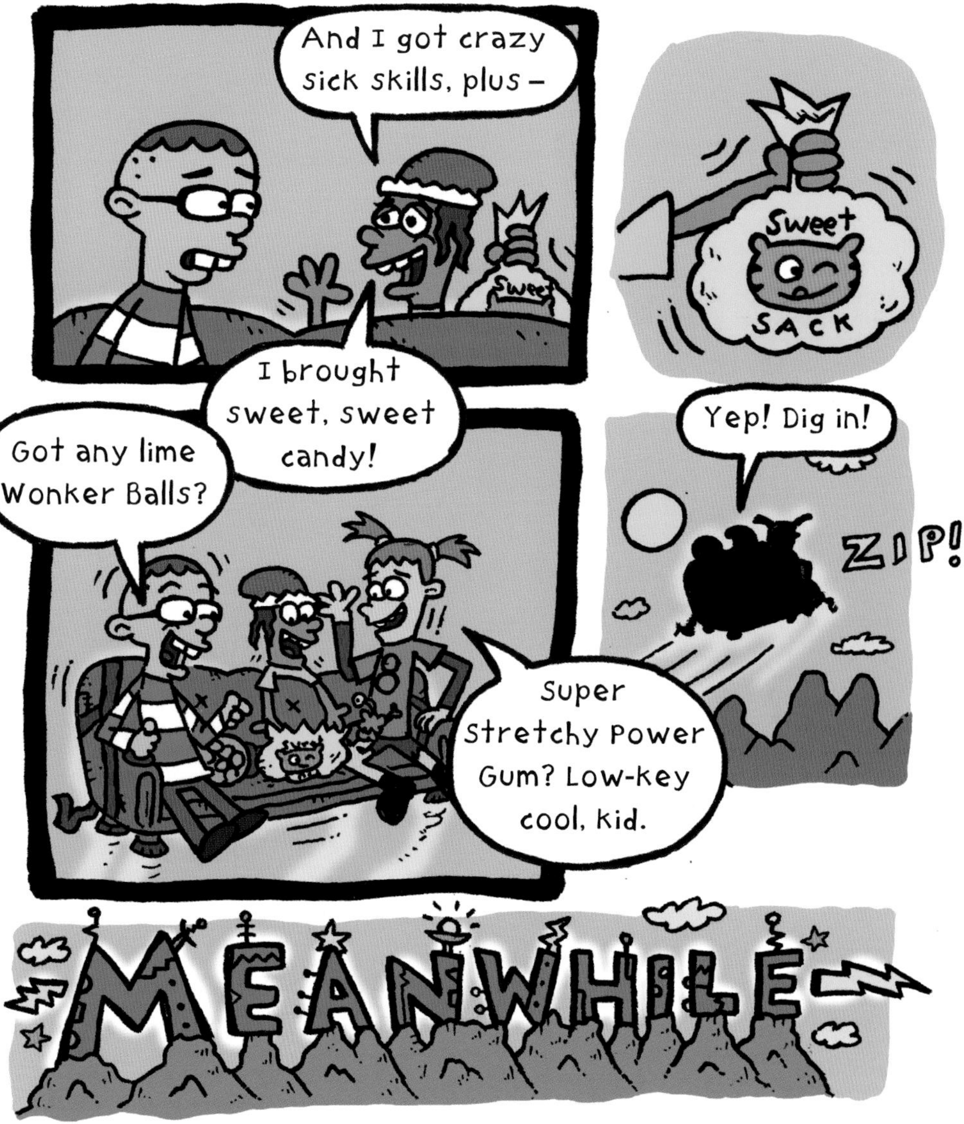
And I got crazy sick skills, plus –
I brought sweet, sweet candy!
Sweet
Sweet SACK
Got any lime Wonker Balls?
Super Stretchy Power Gum? Low-key cool, kid.
Yep! Dig in!
ZIP!
MEANWHILE

CHAPTER

5

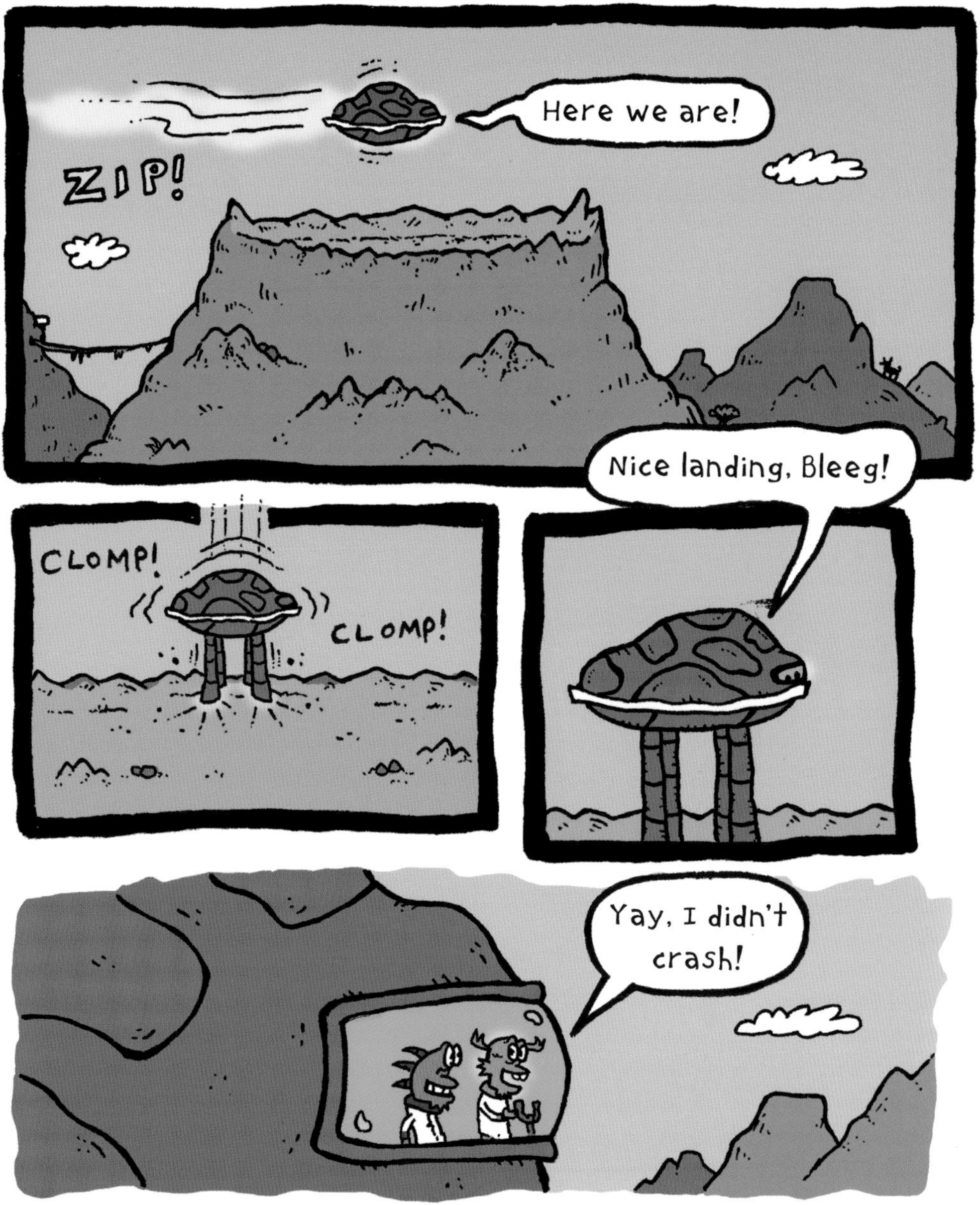
Here we are!
ZIP!
CLOMP!
CLOMP!
Nice landing, Bleeg!
Yay, I didn't crash!

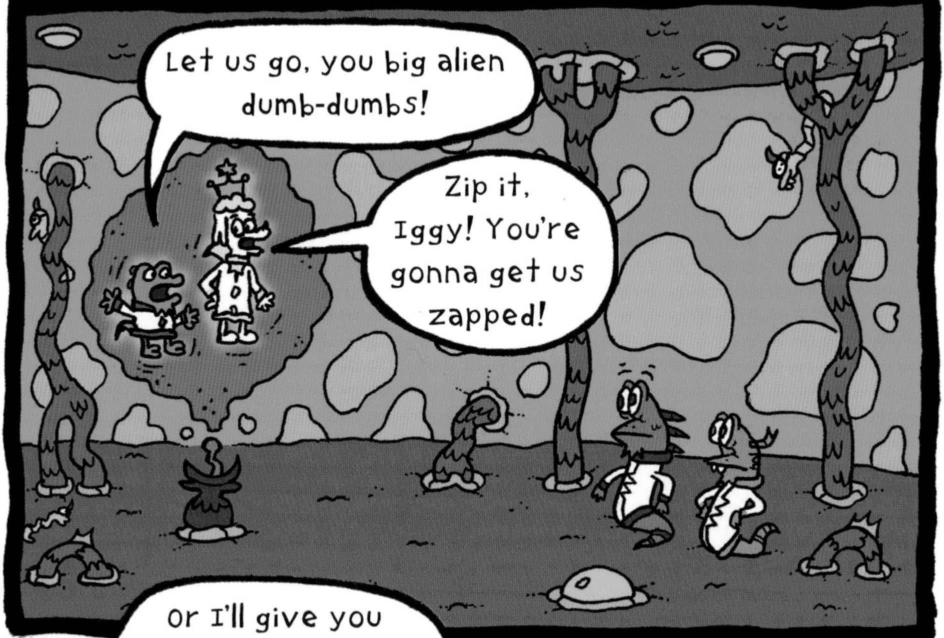
Let us go, you big alien dumb-dumbs!
Zip it, Iggy! You're gonna get us zapped!

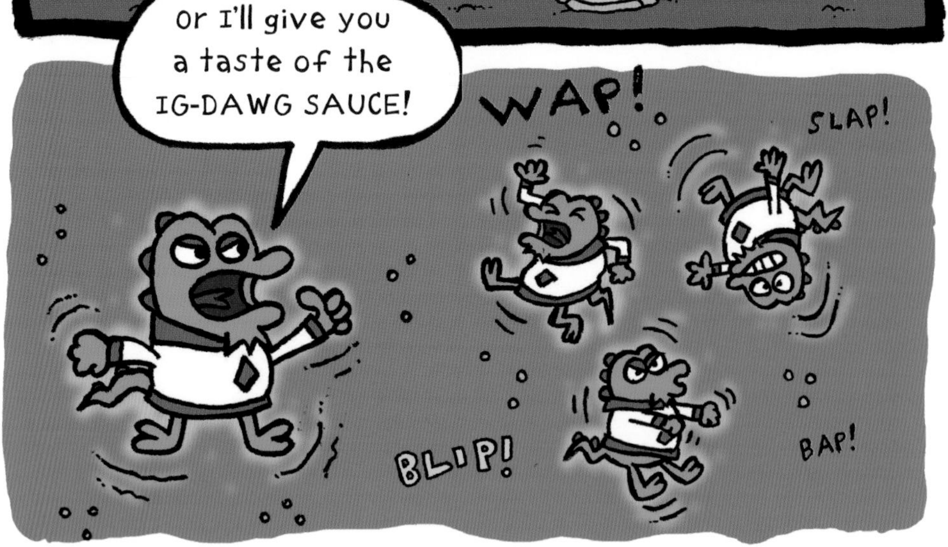
Or I'll give you a taste of the IG-DAWG SAUCE!
WAP!
SLAP!
BLIP!
BAP!

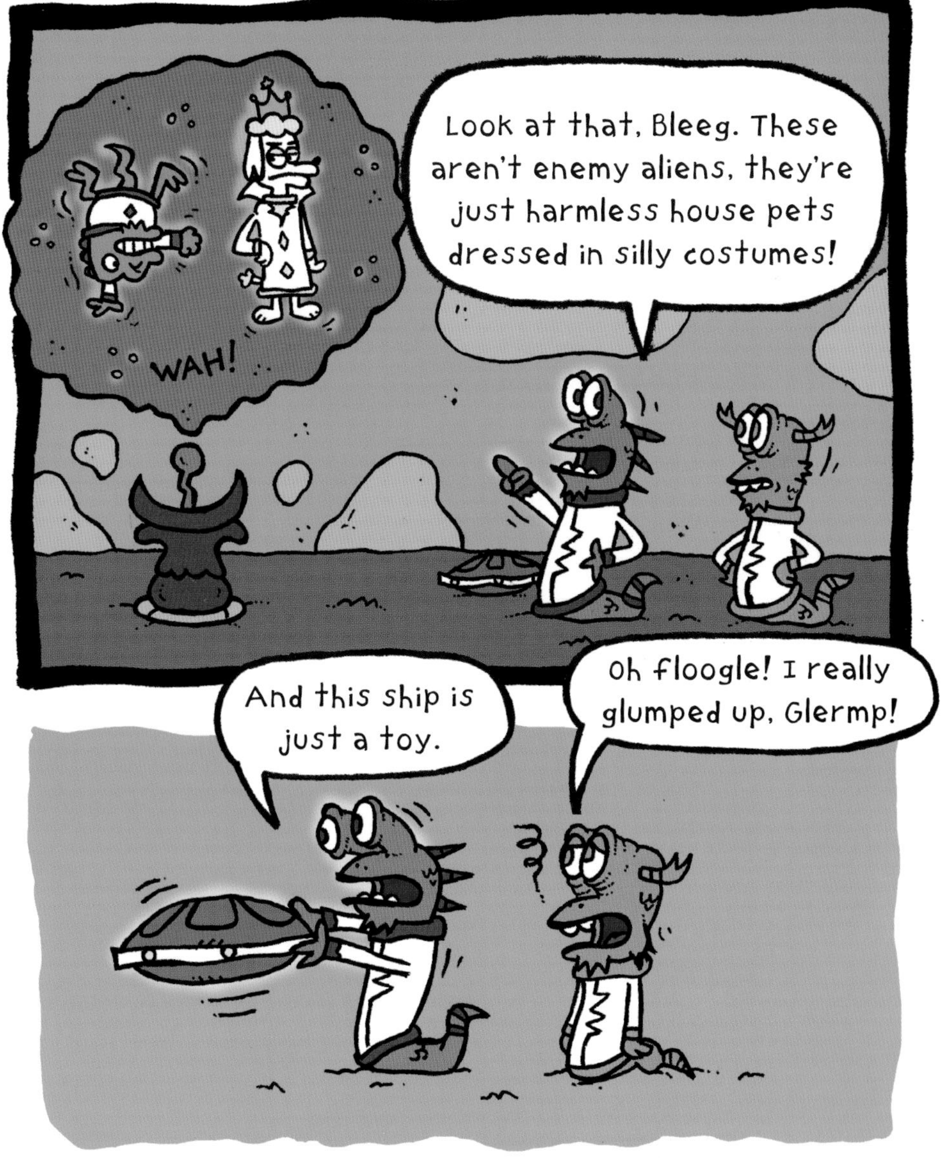
WAH!
Look at that, Bleeg. These aren't enemy aliens, they're just harmless house pets dressed in silly costumes!
And this ship is just a toy.
Oh floogle! I really glumped up, Glermp!

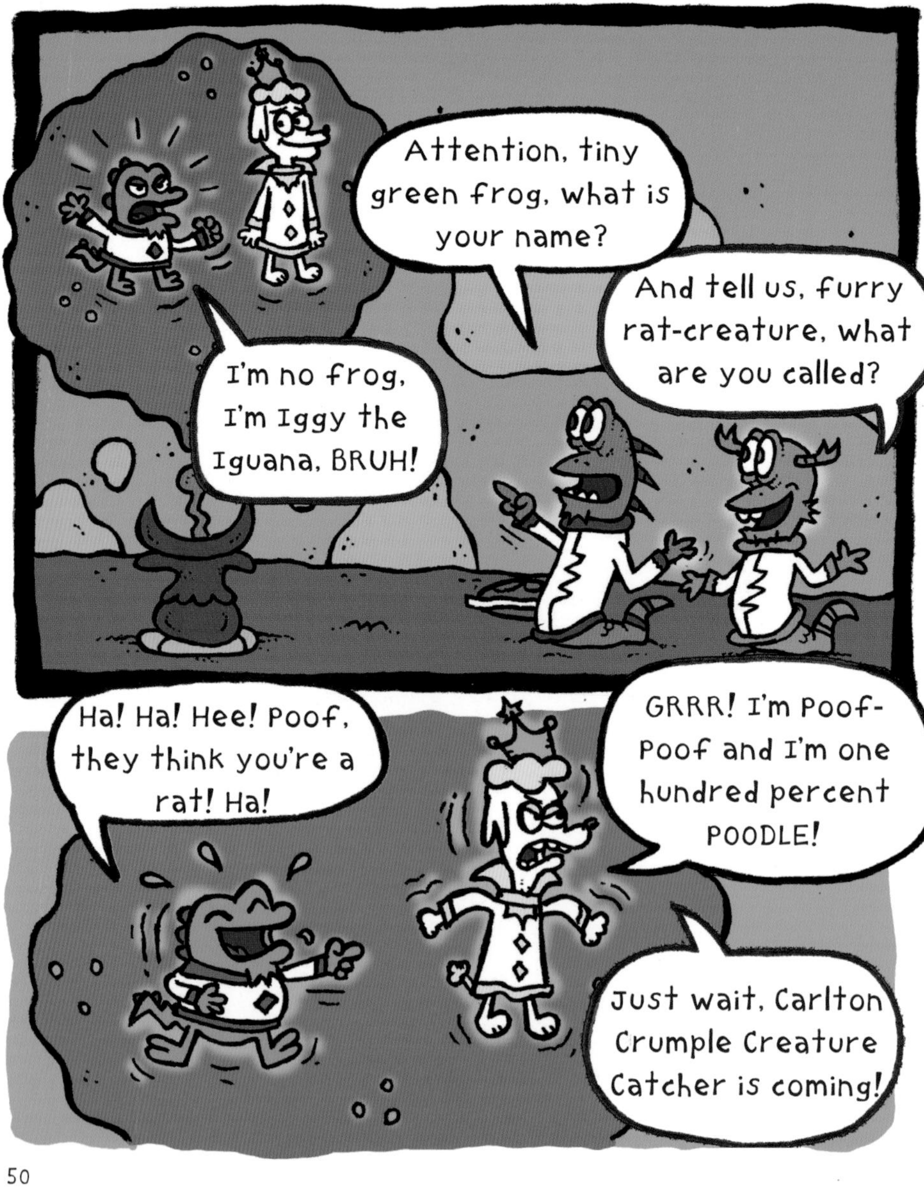
Attention, tiny green frog, what is your name?
I'm no frog, I'm Iggy the Iguana, BRUH!
And tell us, furry rat-creature, what are you called?
Ha! Ha! Hee! Poof, they think you're a rat! Ha!
GRRR! I'm Poof-Poof and I'm one hundred percent POODLE!
Just wait, Carlton Crumple Creature Catcher is coming!

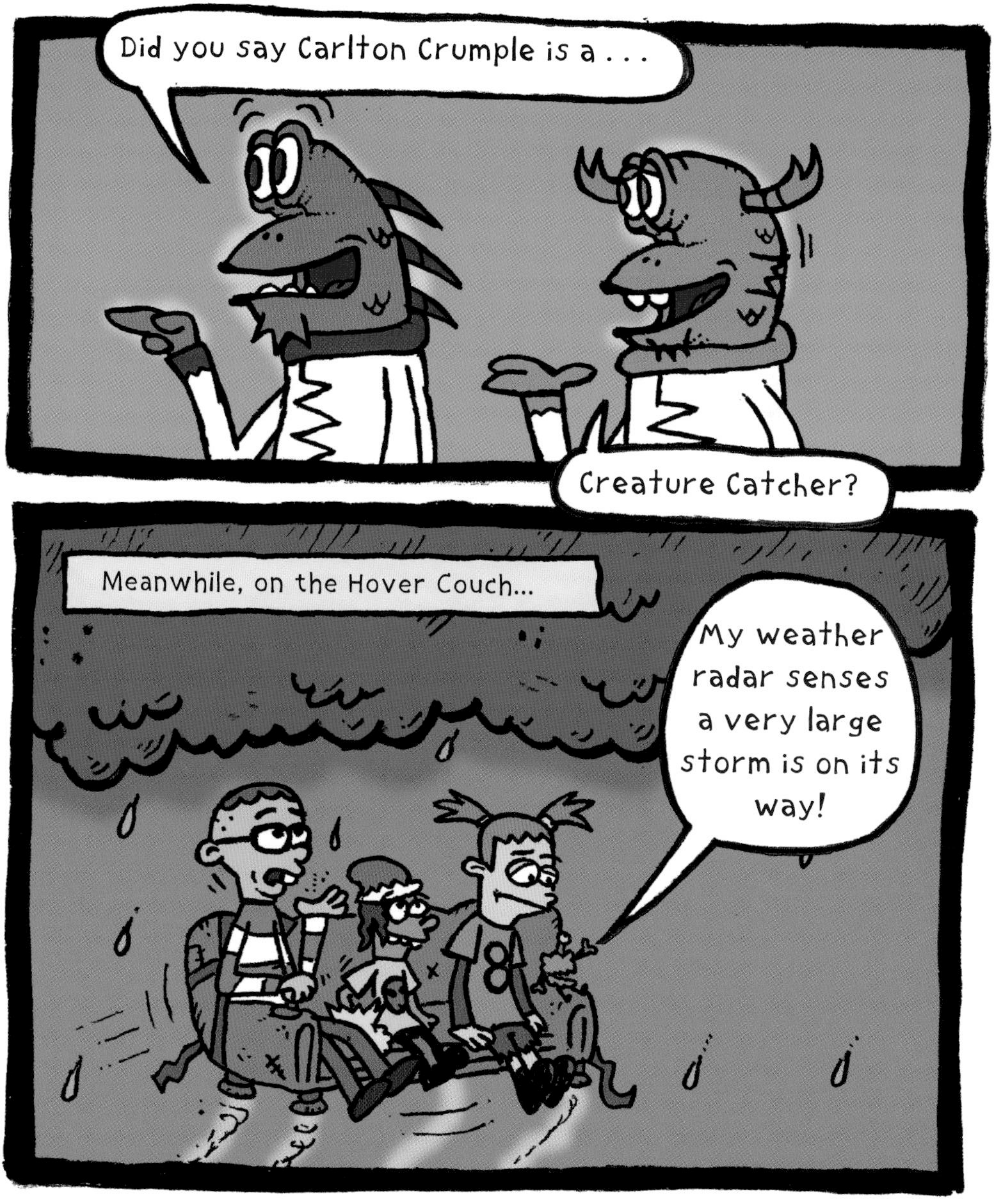
Did you say Carlton Crumple is a . . .
Creature Catcher?
Meanwhile, on the Hover Couch...
My weather radar senses a very large storm is on its way!

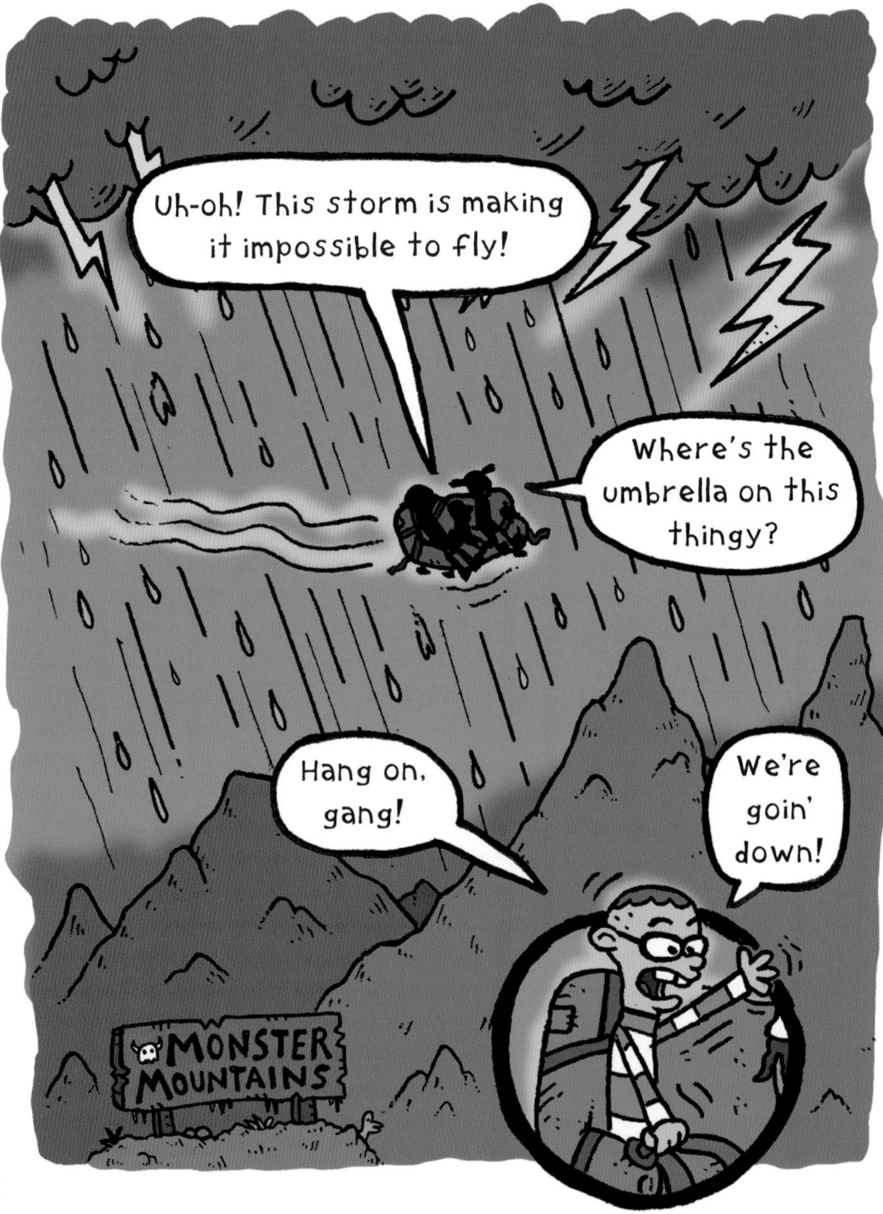
Uh-oh! This storm is making it impossible to fly!
Where's the umbrella on this thingy?
Hang on, gang!
We're goin' down!
MONSTER MOUNTAINS

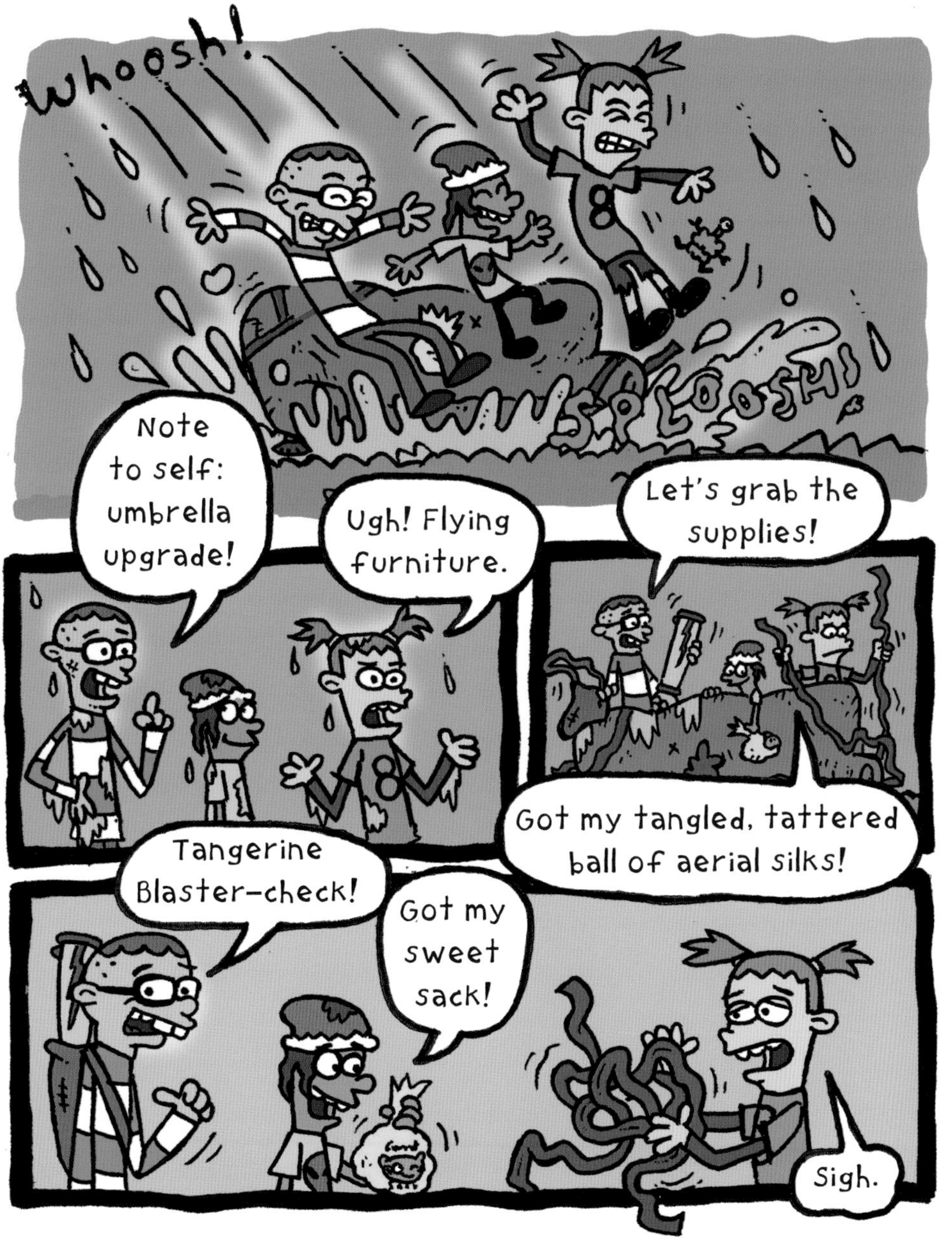
Whoosh!
SPLOOSH!
Note to self: umbrella upgrade!
Ugh! Flying furniture.
Let's grab the supplies!
Got my tangled, tattered ball of aerial silks!
Tangerine Blaster-check!
Got my sweet sack!
Sigh.

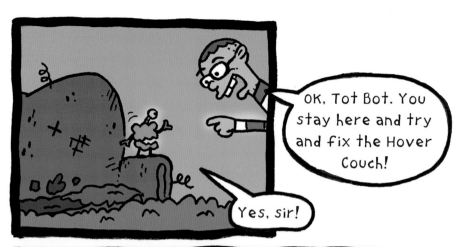

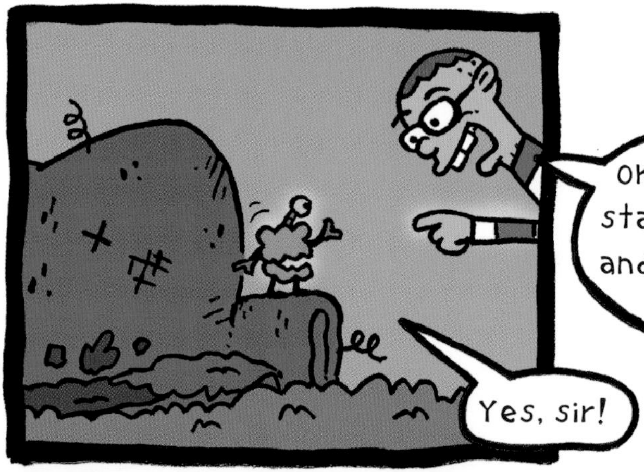
OK, Tot Bot. You stay here and try and fix the Hover Couch!
Yes, sir!

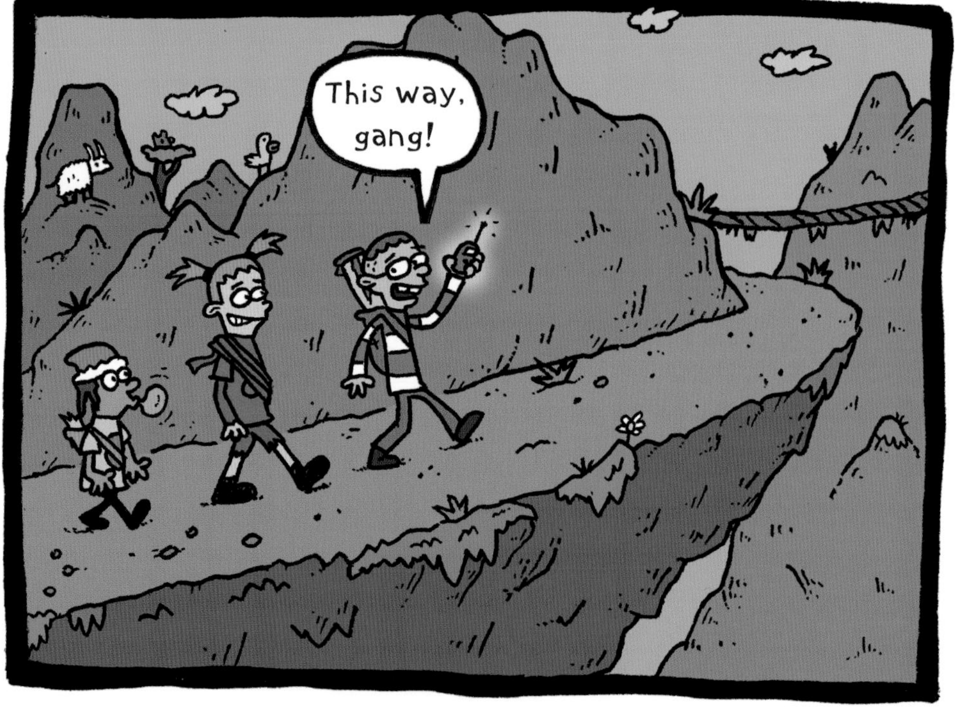
This way, gang!

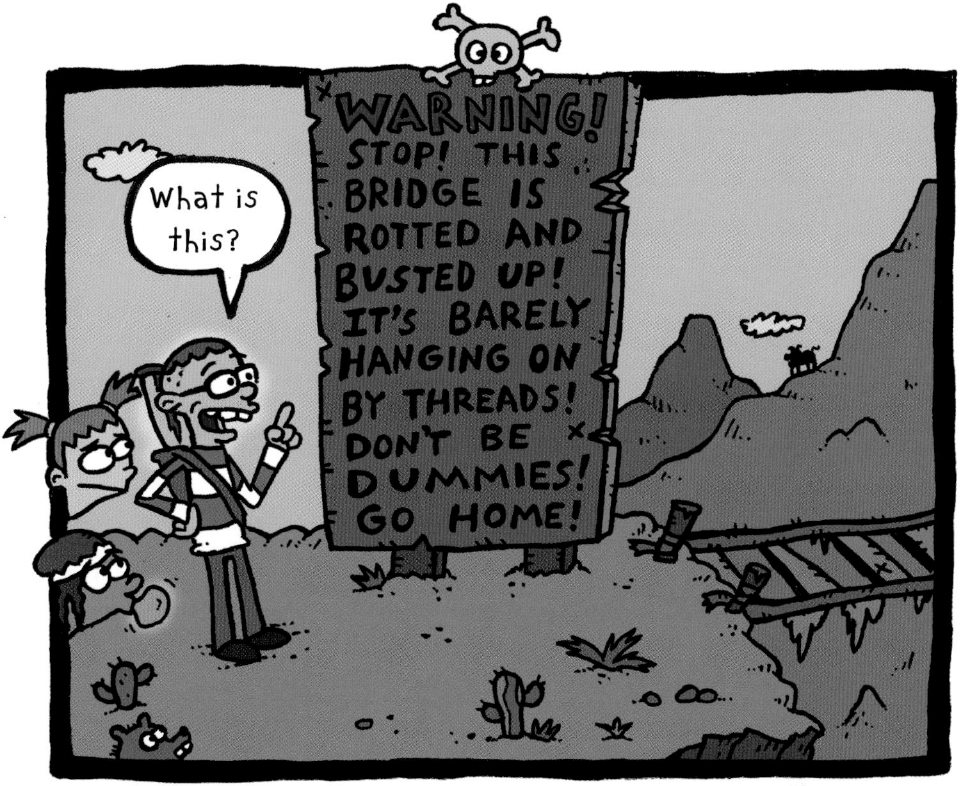

What is this?
WARNING!
STOP! THIS BRIDGE IS ROTTED AND BUSTED UP! IT'S BARELY HANGING ON BY THREADS! DON'T BE DUMMIES! GO HOME!

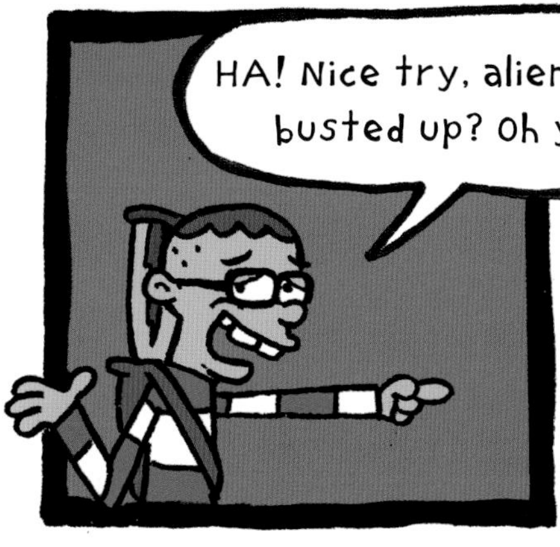

HA! Nice try, aliens! Rotted and busted up? Oh yeah, right!

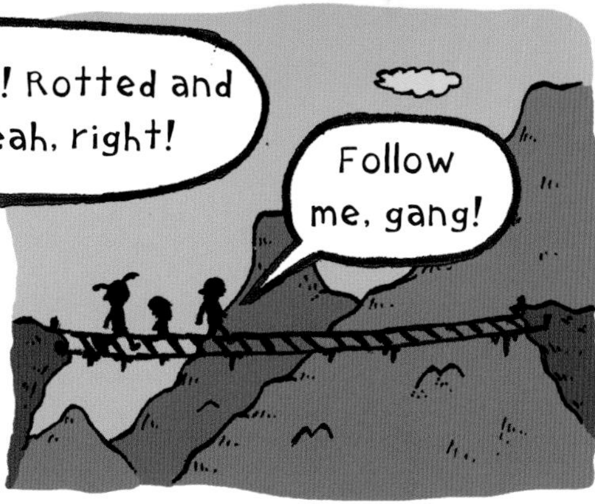

Follow me, gang!

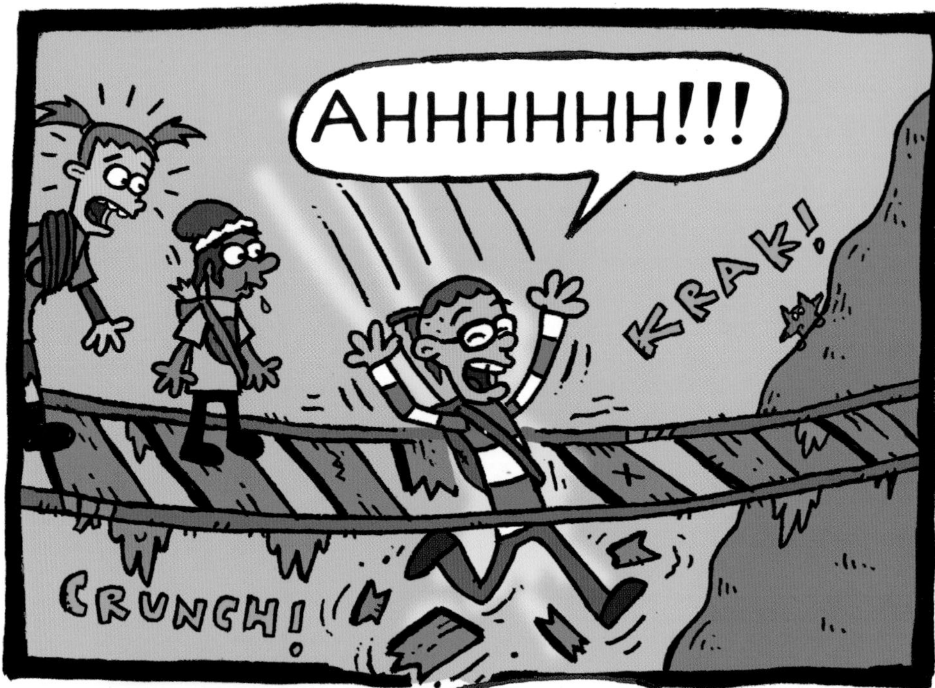
AHHHHHH!!!
KRAK!
CRUNCH!

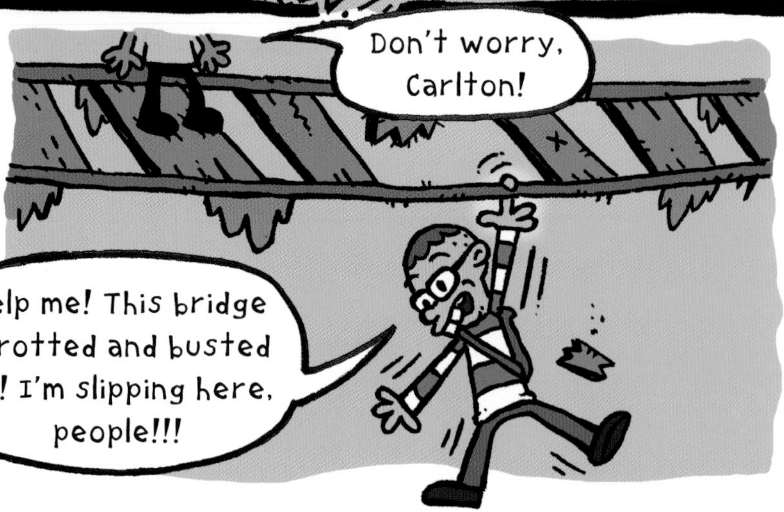
Don't worry, Carlton!
Help me! This bridge is rotted and busted up! I'm slipping here, people!!!

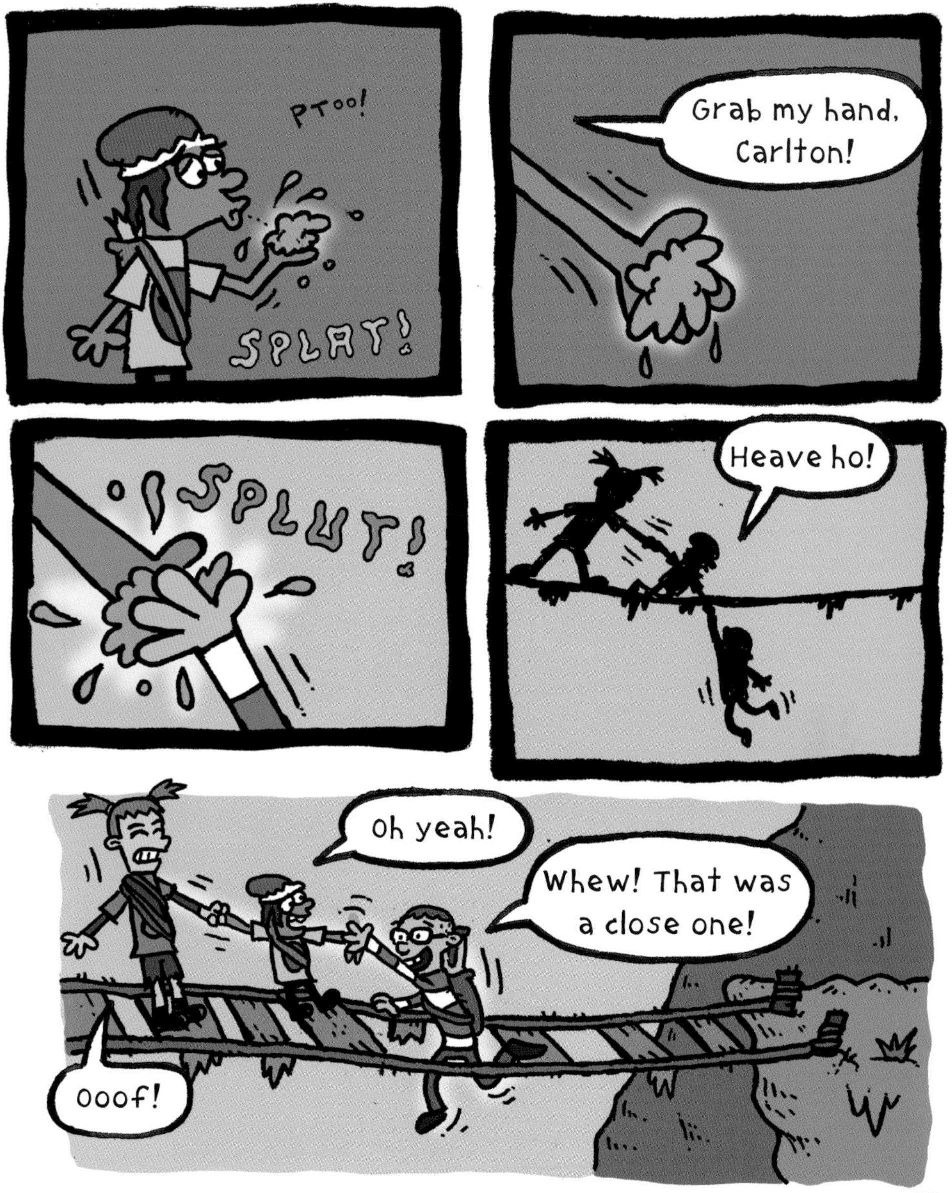
PTOO!
SPLAT!
Grab my hand, Carlton!
SPLUT!
Heave ho!
Oh yeah!
Whew! That was a close one!
ooof!

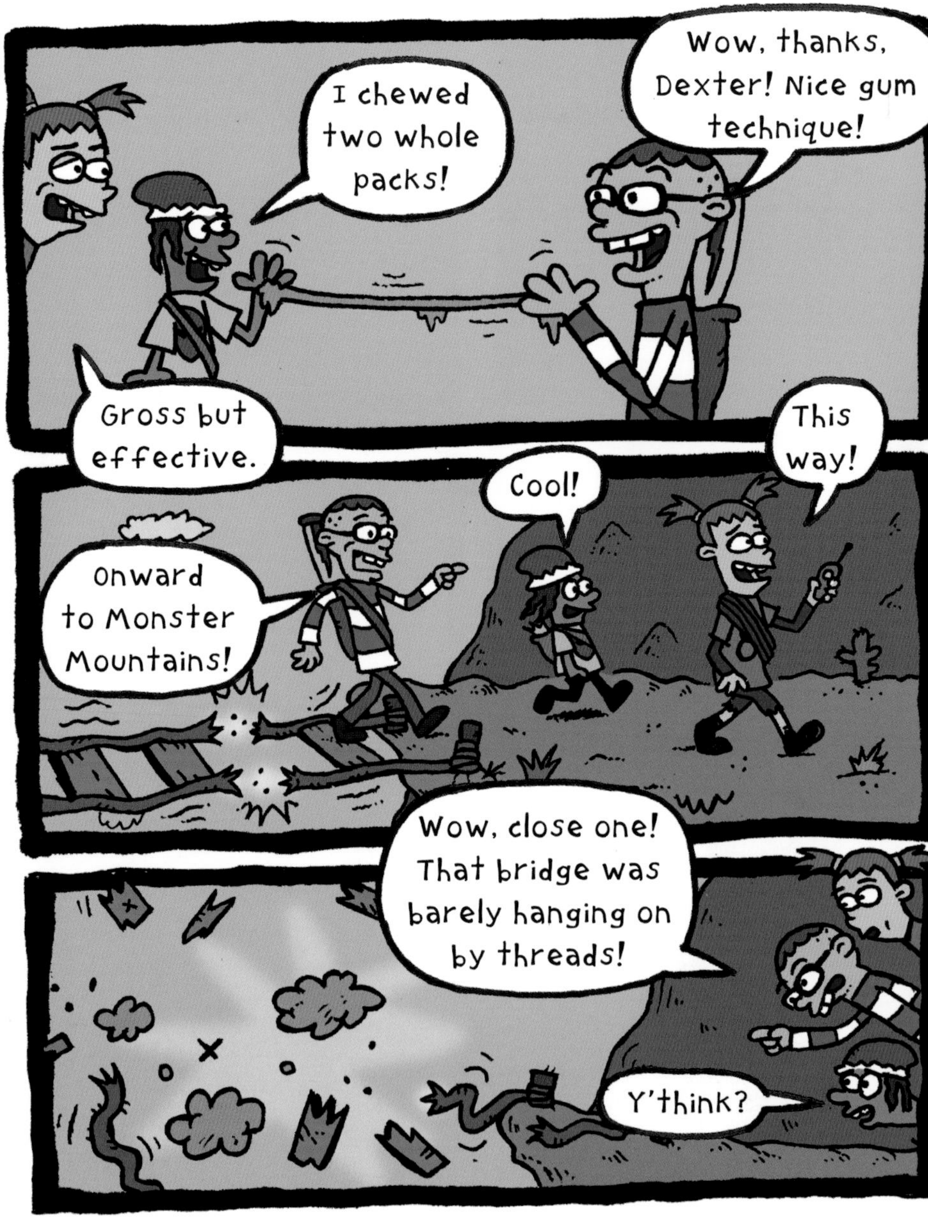
I chewed two whole packs!
Wow, thanks, Dexter! Nice gum technique!
Gross but effective.
Onward to Monster Mountains!
Cool!
This way!
Wow, close one! That bridge was barely hanging on by threads!
Y'think?

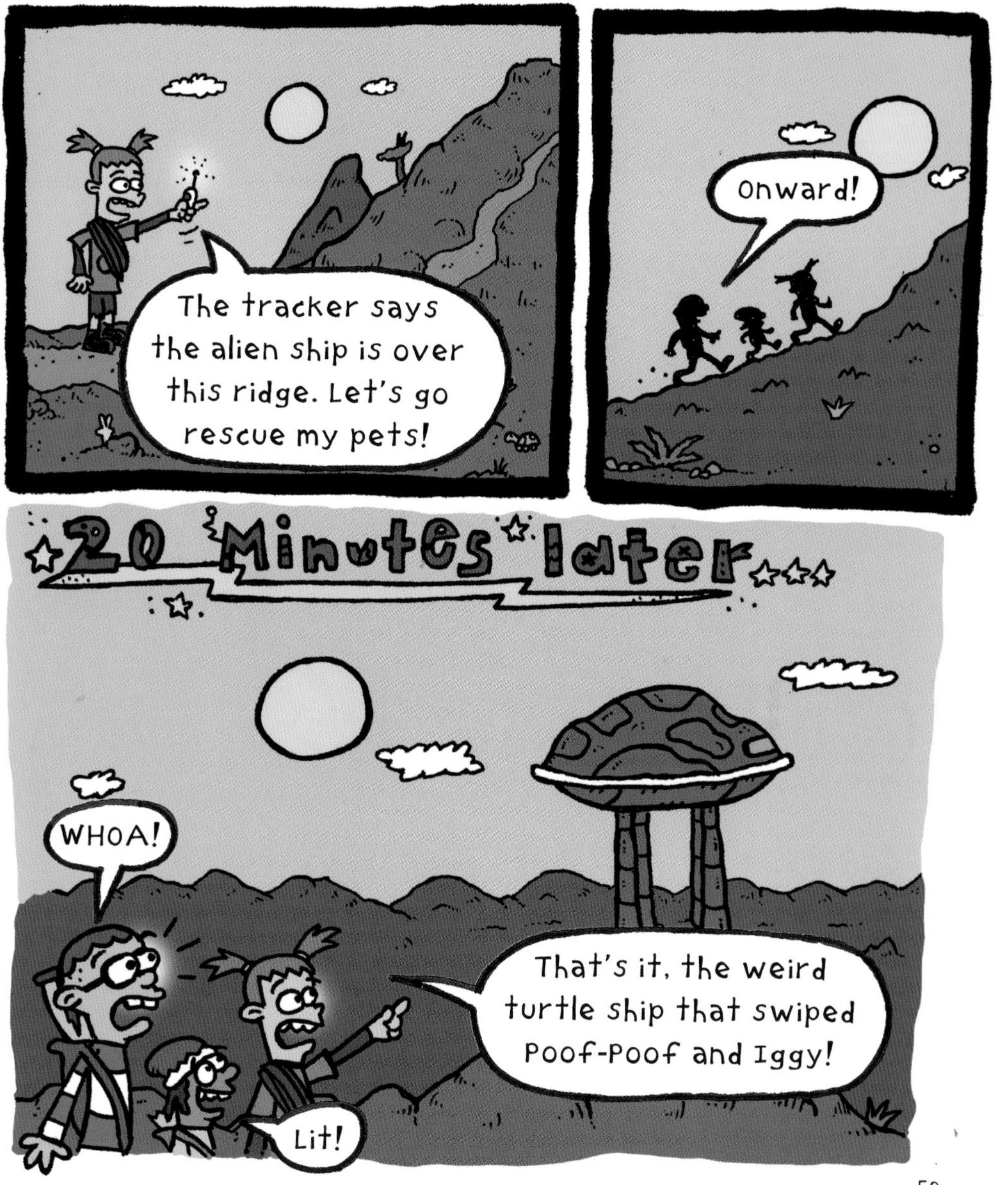
The tracker says the alien ship is over this ridge. Let's go rescue my pets!
Onward!
20 Minutes later
WHOA!
That's it, the weird turtle ship that swiped Poof-Poof and Iggy!
Lit!

CHAPTER 6

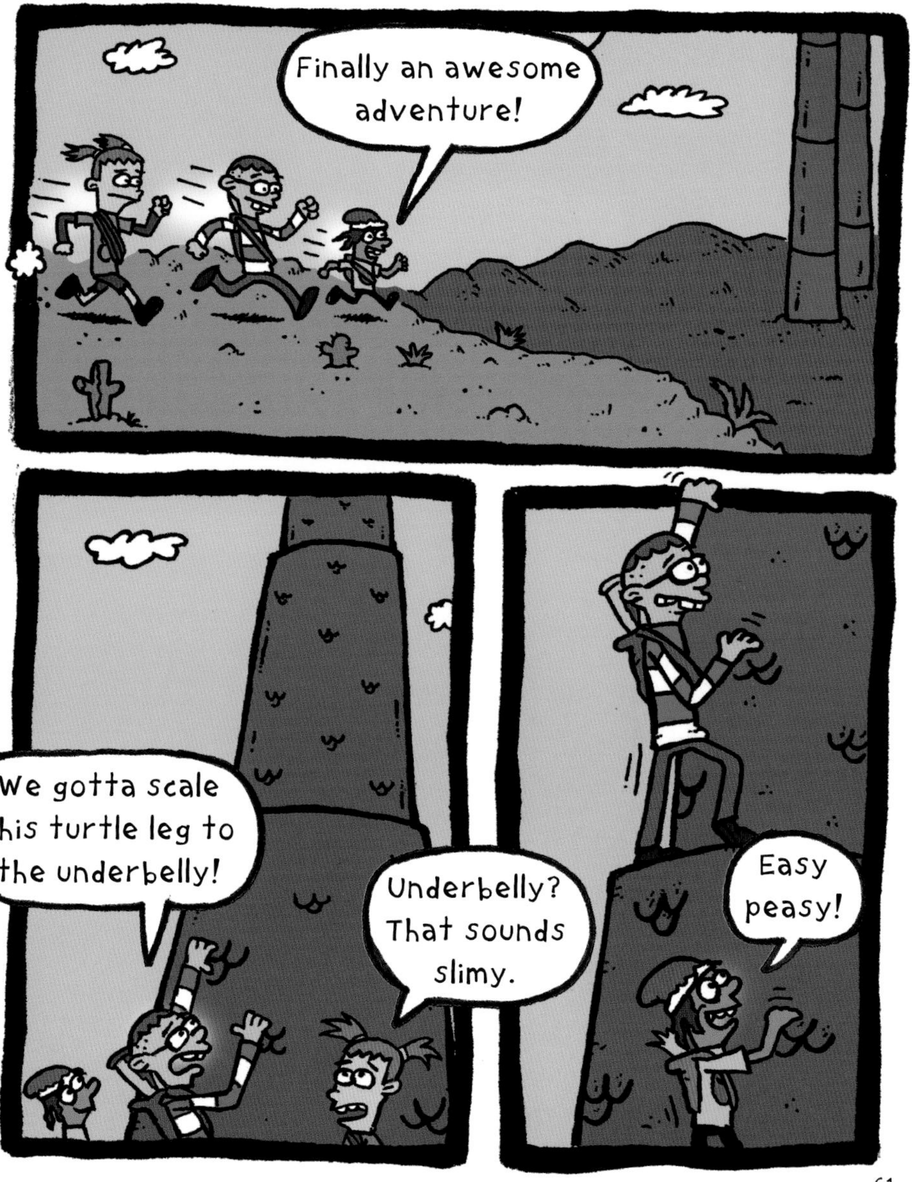
Finally an awesome adventure!
We gotta scale this turtle leg to the underbelly!
Underbelly? That sounds slimy.
Easy peasy!

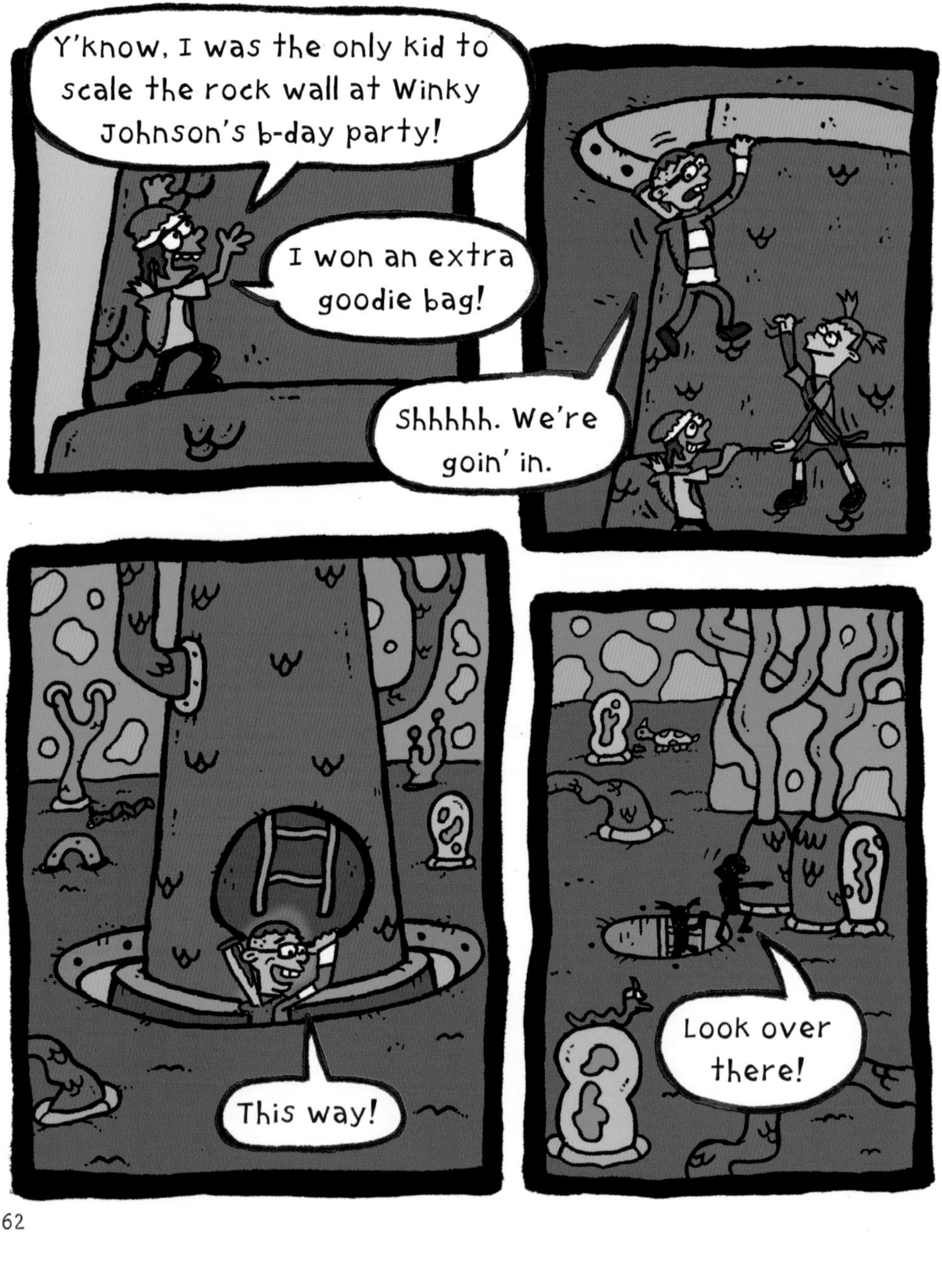
Y'know, I was the only kid to scale the rock wall at Winky Johnson's b-day party!
I won an extra goodie bag!
Shhhhh. We're goin' in.
This way!
Look over there!

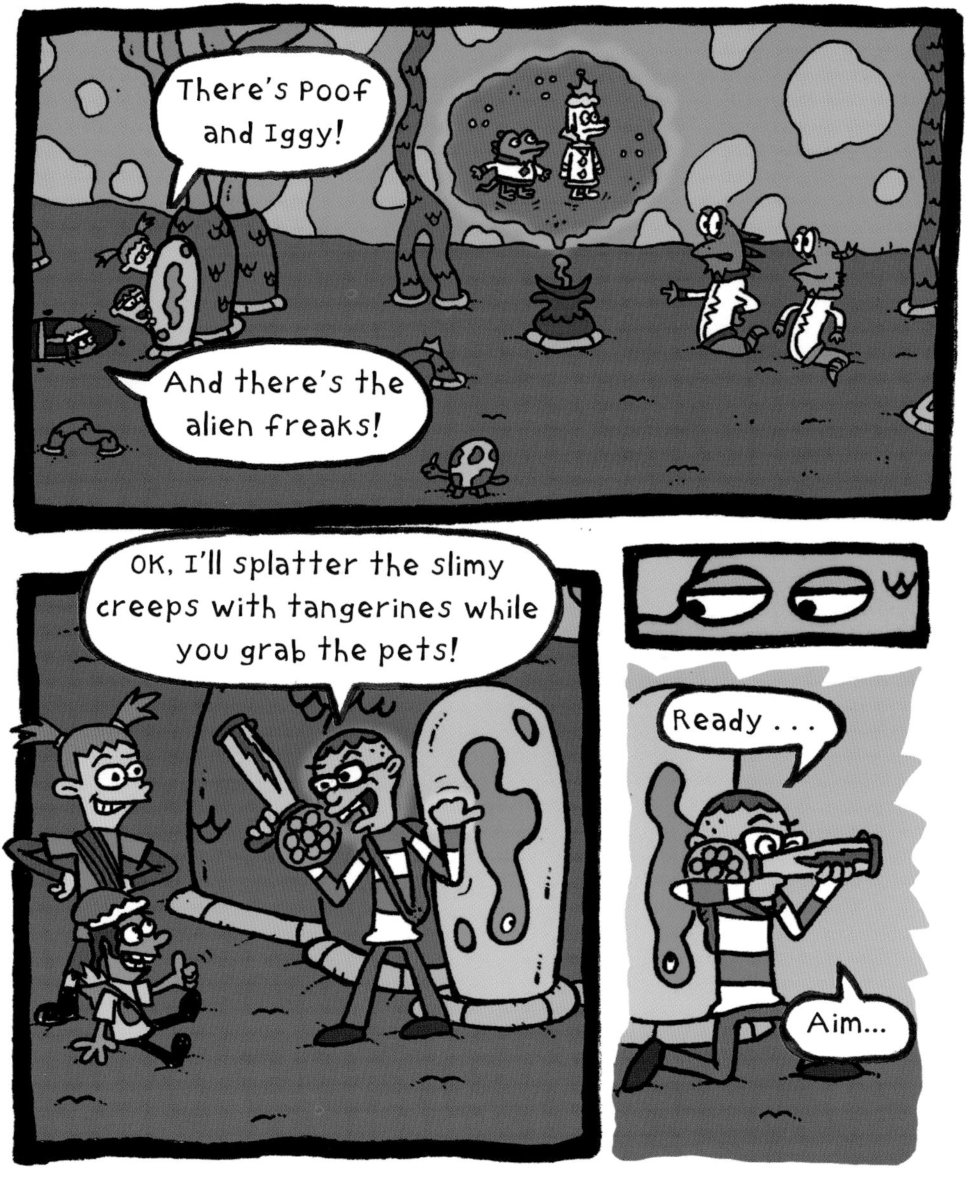
There's Poof and Iggy!
And there's the alien freaks!
OK, I'll splatter the slimy creeps with tangerines while you grab the pets!
Ready . . .
Aim...

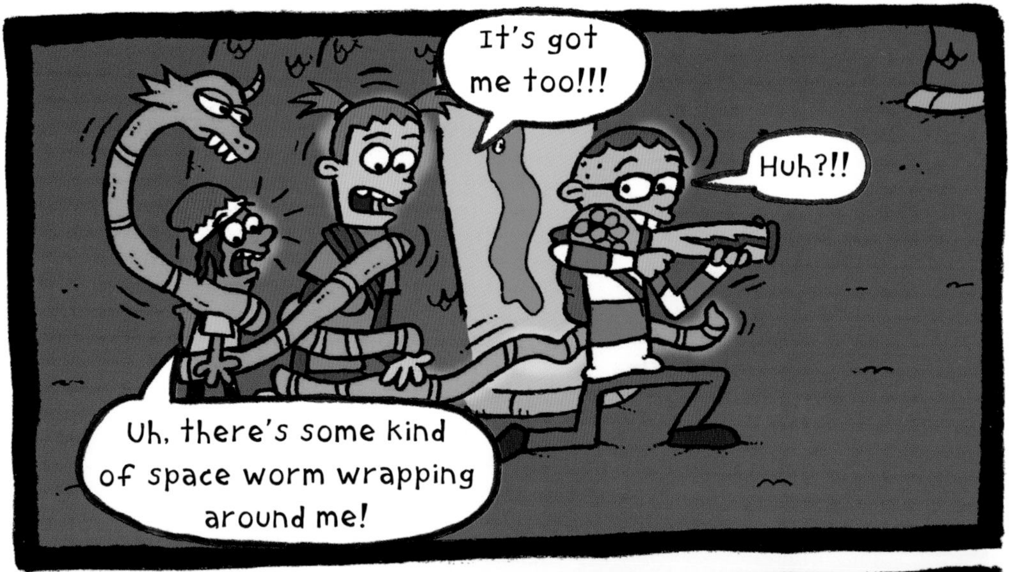
It's got me too!!!
Huh?!!
Uh, there's some kind of space worm wrapping around me!

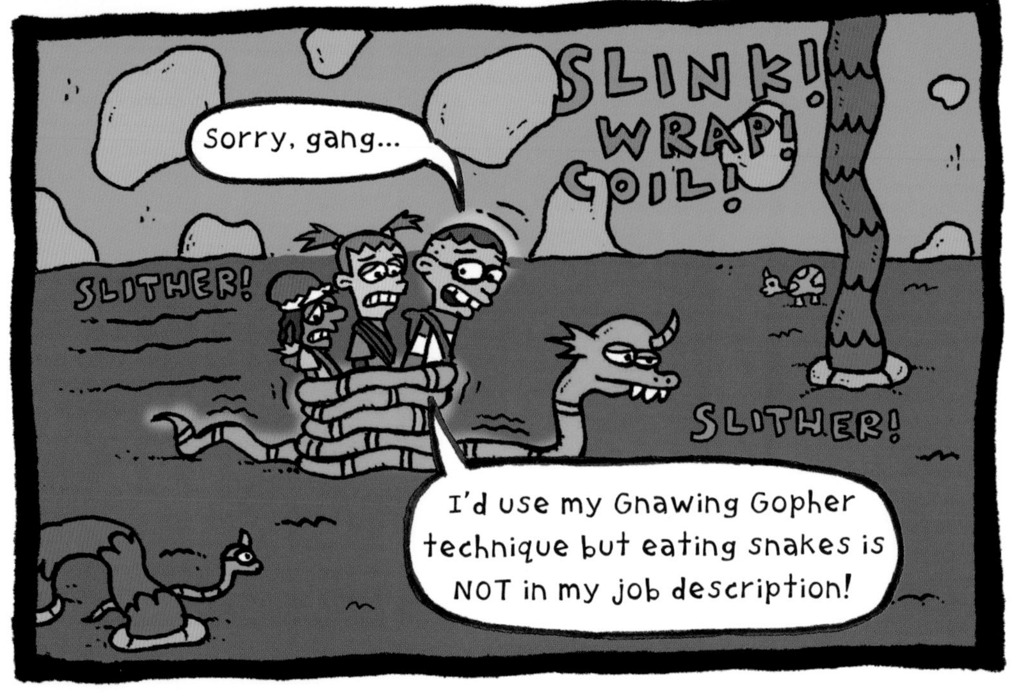
SLINK!
WRAP!
COIL!
Sorry, gang...
SLITHER!
SLITHER!
I'd use my Gnawing Gopher technique but eating snakes is NOT in my job description!

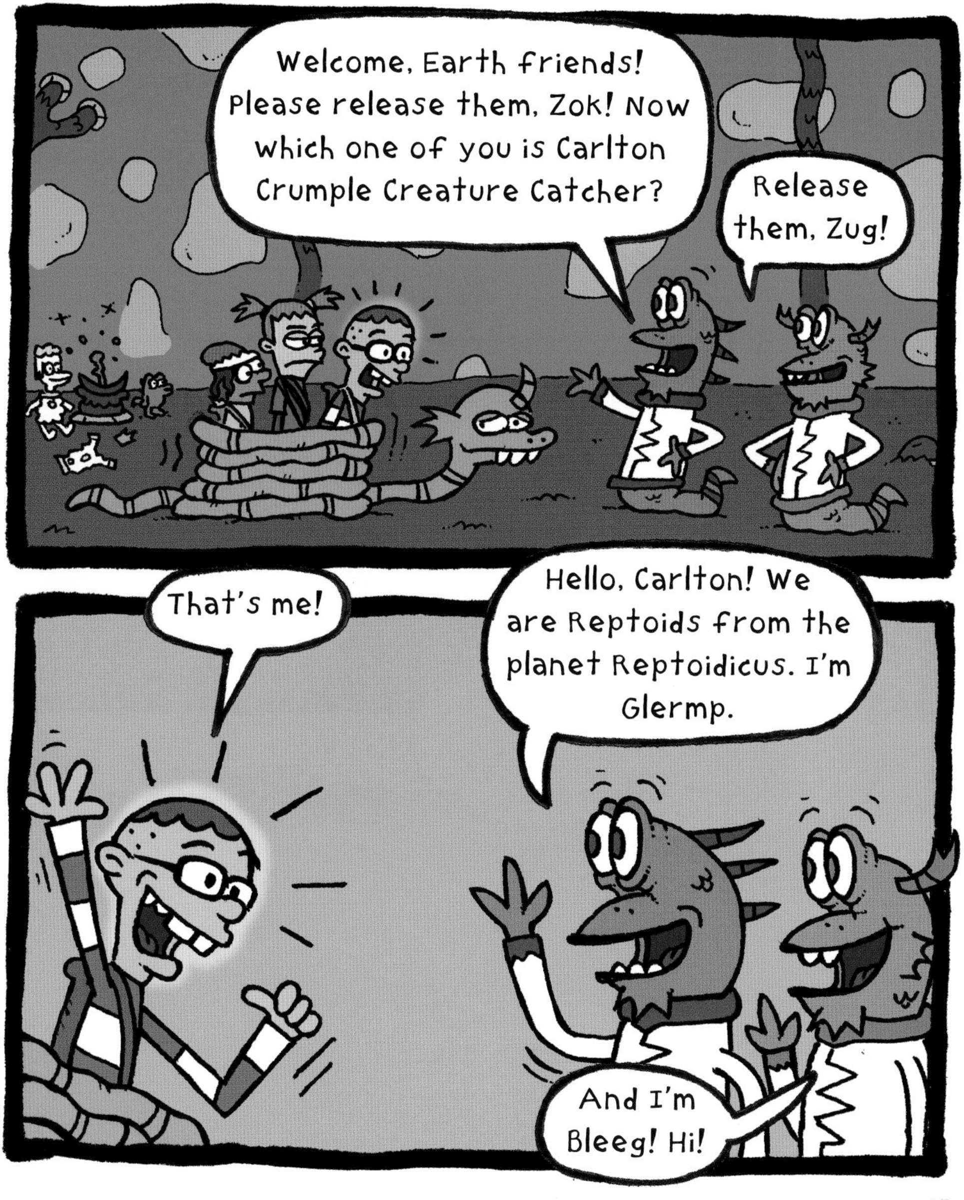
Welcome, Earth friends! Please release them, Zok! Now which one of you is Carlton Crumple Creature Catcher?
Release them, Zug!
That's me!
Hello, Carlton! We are Reptoids from the planet Reptoidicus. I'm Glermp.
And I'm Bleeg! Hi!

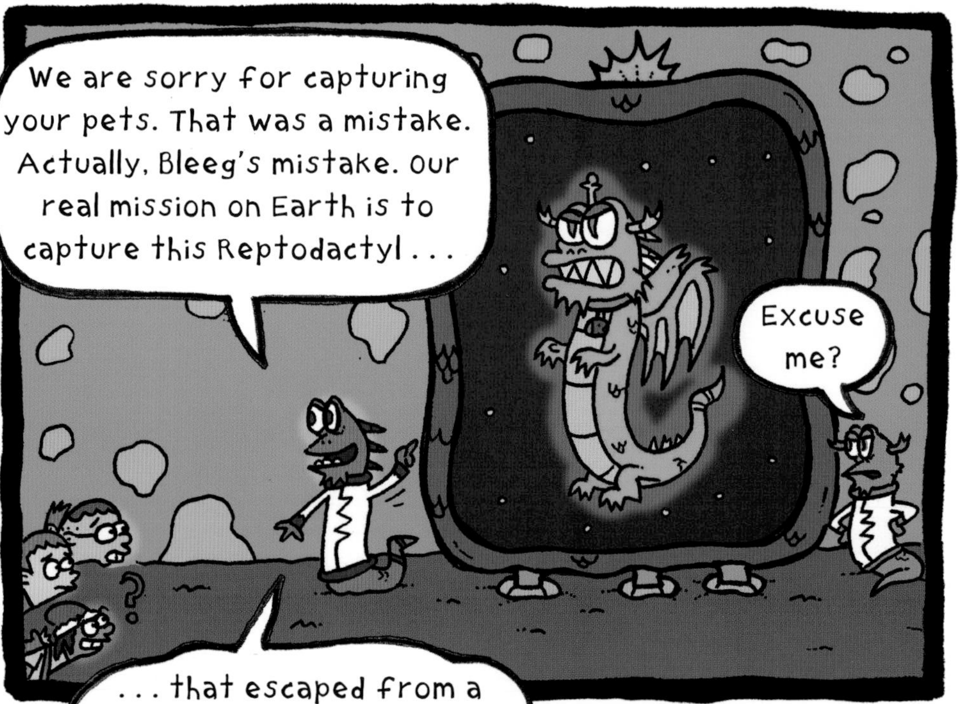
We are sorry for capturing your pets. That was a mistake. Actually, Bleeg's mistake. Our real mission on Earth is to capture this Reptodactyl . . .
Excuse me?
?

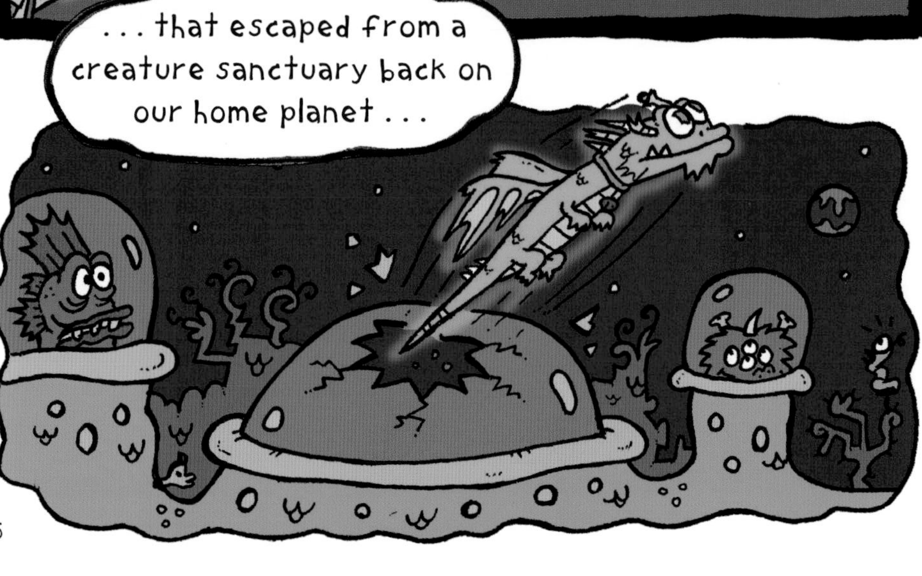
. . . that escaped from a creature sanctuary back on our home planet . . .

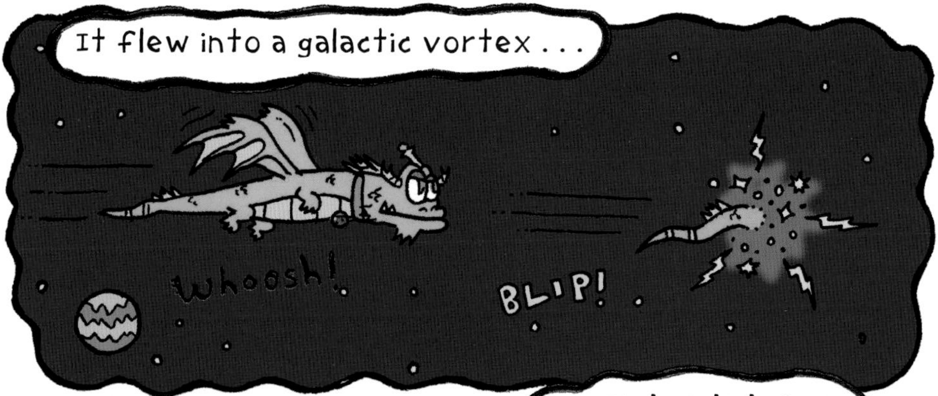
It flew into a galactic vortex . . .
Whoosh!
BLIP!

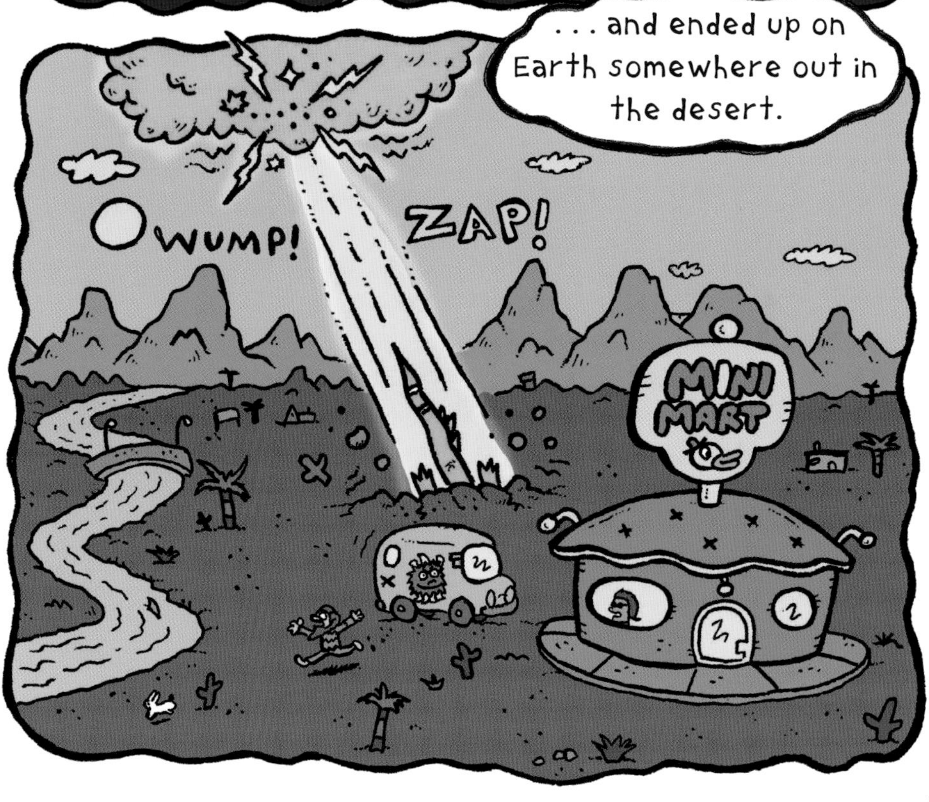
. . . and ended up on Earth somewhere out in the desert.
WUMP!
ZAP!
MINI MART

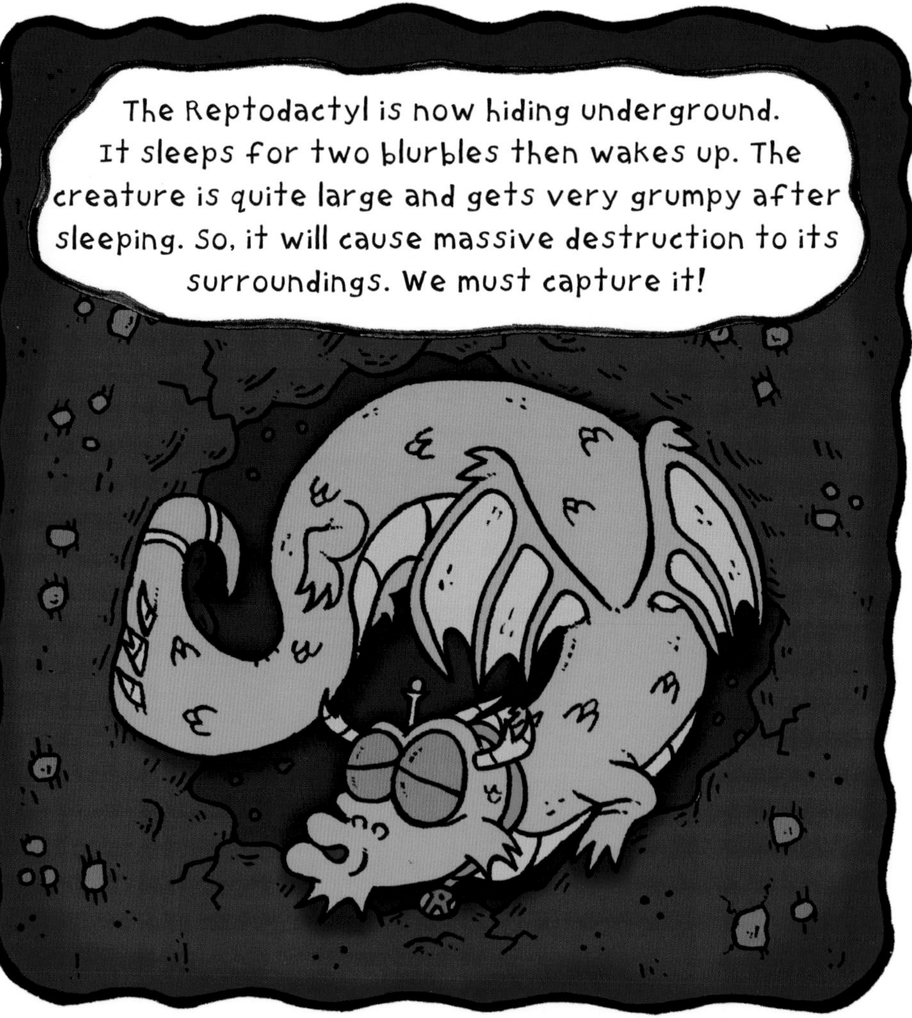
The Reptodactyl is now hiding underground. It sleeps for two blurbles then wakes up. The creature is quite large and gets very grumpy after sleeping. So, it will cause massive destruction to its surroundings. We must capture it!

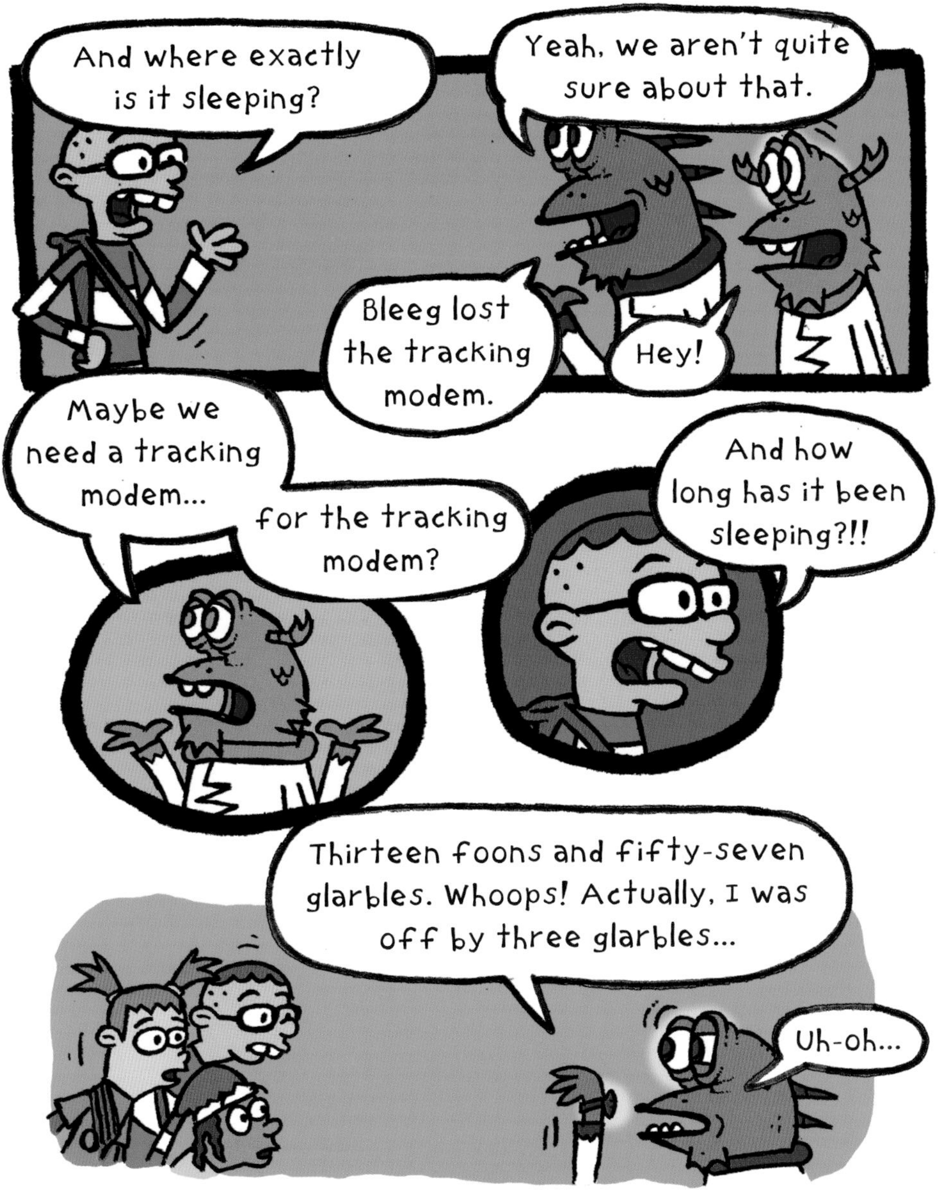
And where exactly is it sleeping?
Yeah, we aren't quite sure about that.
Bleeg lost the tracking modem.
Hey!
Maybe we need a tracking modem...
for the tracking modem?
And how long has it been sleeping?!!
Thirteen foons and fifty-seven glarbles. Whoops! Actually, I was off by three glarbles...
Uh-oh...

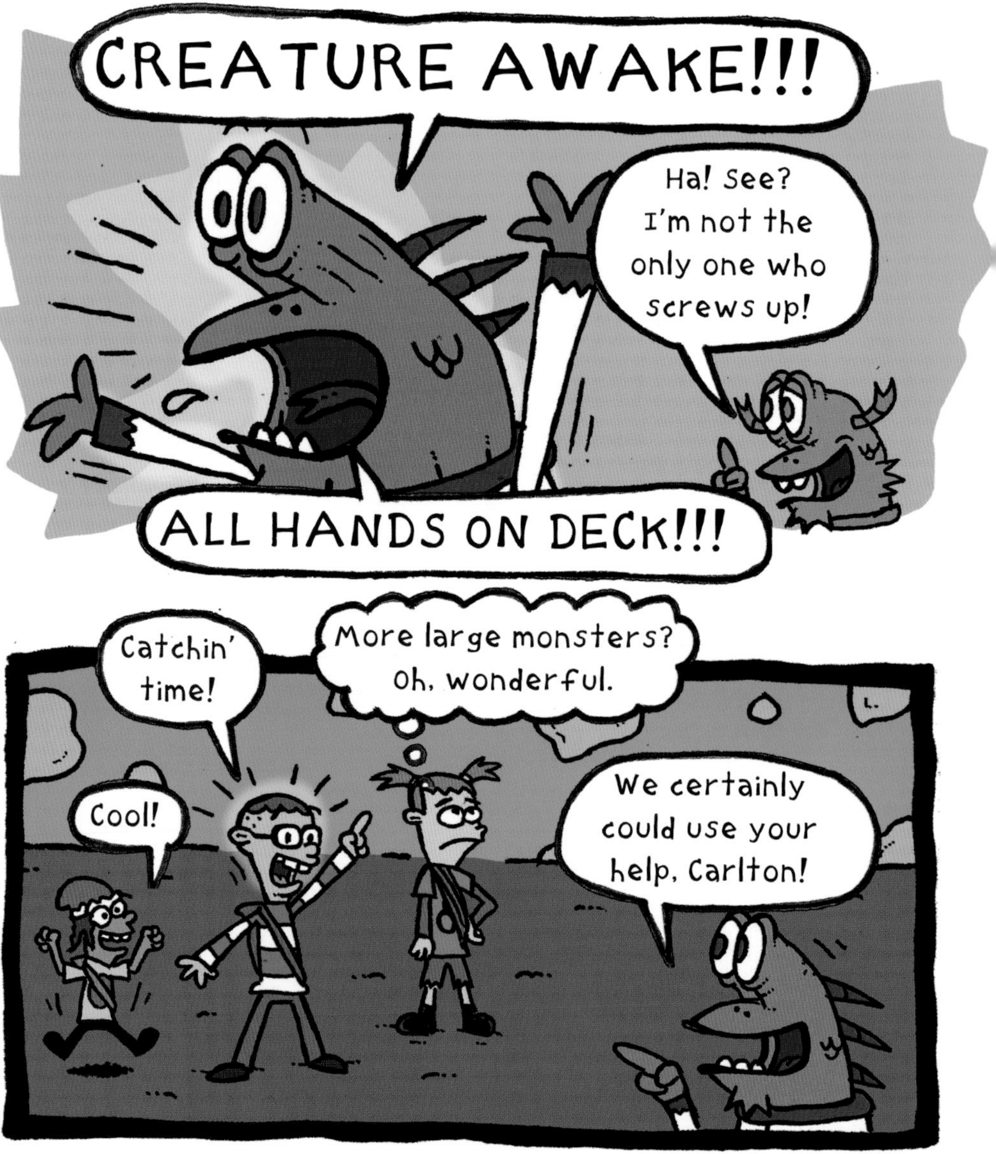
CREATURE AWAKE!!!
Ha! See? I'm not the only one who screws up!
ALL HANDS ON DECK!!!
Catchin' time!
More large monsters? Oh, wonderful.
Cool!
We certainly could use your help, Carlton!

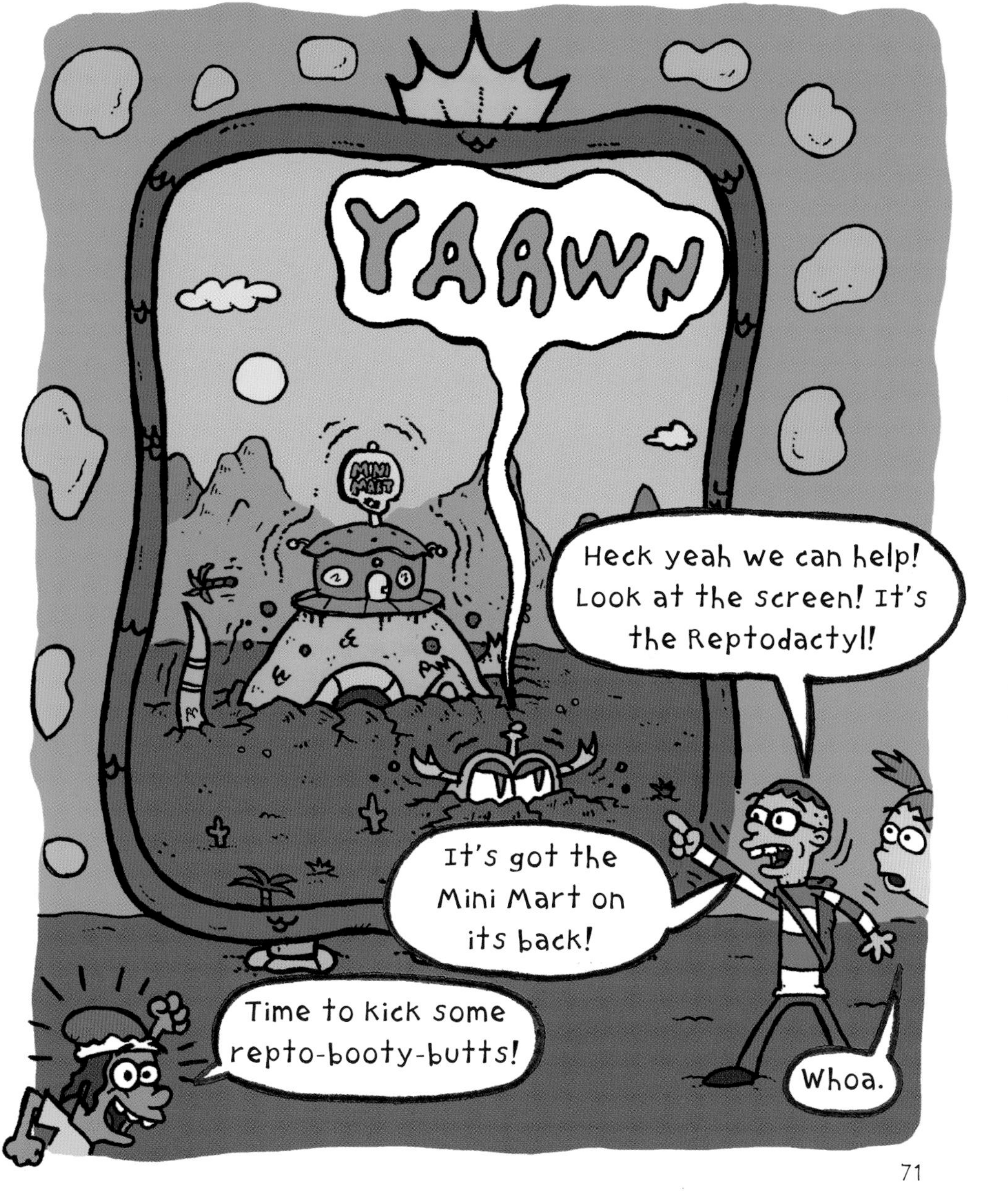

YAAWN
MINI MART
Heck yeah we can help! Look at the screen! It's the Reptodactyl!
It's got the Mini Mart on its back!
Time to kick some repto-booty-butts!
Whoa.

CHAPTER 7

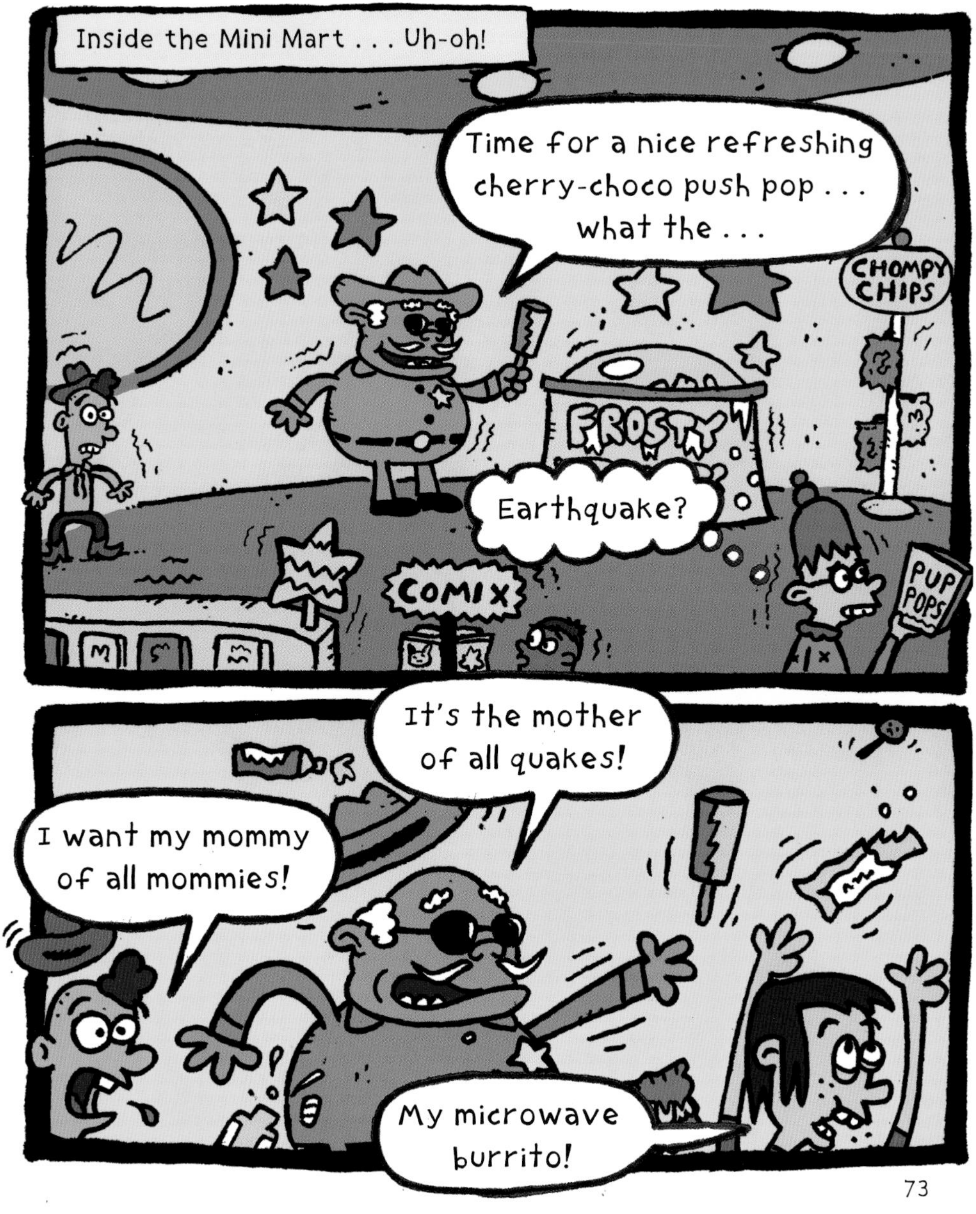
Inside the Mini Mart . . . Uh-oh!
Time for a nice refreshing cherry-choco push pop . . . what the . . .
CHOMPY CHIPS
FROSTY
Earthquake?
COMIX
PUP POPS
I want my mommy of all mommies!
It's the mother of all quakes!
My microwave burrito!

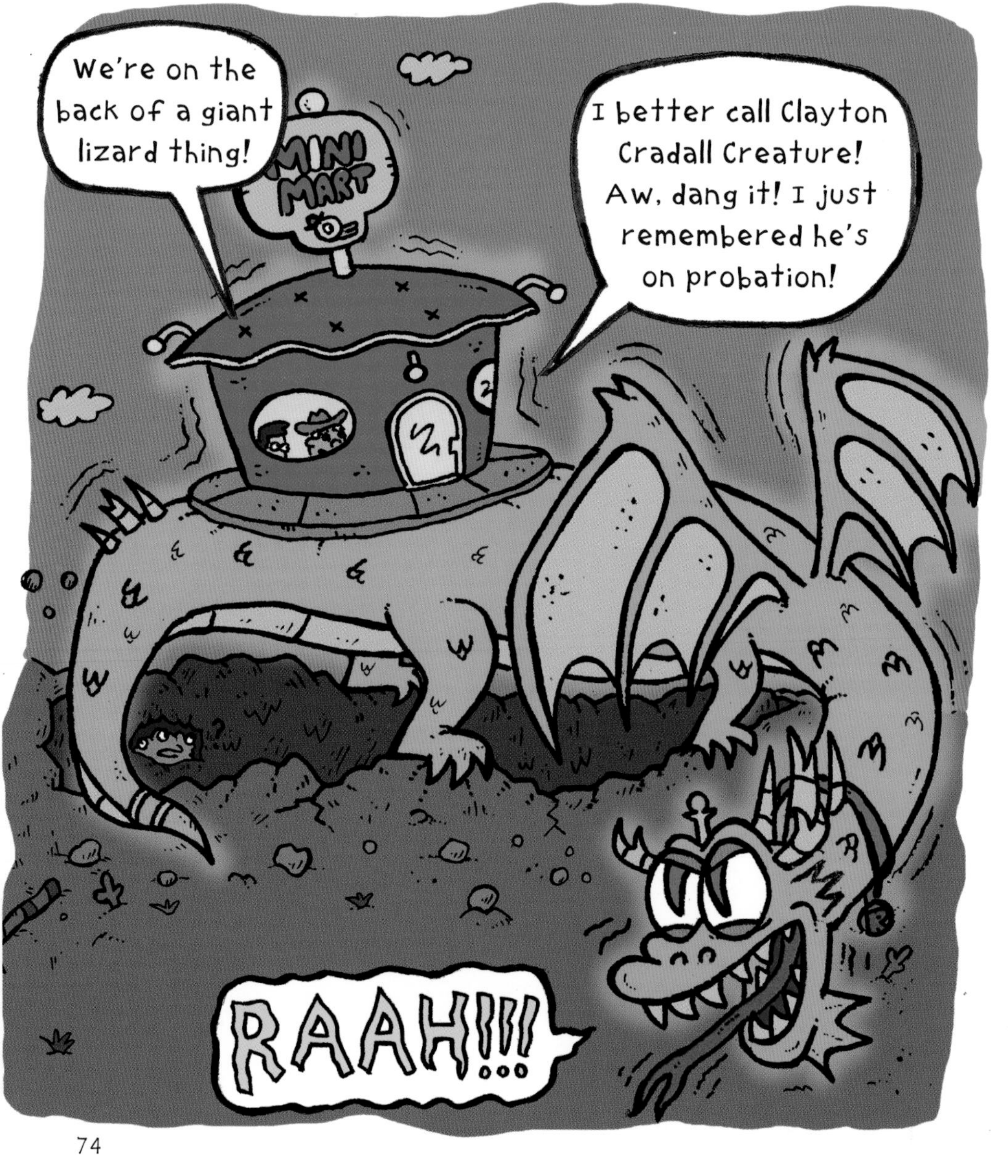
We're on the back of a giant lizard thing!
MINI MART
I better call Clayton Cradall Creature! Aw, dang it! I just remembered he's on probation!
RAAH!!!

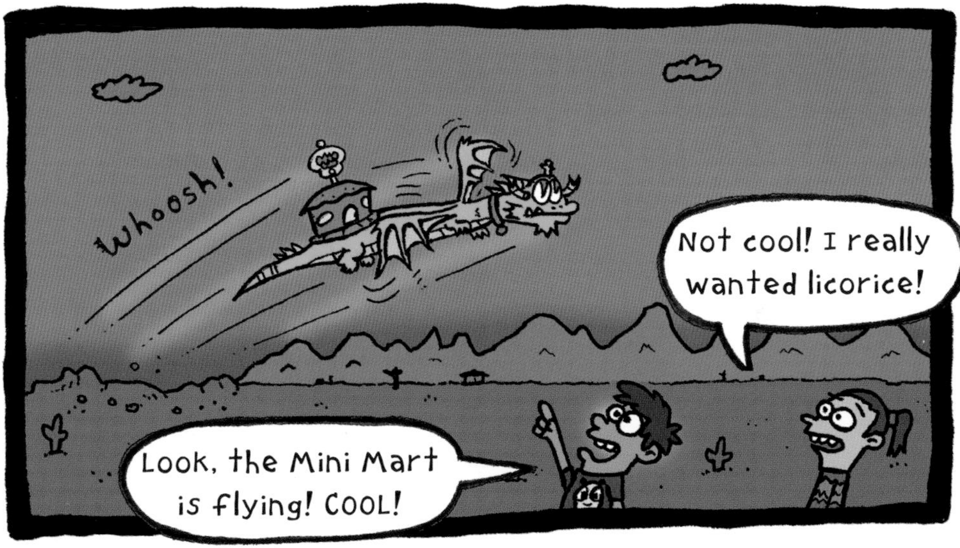
Whoosh!
Not cool! I really wanted licorice!
Look, the Mini Mart is flying! COOL!

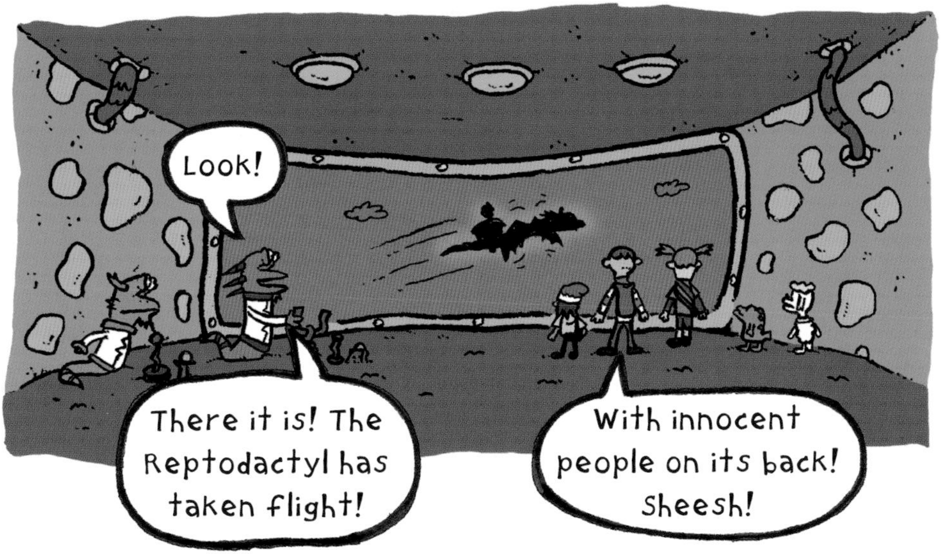
Look!
There it is! The Reptodactyl has taken flight!
With innocent people on its back! Sheesh!

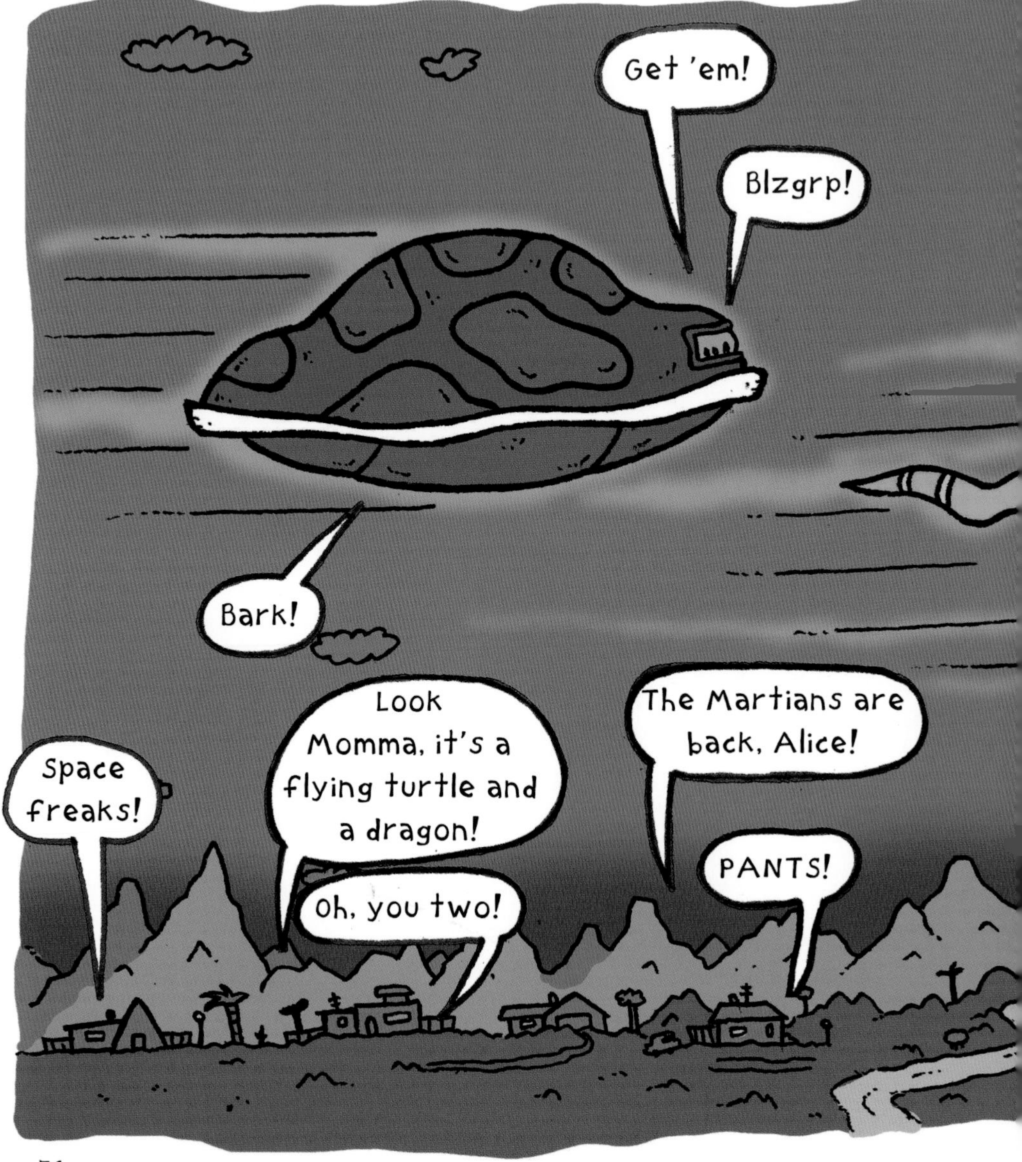
Get 'em!
Blzgrp!
Bark!
Space freaks!
Look Momma, it's a flying turtle and a dragon!
Oh, you two!
The Martians are back, Alice!
PANTS!

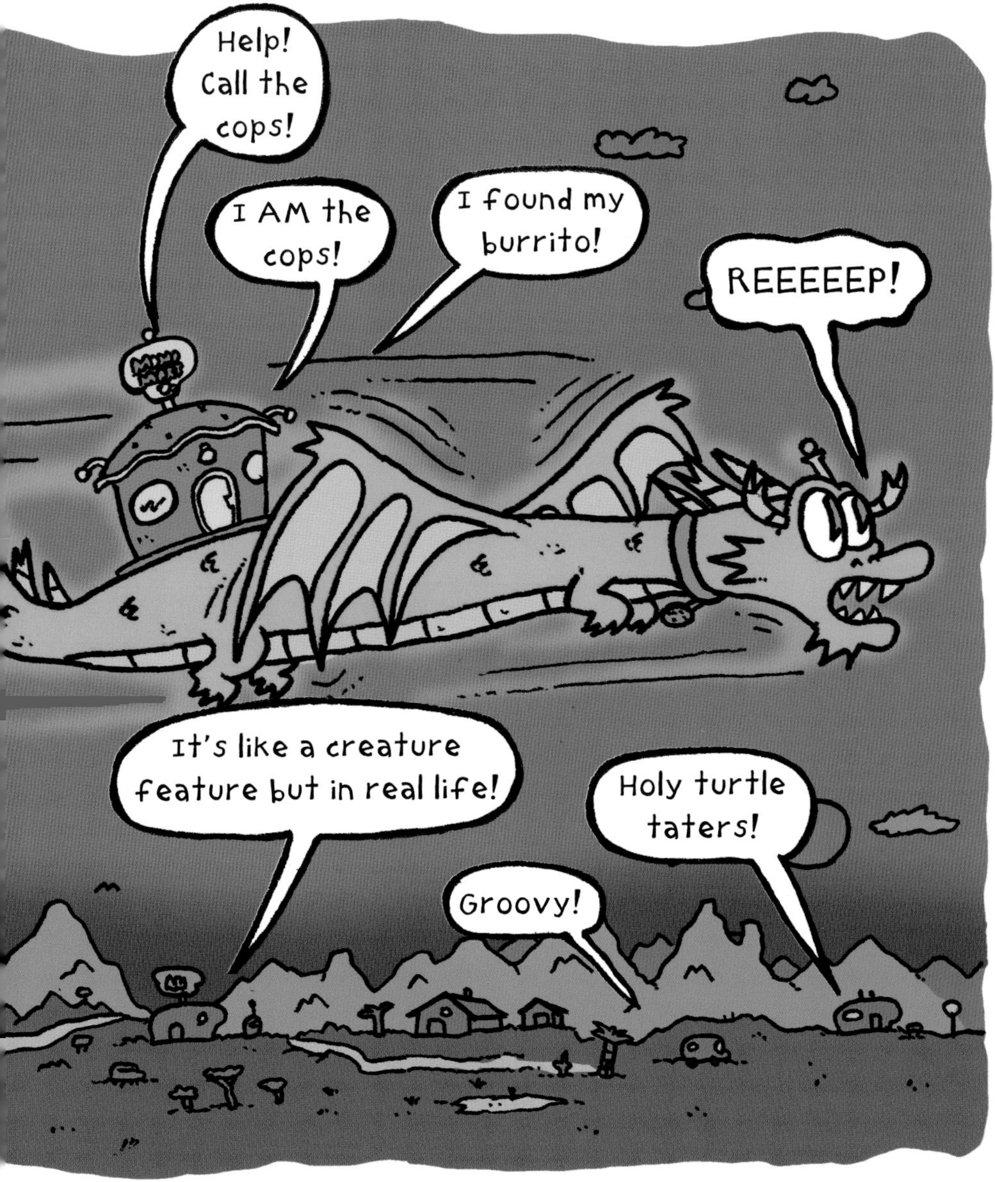
Help! Call the cops!
I AM the cops!
I found my burrito!
REEEEEP!
It's like a creature feature but in real life!
Groovy!
Holy turtle taters!

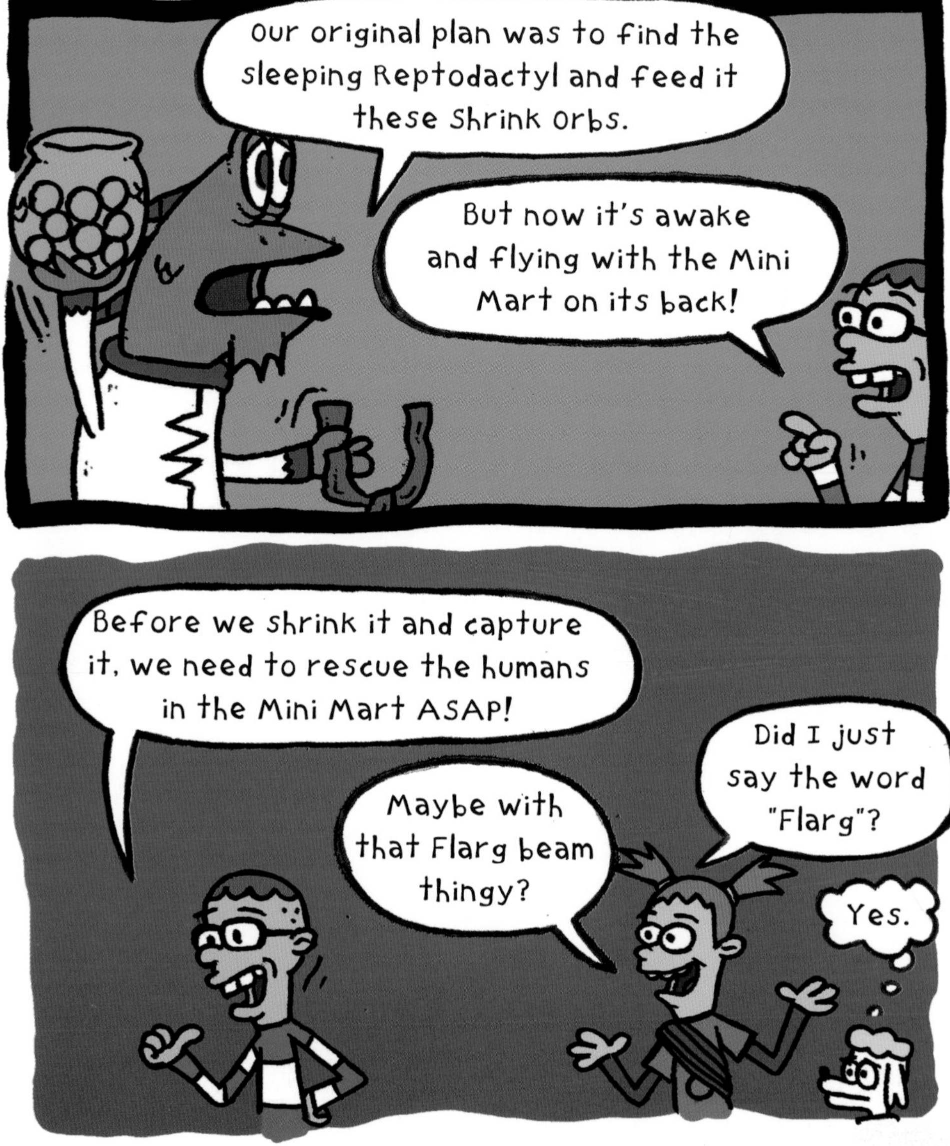
Our original plan was to find the sleeping Reptodactyl and feed it these Shrink Orbs.
But now it's awake and flying with the Mini Mart on its back!
Before we shrink it and capture it, we need to rescue the humans in the Mini Mart ASAP!
Maybe with that Flarg beam thingy?
Did I just say the word "Flarg"?
Yes.

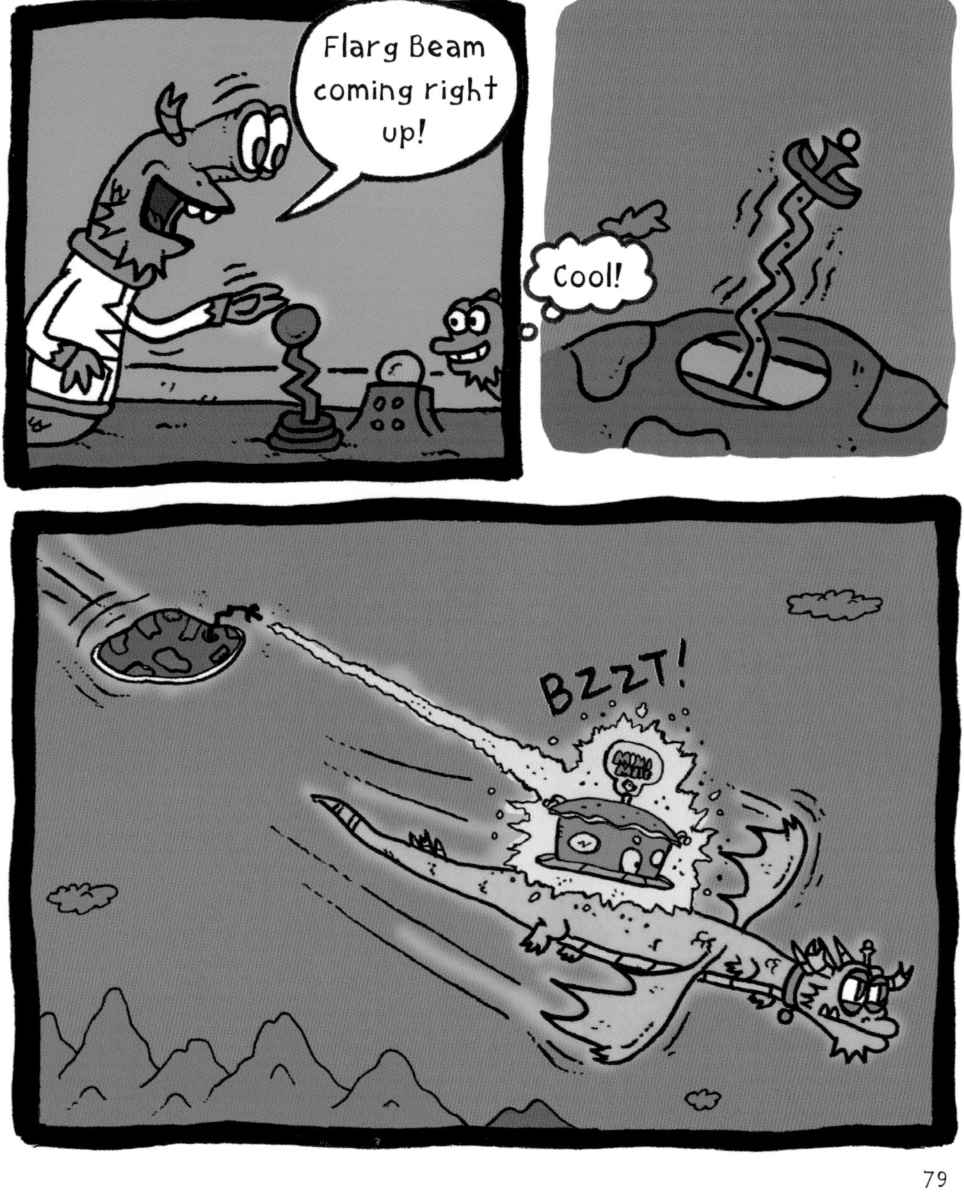
Flarg Beam coming right up!
Cool!
BZZT!

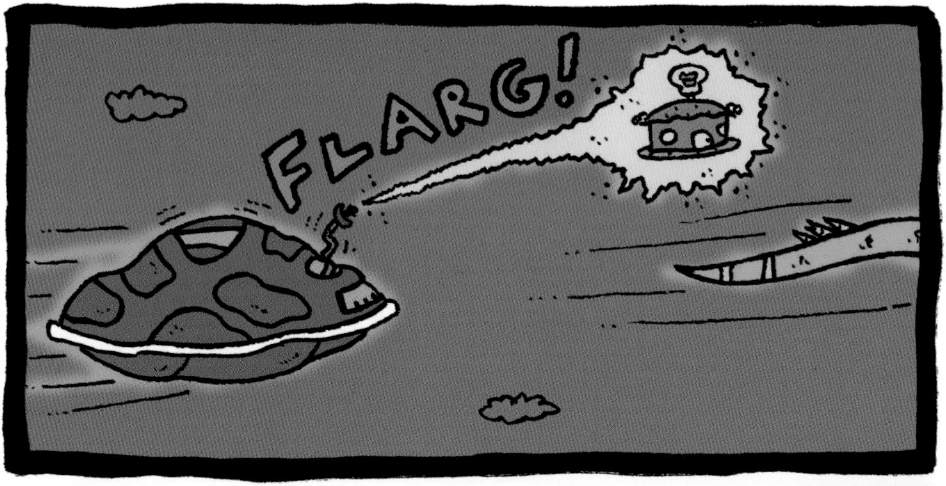
FLARG!

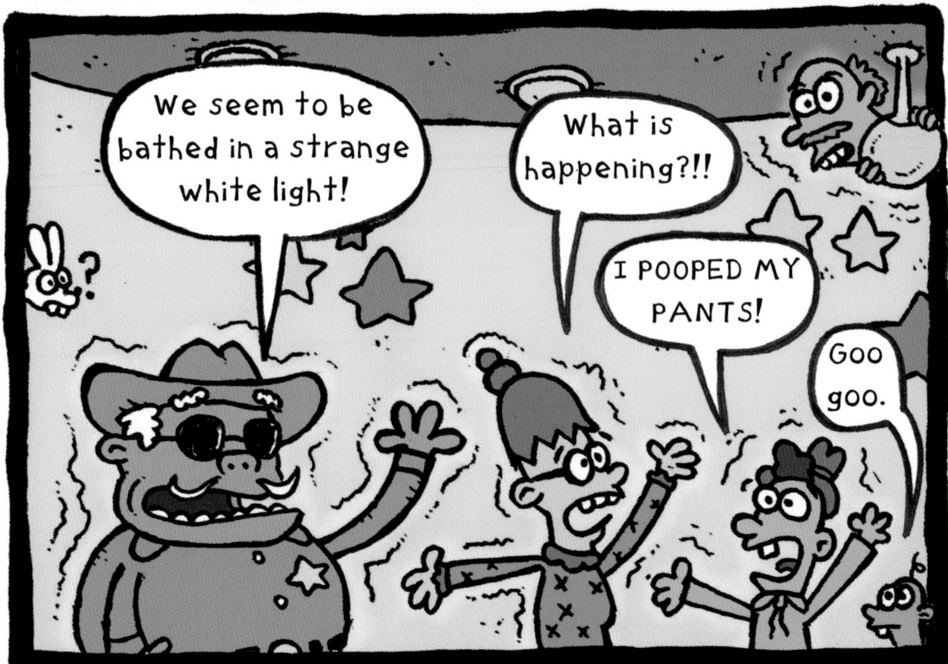
We seem to be bathed in a strange white light!
What is happening?!!
I POOPED MY PANTS!
Goo goo.
?

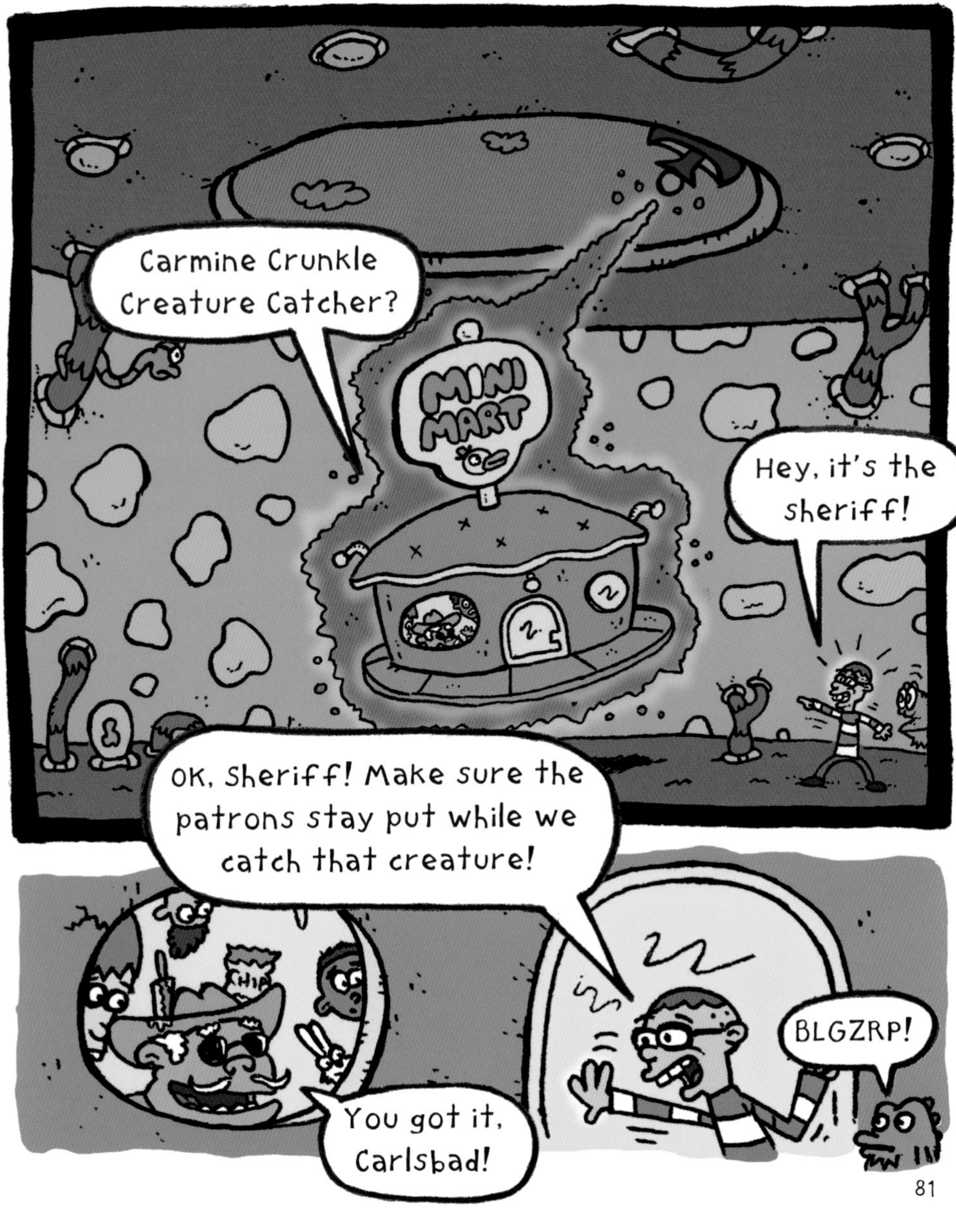
MINI MART
Carmine Crunkle Creature Catcher?
Hey, it's the sheriff!
OK, Sheriff! Make sure the patrons stay put while we catch that creature!
CHIP
You got it, Carlsbad!
BLGZRP!

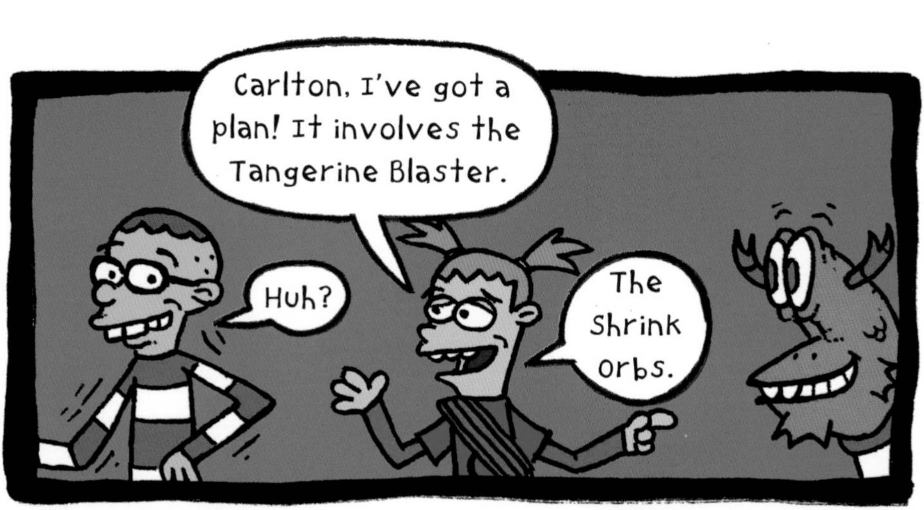
Carlton, I've got a plan! It involves the Tangerine Blaster.
Huh?
The Shrink orbs.

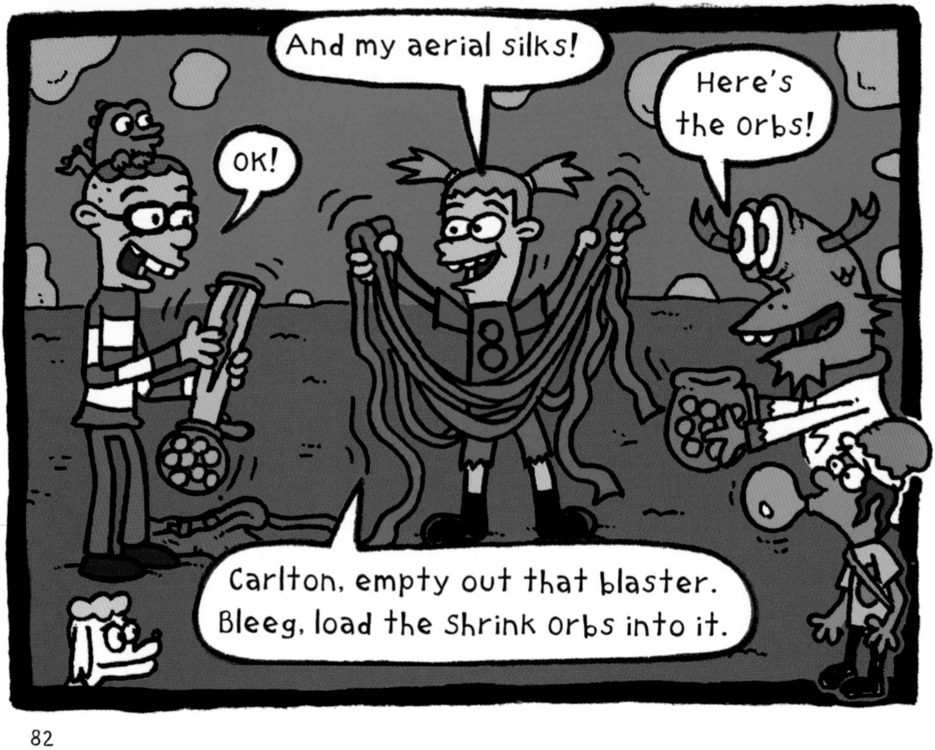
And my aerial silks!
OK!
Here's the orbs!
8
Carlton, empty out that blaster. Bleeg, load the Shrink orbs into it.

CHAPTER

8

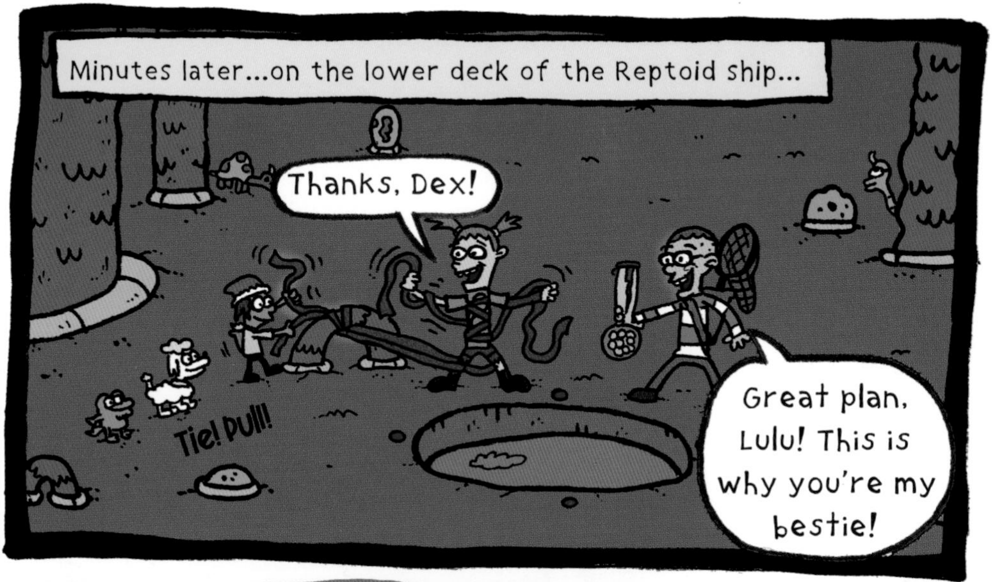
Minutes later...on the lower deck of the Reptoid ship...
Thanks, Dex!
Great plan, Lulu! This is why you're my bestie!
Tie! Pull!

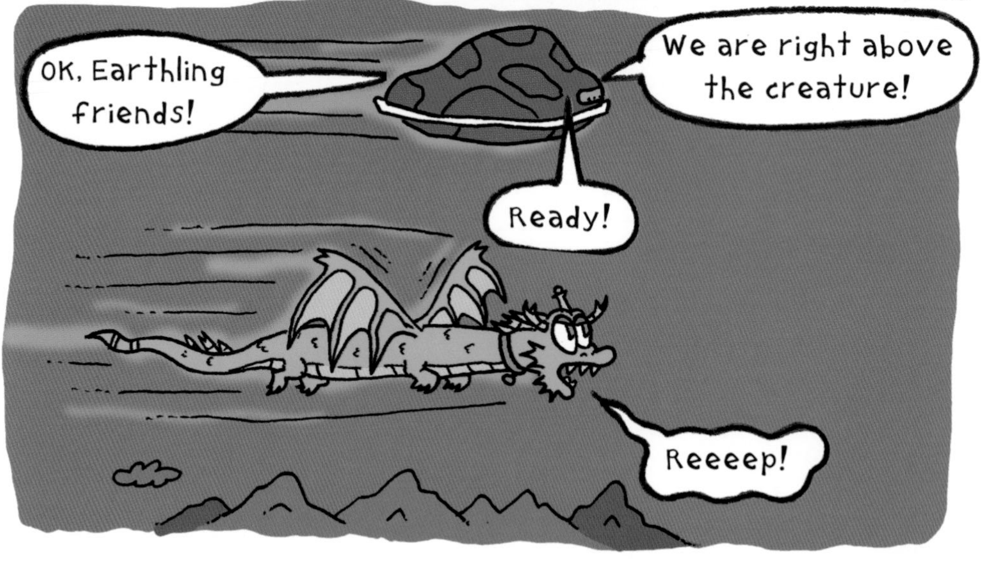
OK, Earthling friends!
We are right above the creature!
Ready!
Reeeep!

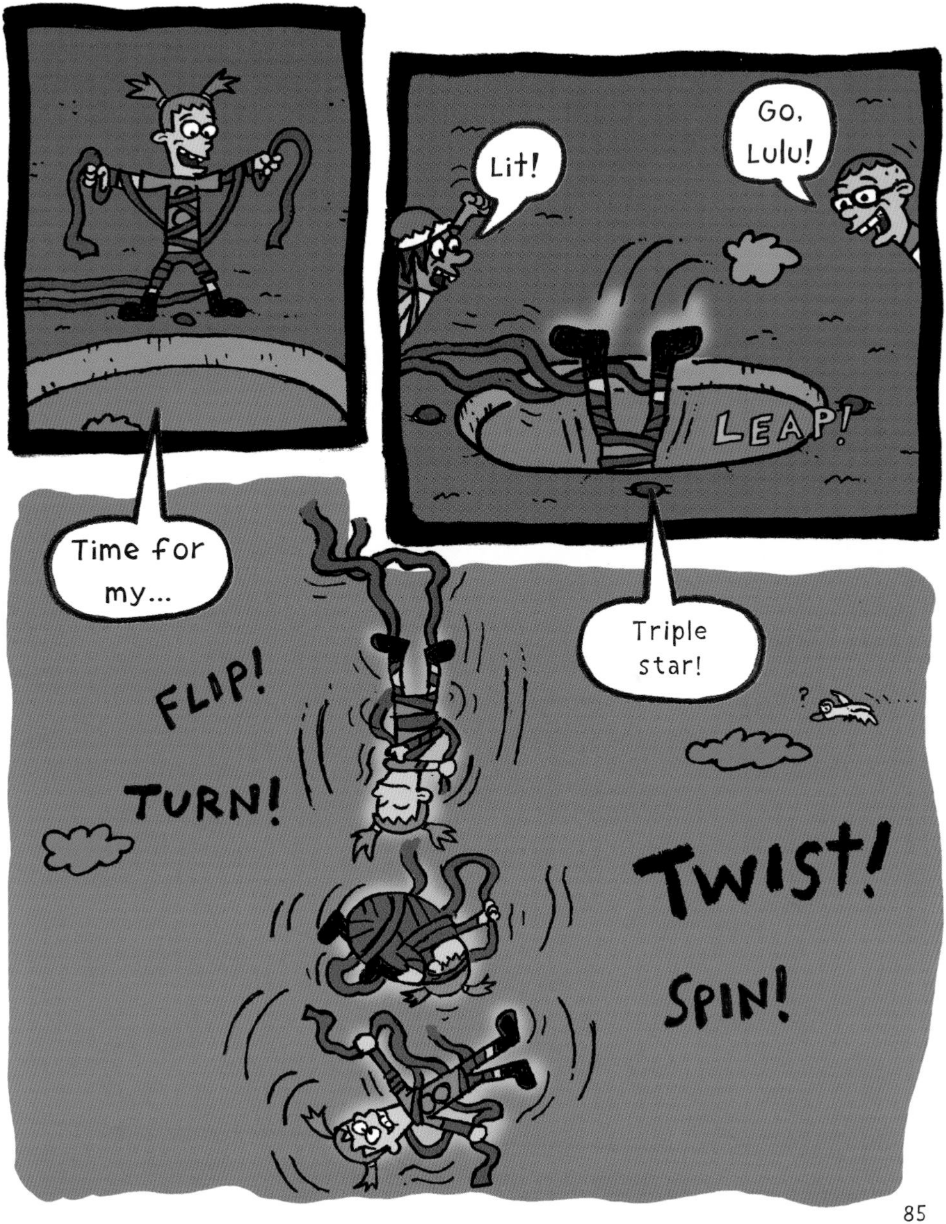
Time for my...
Lit!
Go, Lulu!
LEAP!
Triple star!
FLIP!
TURN!
TWIST!
SPIN!

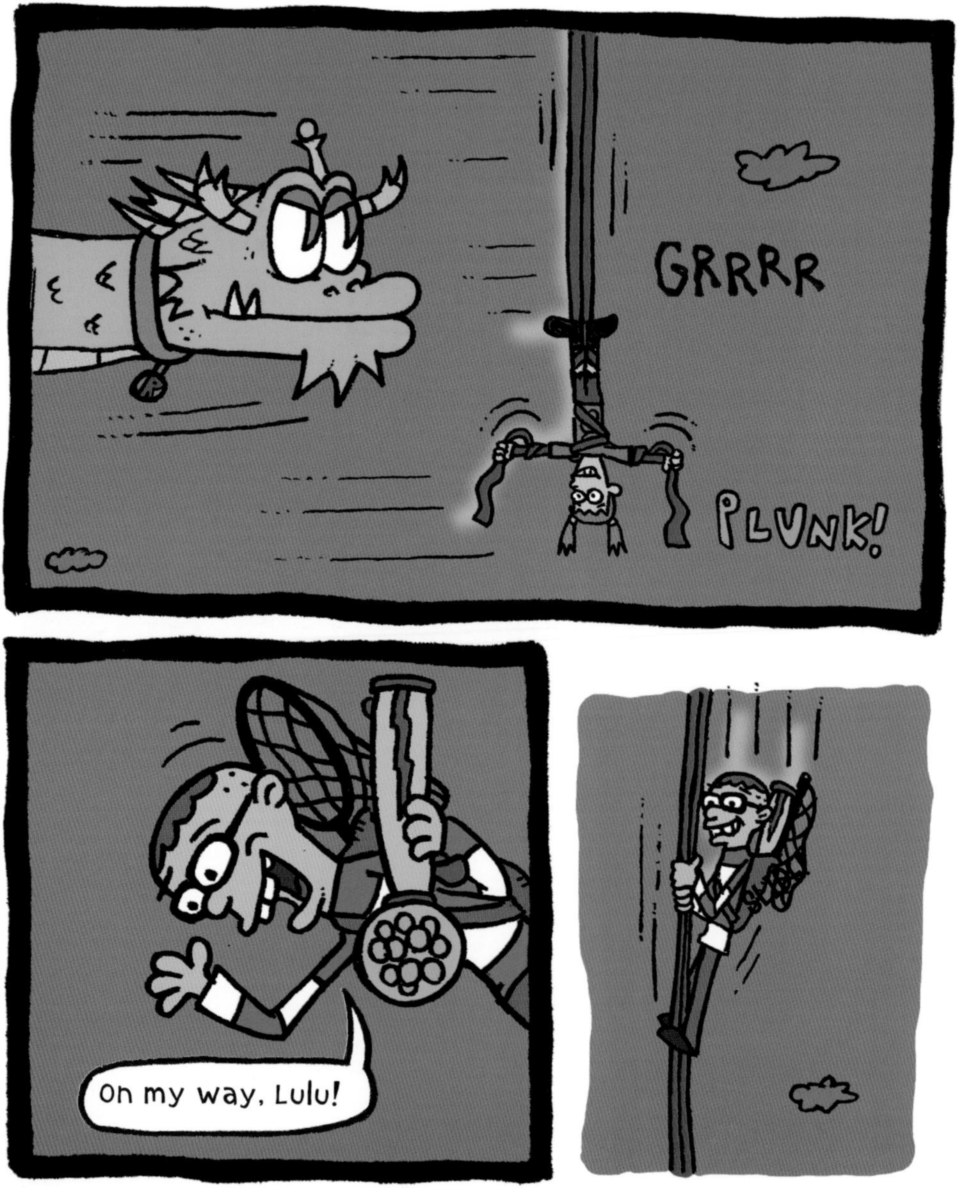
GRRRR
PLUNK!
Oh my way, Lulu!

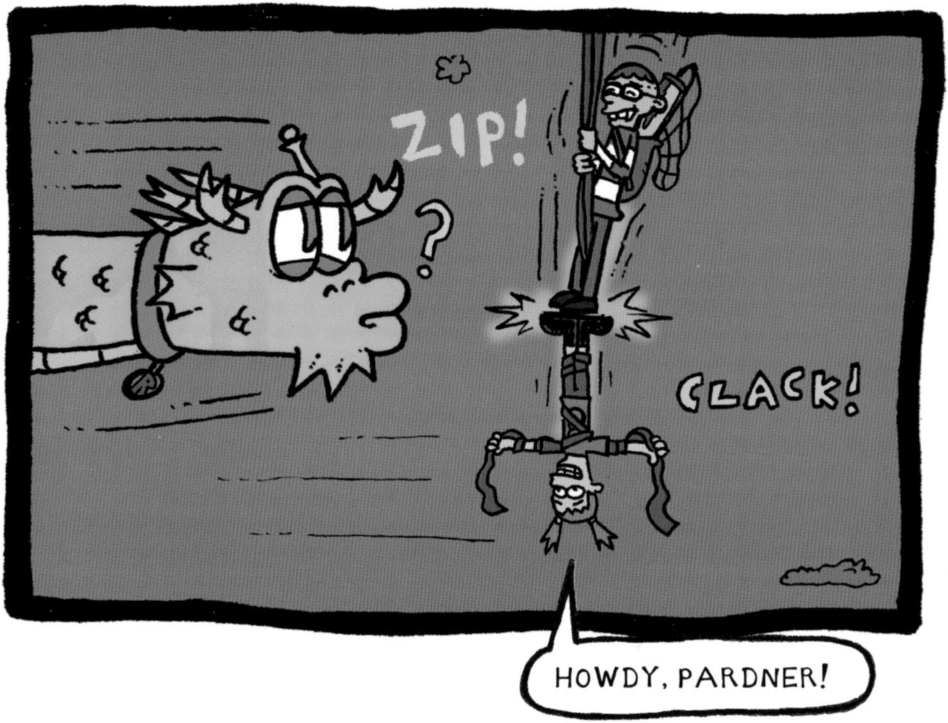
ZIP!
?
CLACK!
HOWDY, PARDNER!

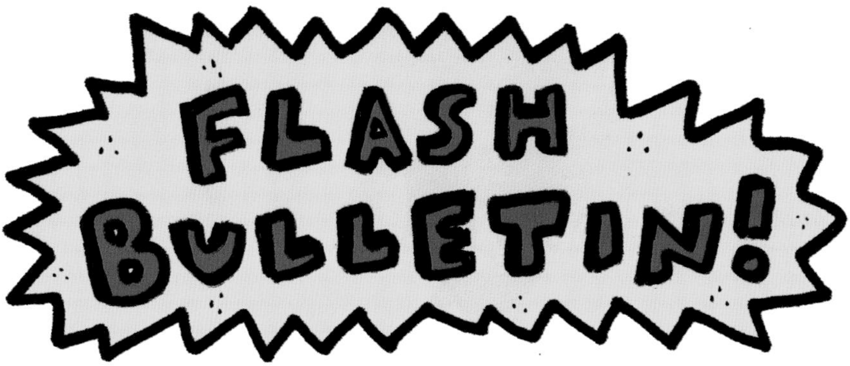
FLASH BULLETIN!

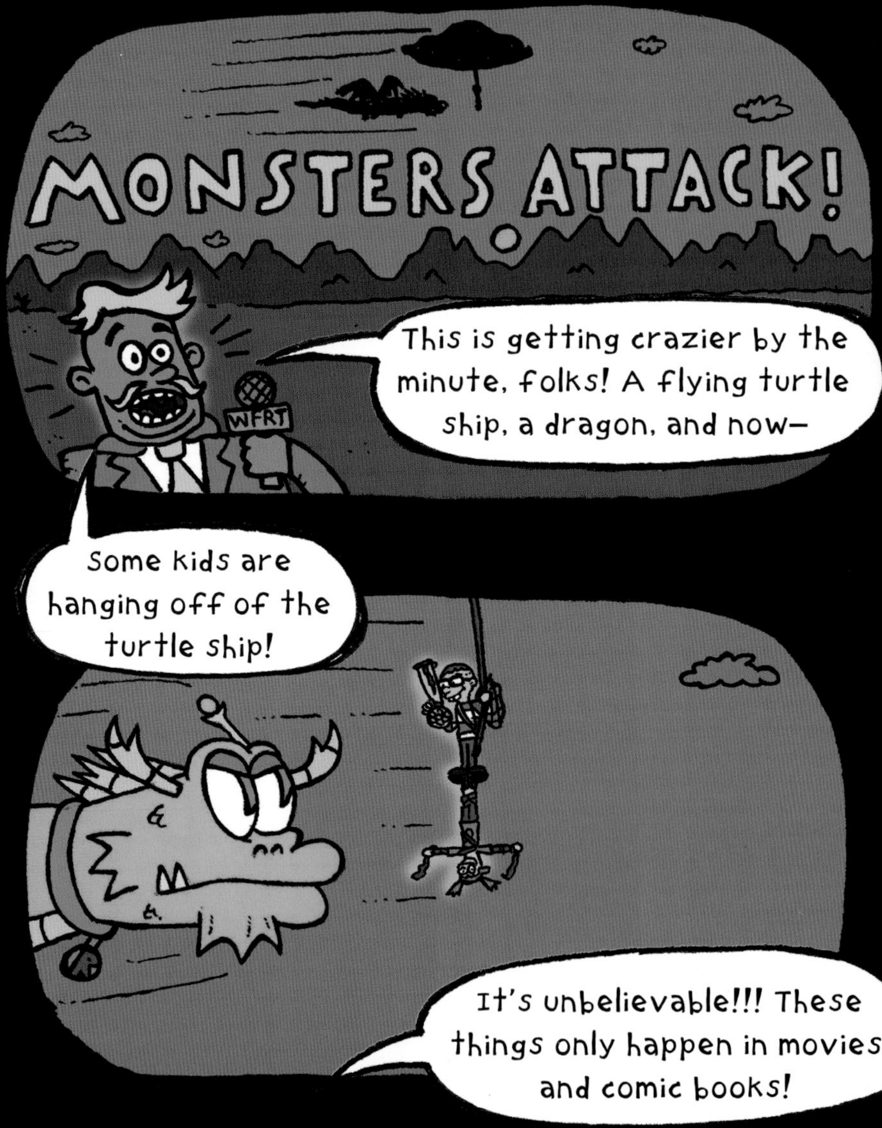
MONSTERS ATTACK!
WFRT
This is getting crazier by the minute, folks! A flying turtle ship, a dragon, and now—
Some kids are hanging off of the turtle ship!
It's unbelievable!!! These things only happen in movies and comic books!

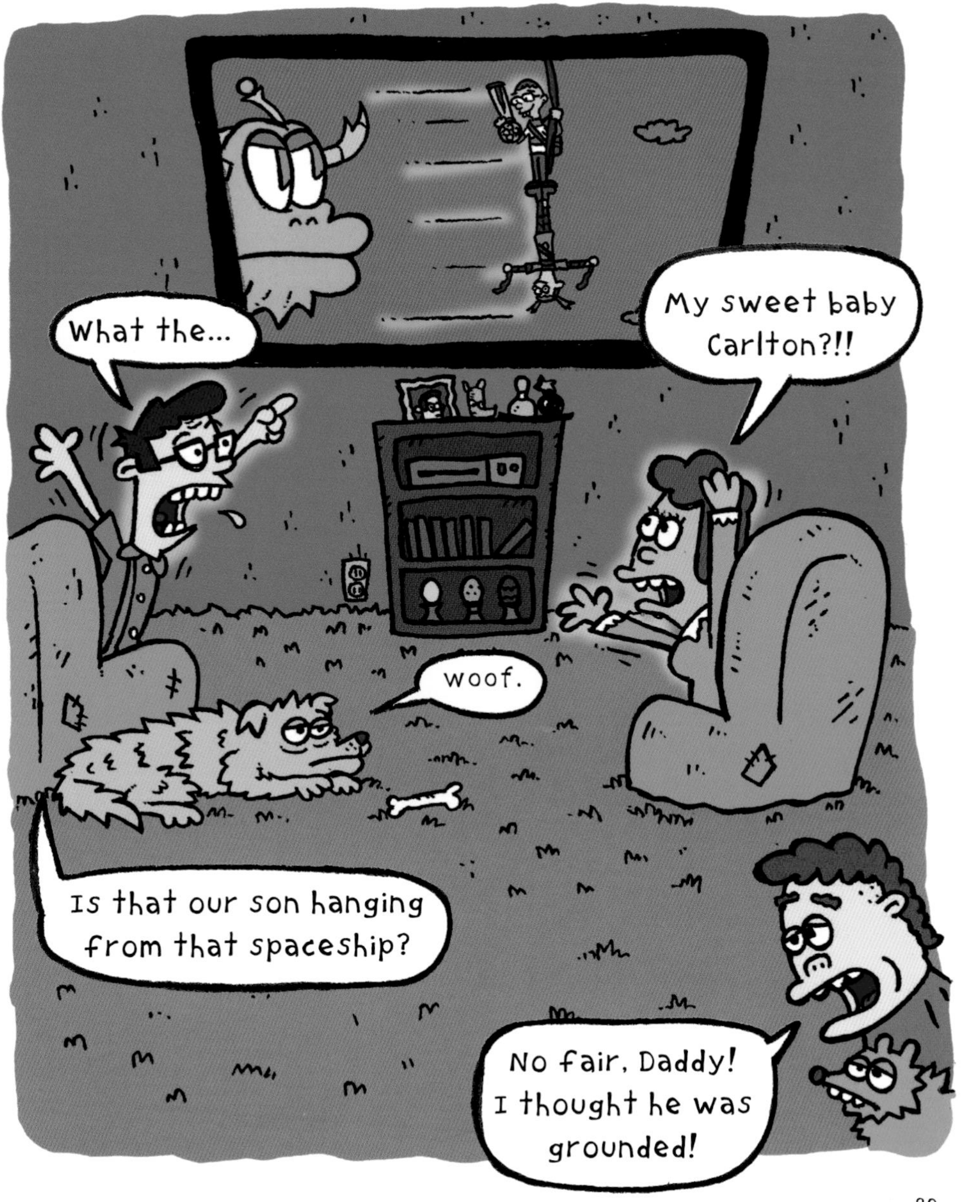
What the...
My sweet baby Carlton?!!
woof.
Is that our son hanging from that spaceship?
No fair, Daddy! I thought he was grounded!

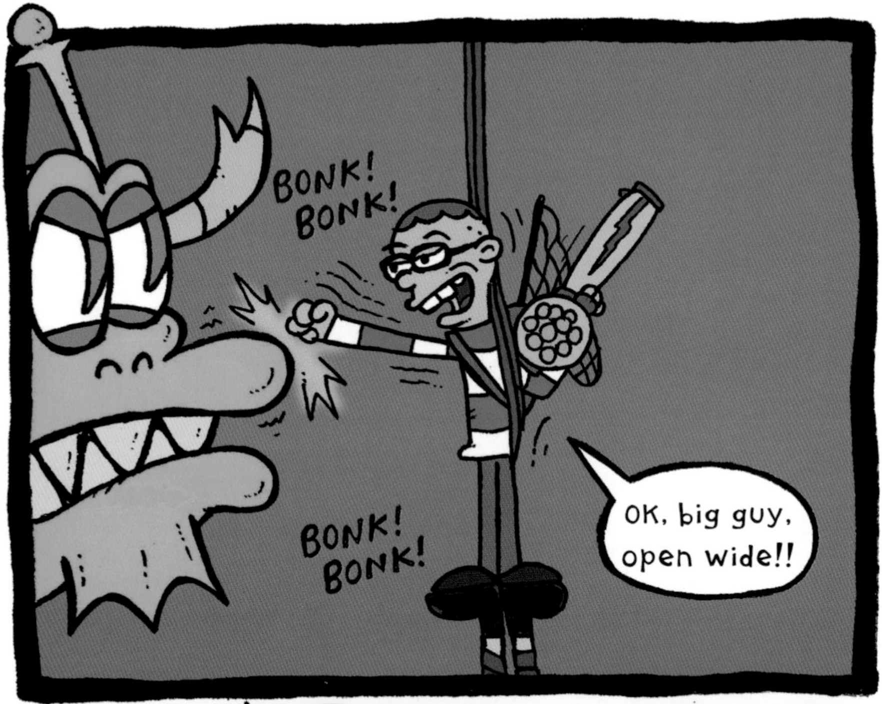
BONK!
BONK!
BONK!
BONK!
OK, big guy, open wide!!

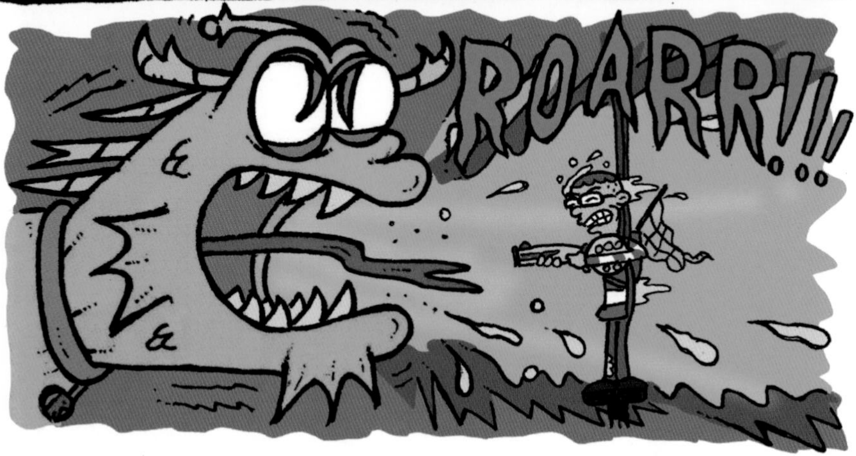
ROARR!!!

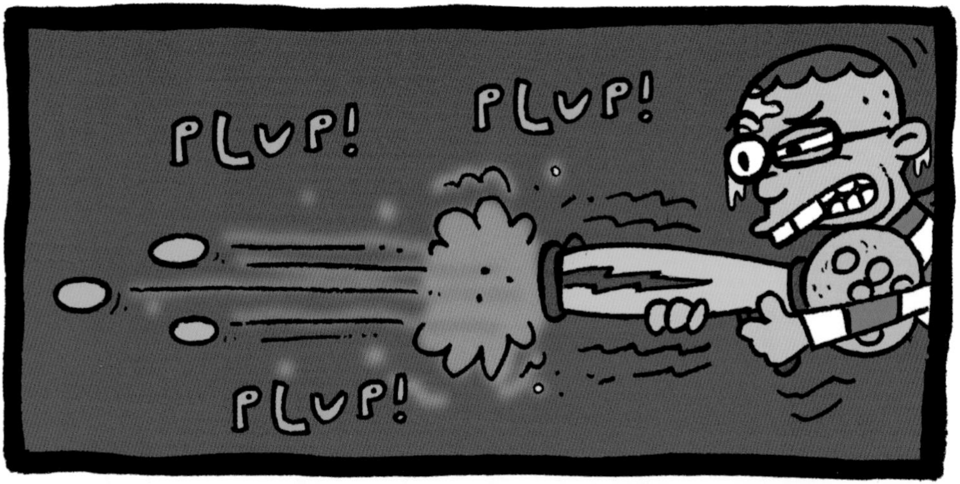
PLUP!
PLUP!
PLUP!

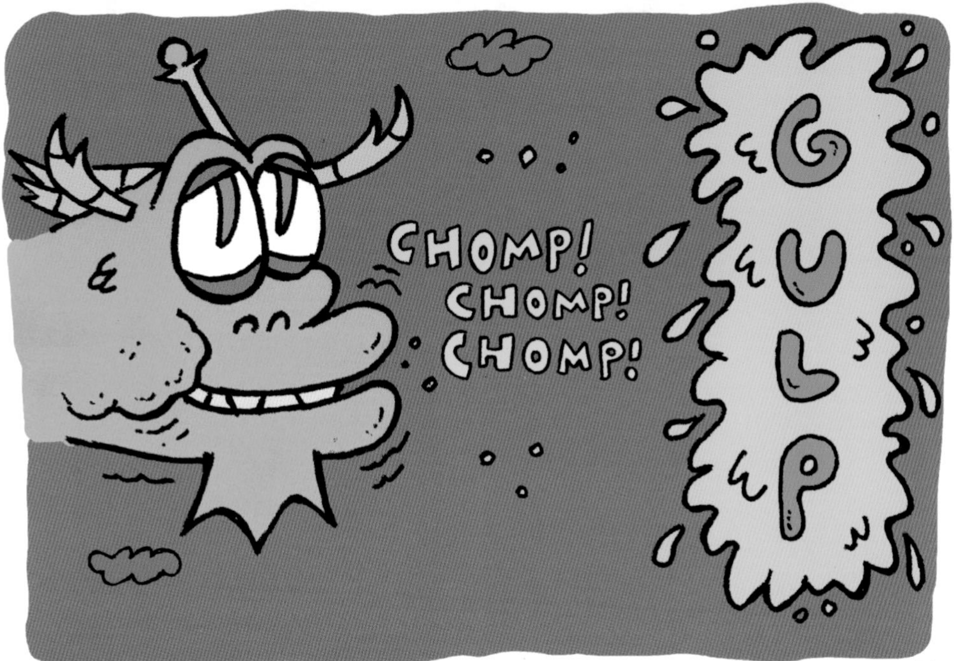
CHOMP!
CHOMP!
CHOMP!
GULP

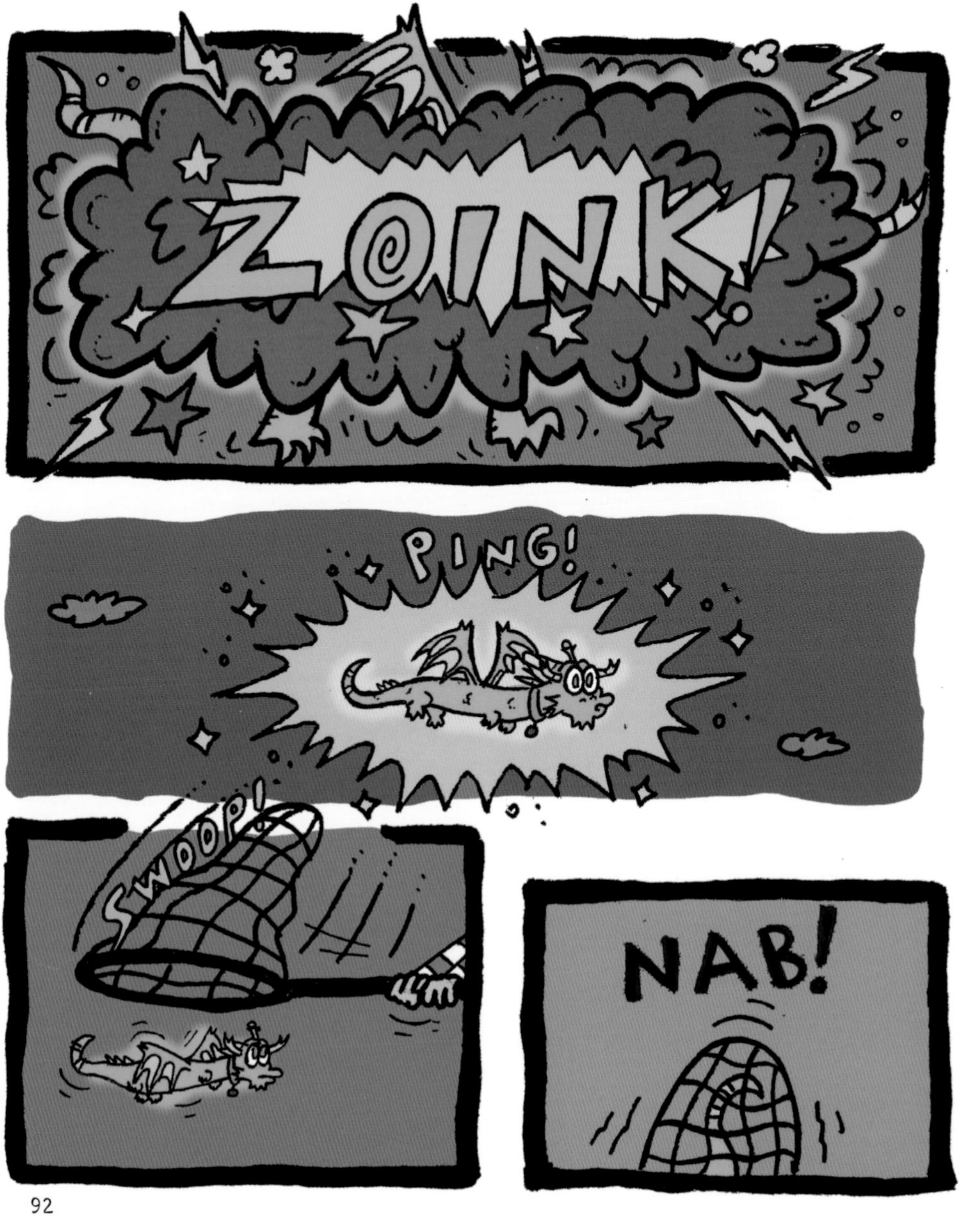
ZOINK!
PING!
SWOOP!
NAB!

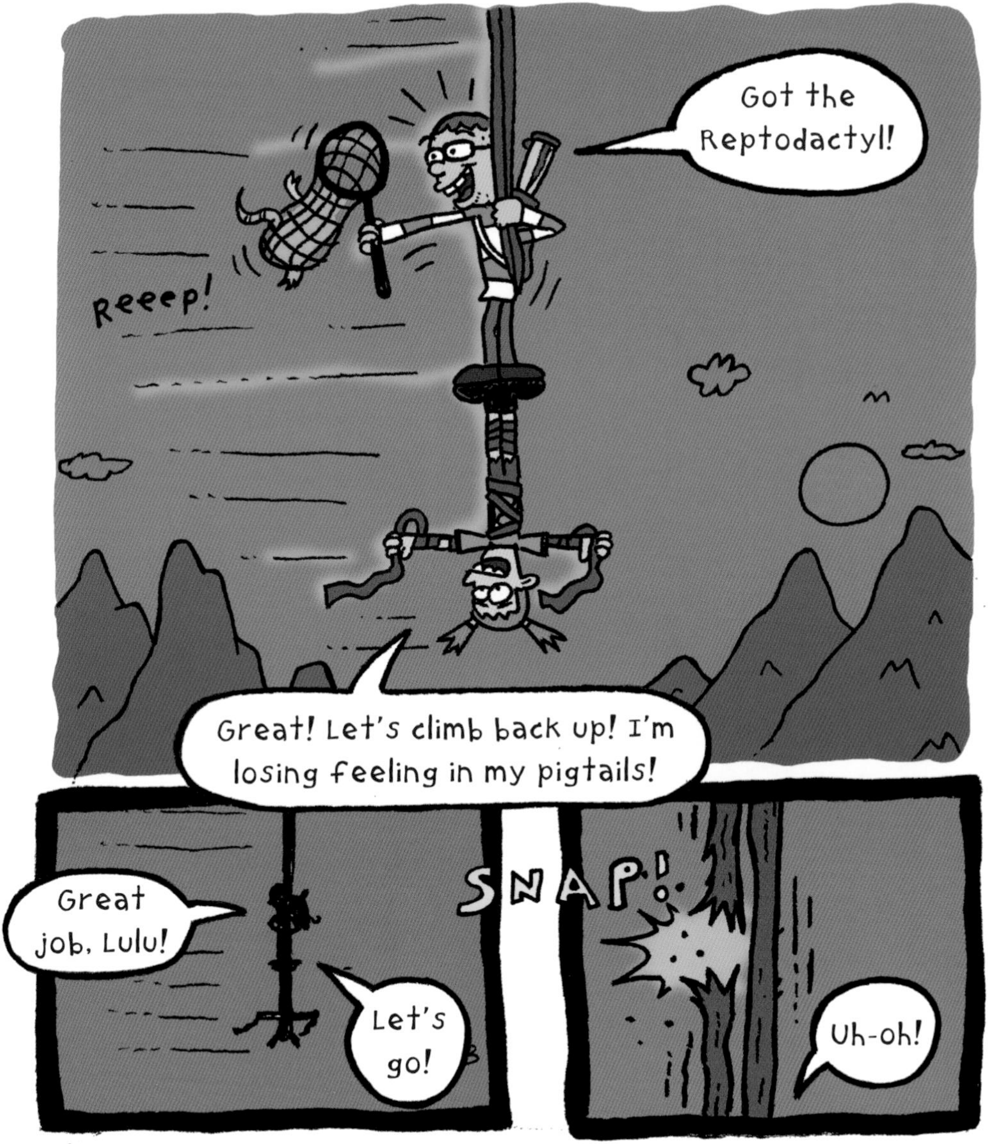
Got the Reptodactyl!
Reeep!
Great! Let's climb back up! I'm losing feeling in my pigtails!
Great job, Lulu!
Let's go!
SNAP!
Uh-oh!

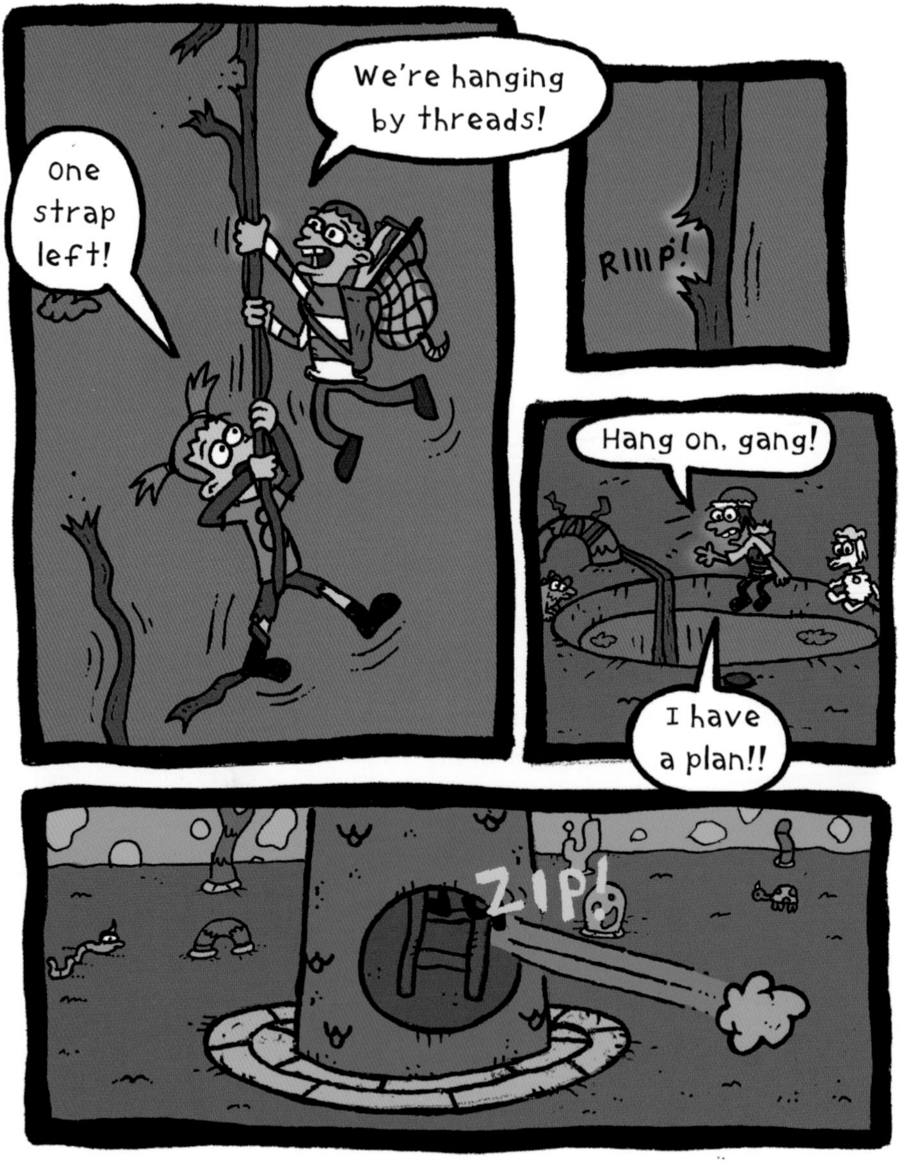
One strap left!
We're hanging by threads!
RIIIP!
Hang on, gang!
I have a plan!!
ZIP!

CHAPTER

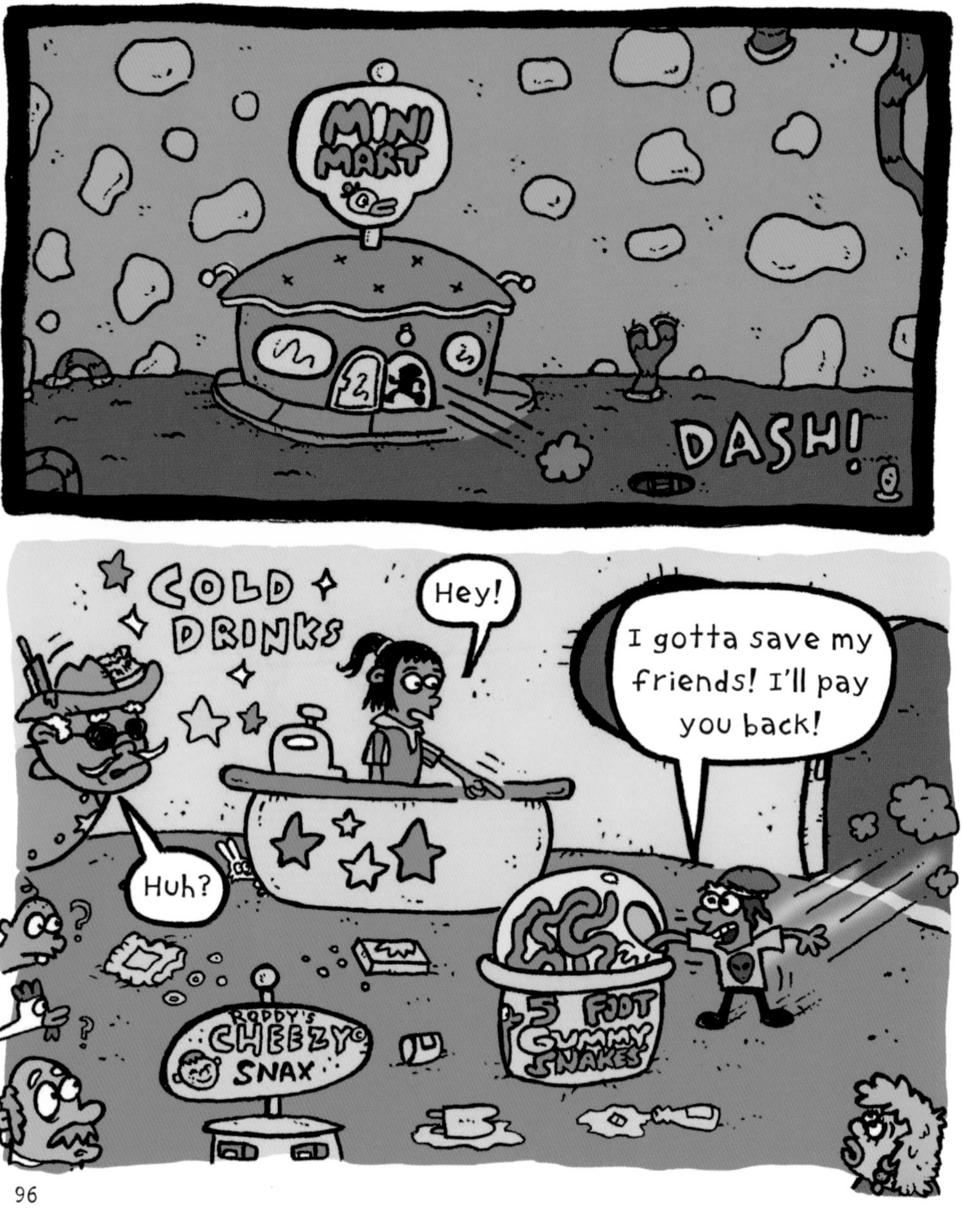
MINI MART
DASH!
COLD DRINKS
Hey!
I gotta save my friends! I'll pay you back!
Huh?
RODDY'S CHEEZY© SNAX
5 FOOT GUMMY SNAKES

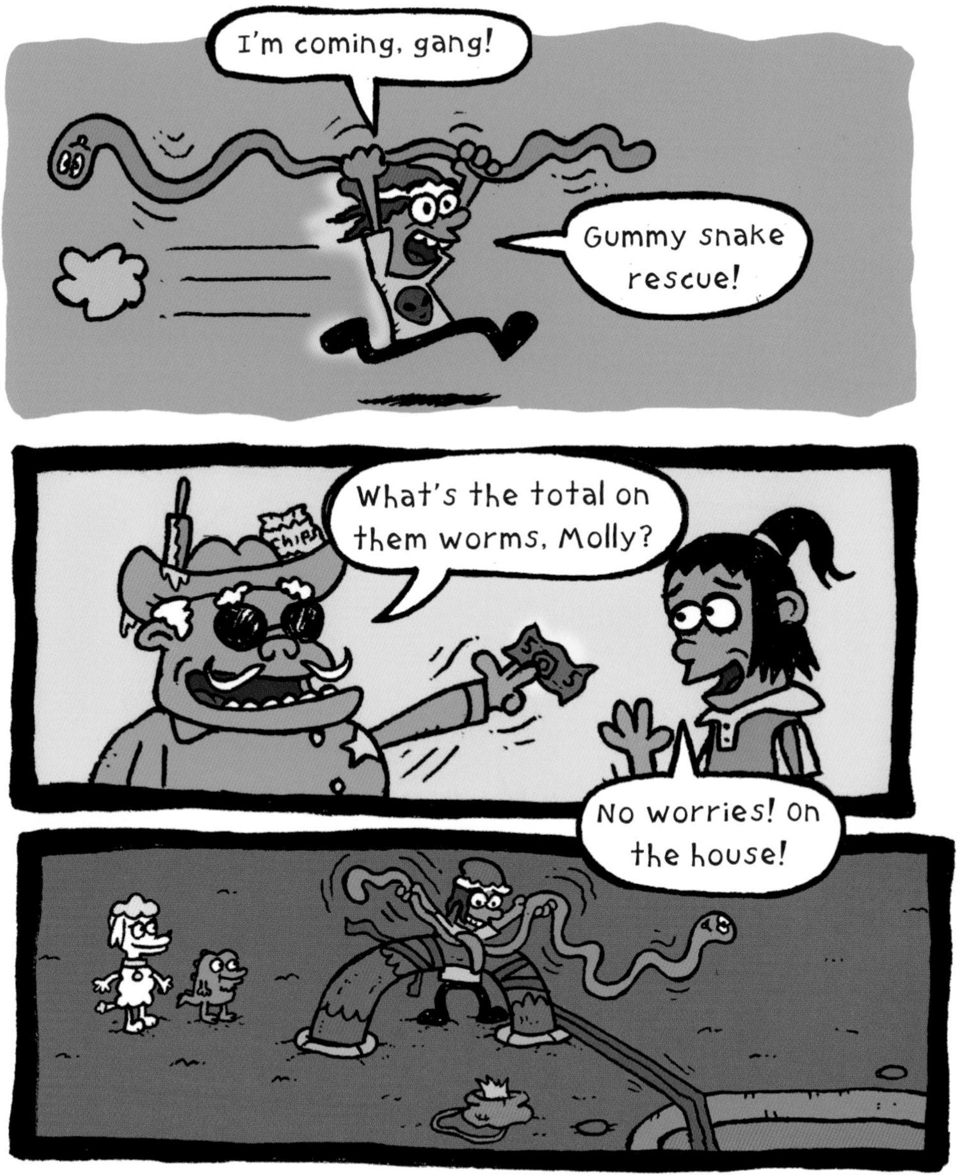
I'm coming, gang!
Gummy snake rescue!
What's the total on them worms, Molly?
No worries! On the house!

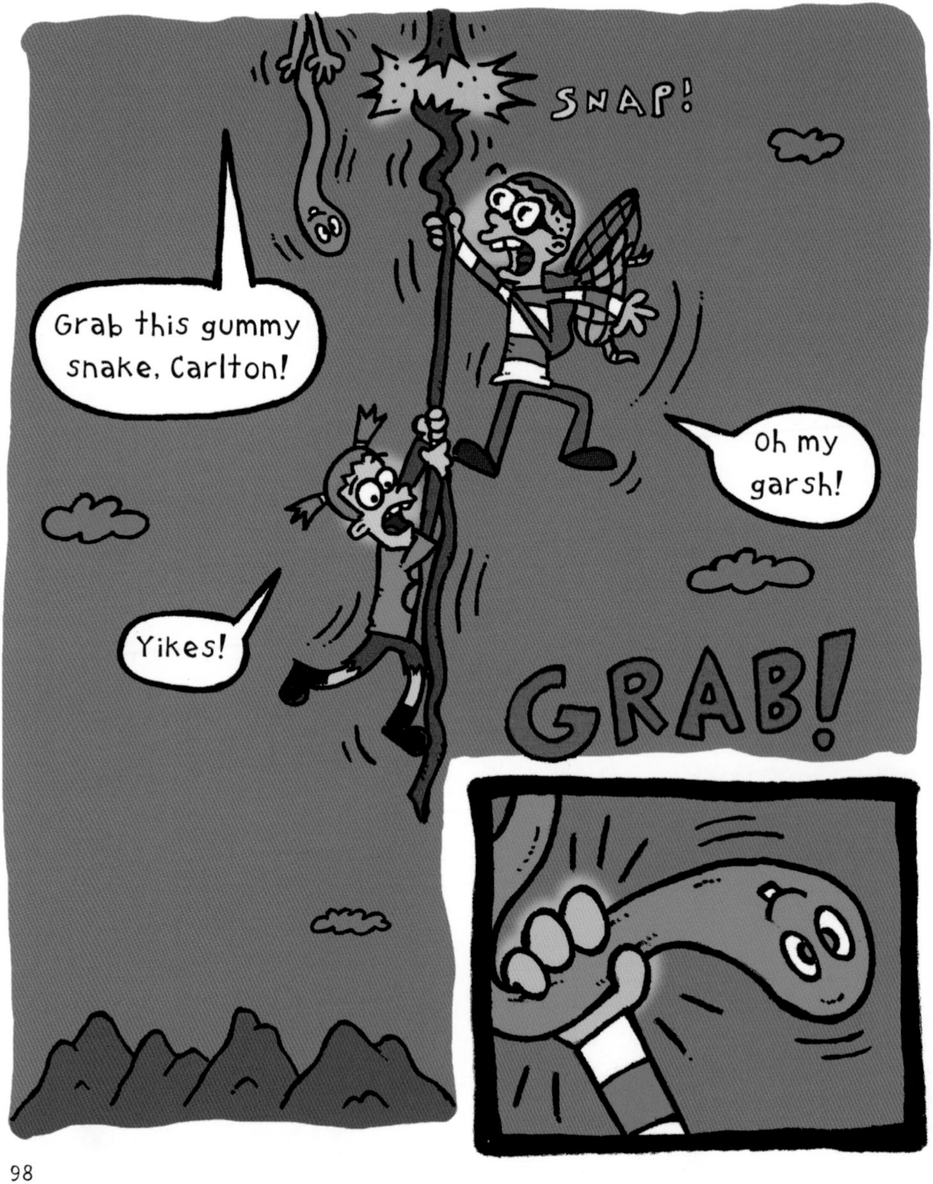
SNAP!
Grab this gummy snake, Carlton!
Oh my garsh!
Yikes!
GRAB!

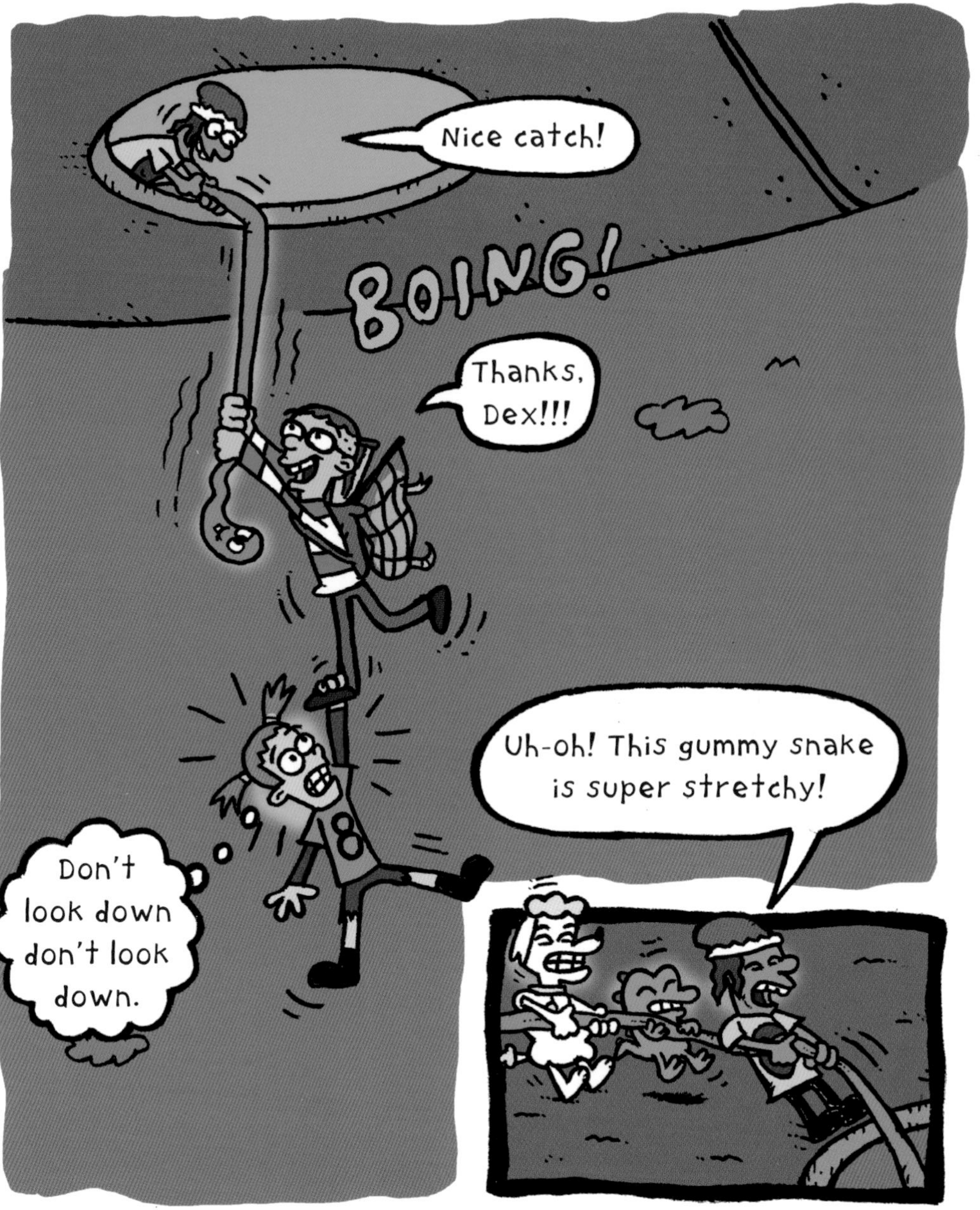
Nice catch!
BOING!
Thanks, Dex!!!
Don't look down don't look don't look down.
Uh-oh! This gummy snake is super stretchy!

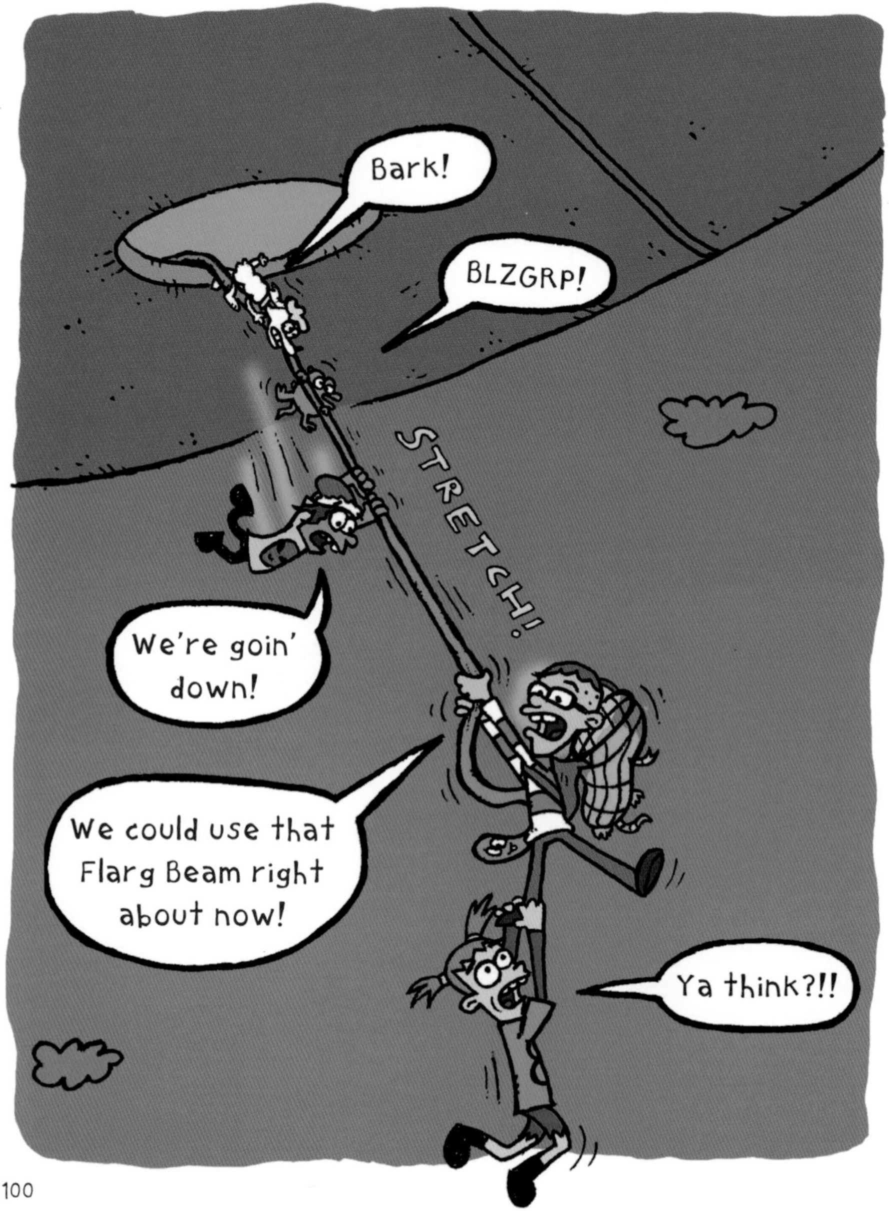
Bark!
BLZGRP!
STRETCH!
We're goin' down!
We could use that Flarg Beam right about now!
Ya think?!!

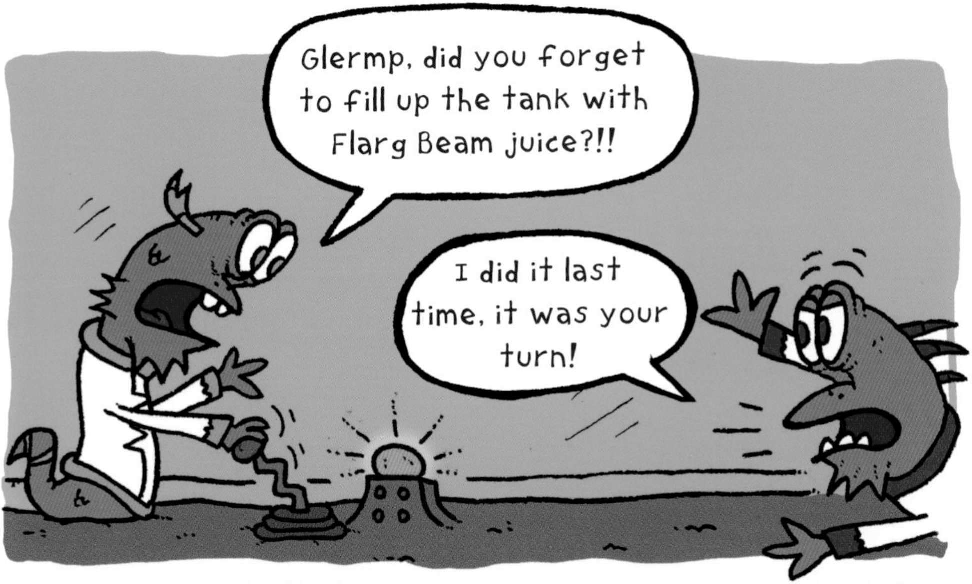
Glermp, did you forget to fill up the tank with Flarg Beam juice?!!
I did it last time, it was your turn!

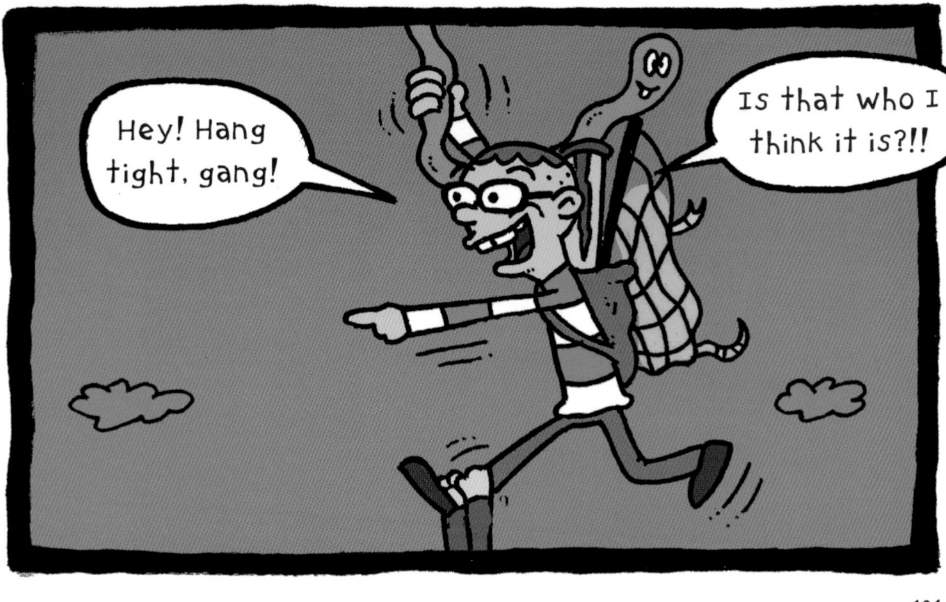
Hey! Hang tight, gang!
Is that who I think it is?!!

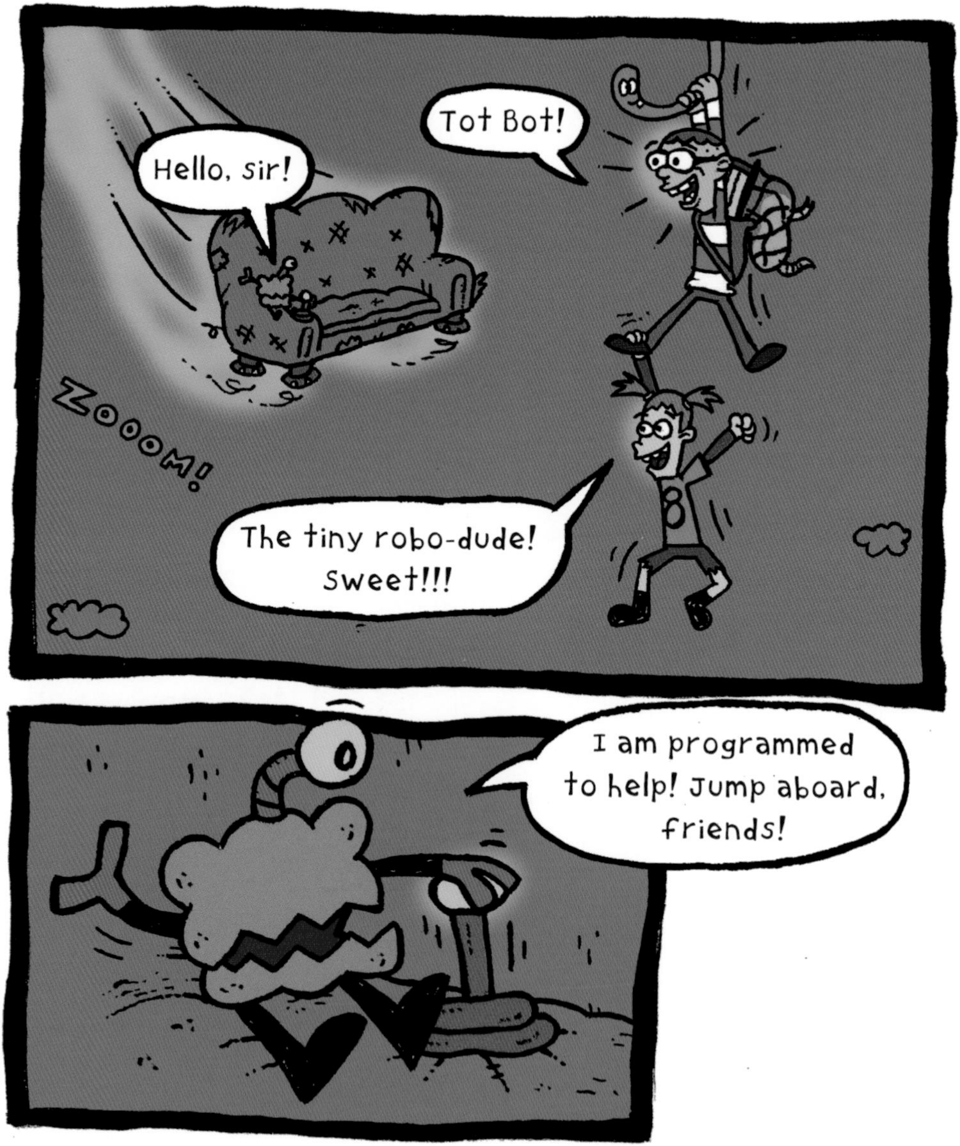
Hello, sir!
Tot Bot!
ZOOOM!
The tiny robo-dude! Sweet!!!
I am programmed to help! Jump aboard, friends!

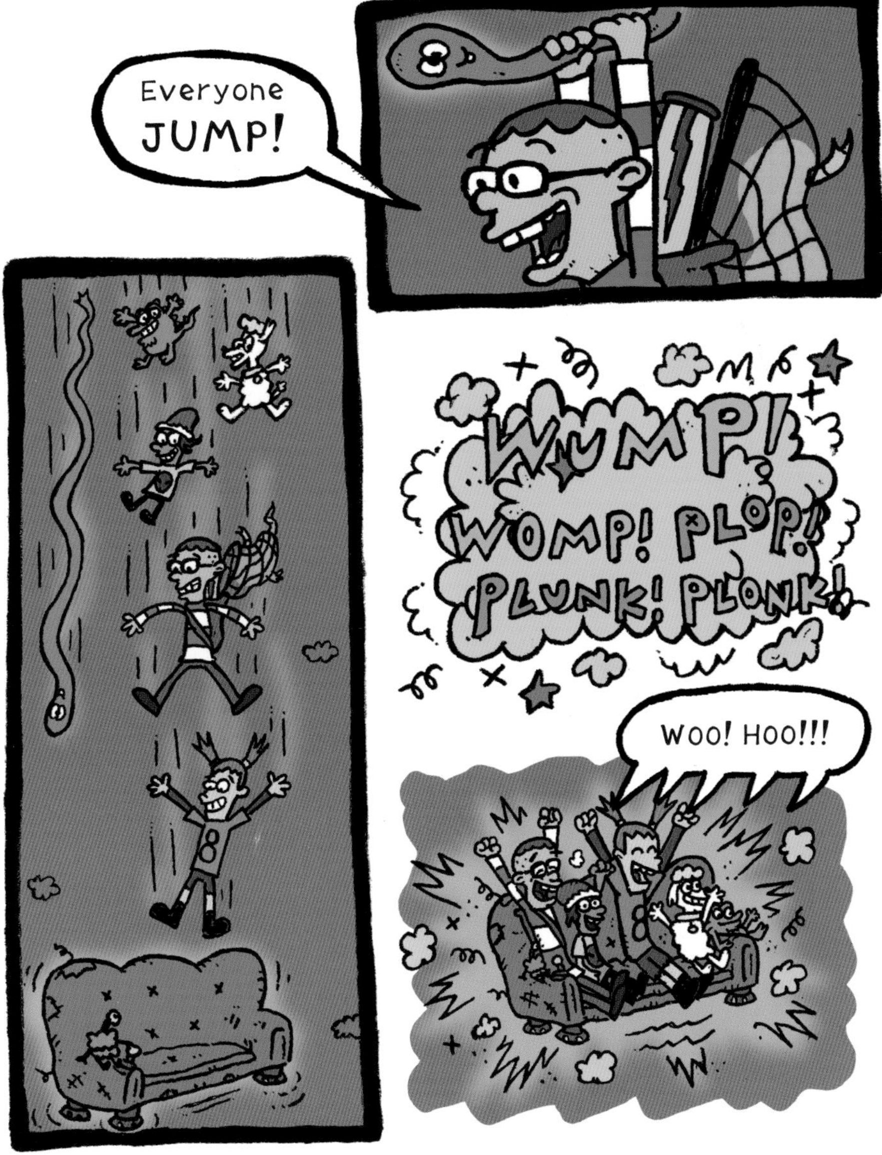
Everyone JUMP!
WUMP! WOMP! PLOP! PLUNK! PLONK!
WOO! HOO!!!

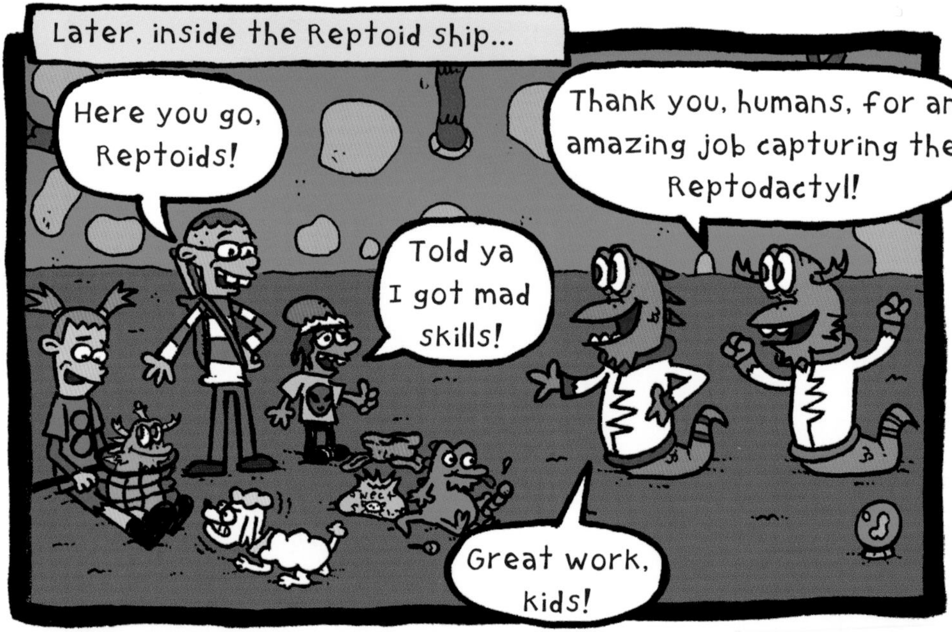
Later, inside the Reptoid ship...
Here you go, Reptoids!
Thank you, humans, for an amazing job capturing the Reptodactyl!
Told ya I got mad skills!
Great work, kids!

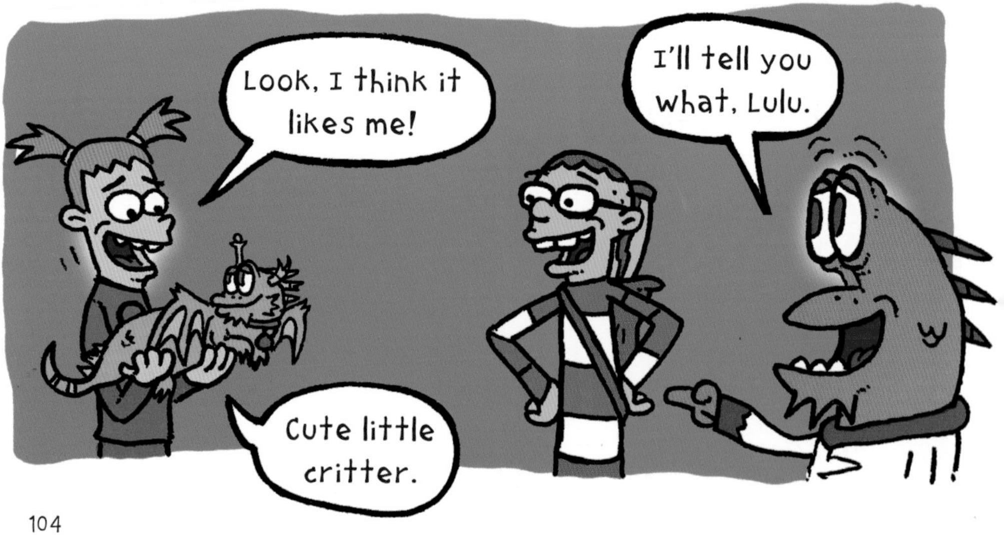
Look, I think it likes me!
I'll tell you what, Lulu.
Cute little critter.

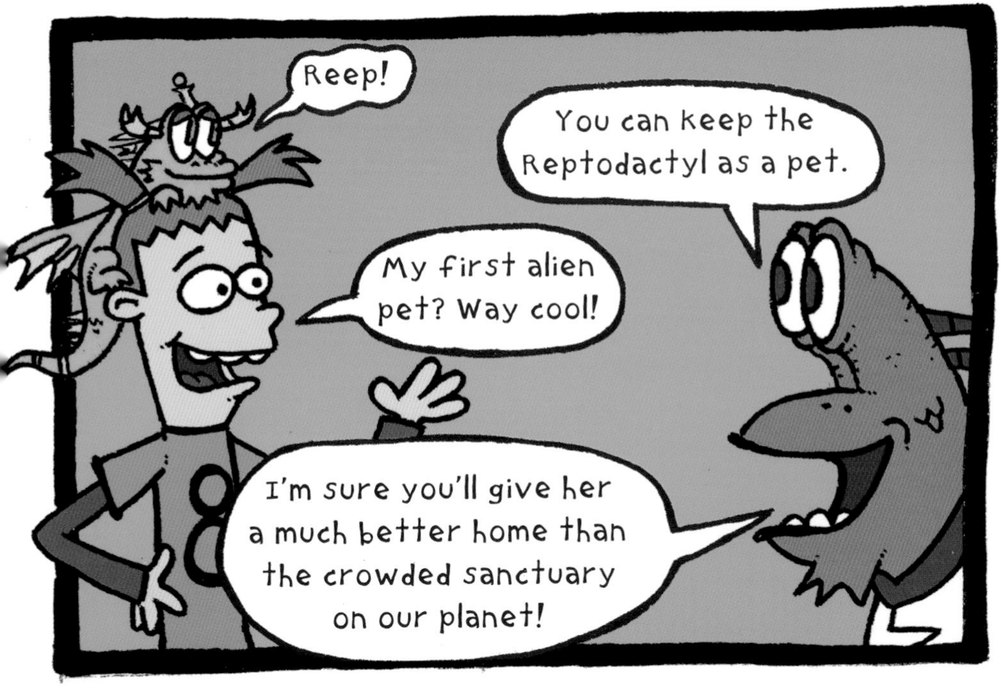
Reep!
You can keep the Reptodactyl as a pet.
My first alien pet? Way cool!
I'm sure you'll give her a much better home than the crowded sanctuary on our planet!

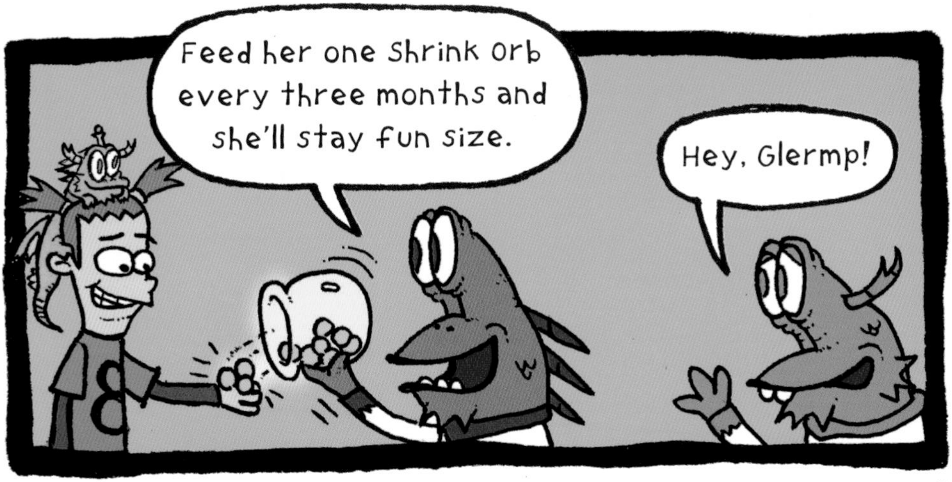
Feed her one Shrink Orb every three months and she'll stay fun size.
Hey, Glermp!

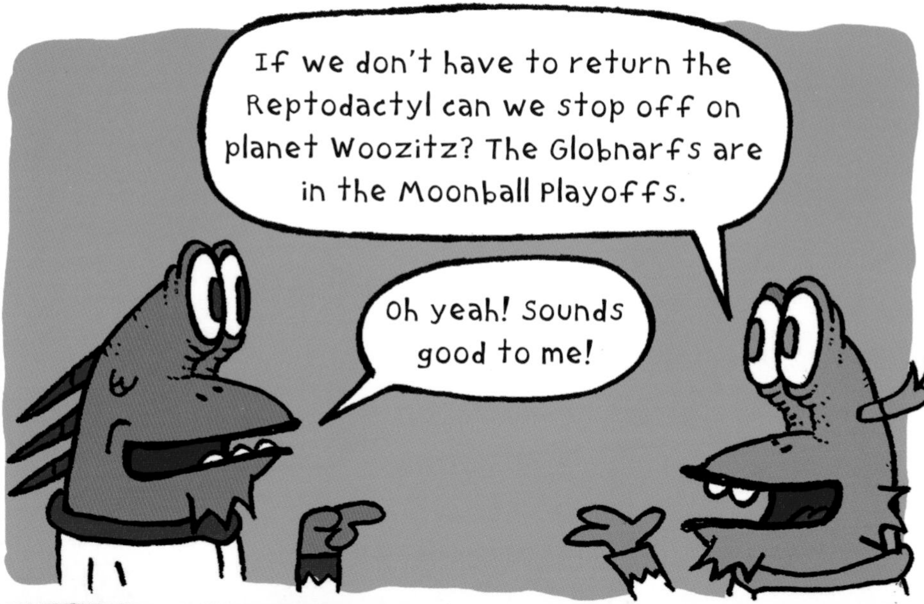
If we don't have to return the Reptodactyl can we stop off on planet Woozitz? The Globnarfs are in the Moonball Playoffs.
Oh yeah! Sounds good to me!

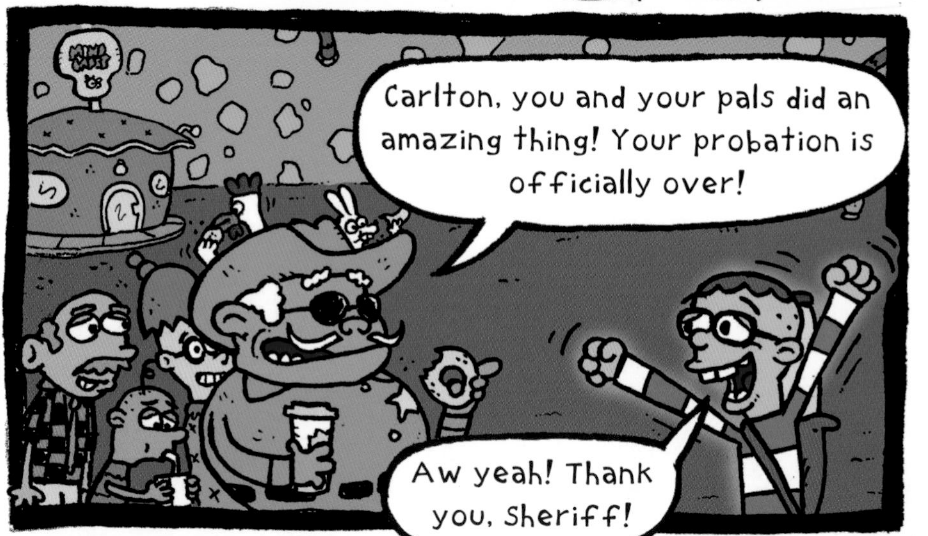
Carlton, you and your pals did an amazing thing! Your probation is officially over!
Aw yeah! Thank you, Sheriff!

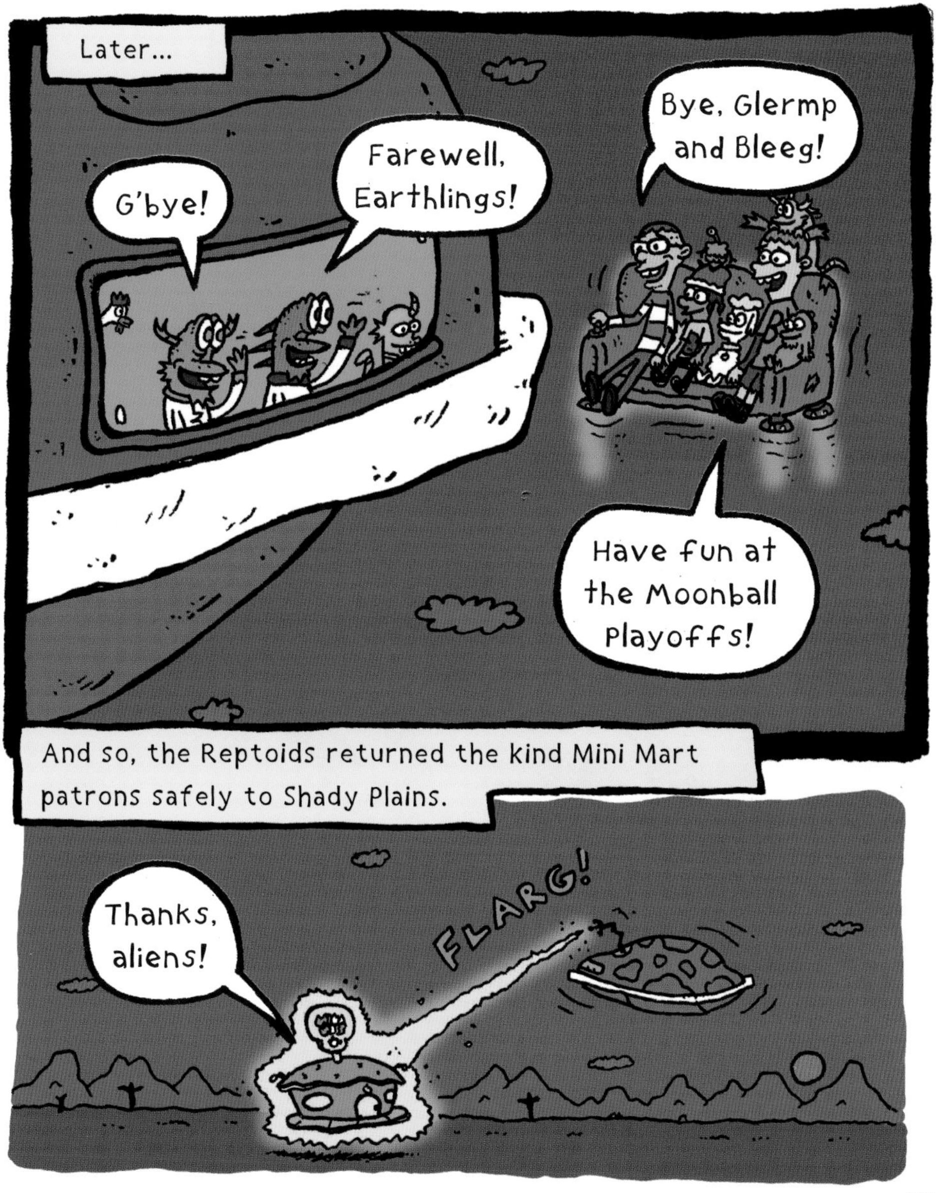
Later...
G'bye!
Farewell, Earthlings!
Bye, Glermp and Bleeg!
Have fun at the Moonball playoffs!
And so, the Reptoids returned the kind Mini Mart patrons safely to Shady Plains.
Thanks, aliens!
FLARG!

CHAPTER 1

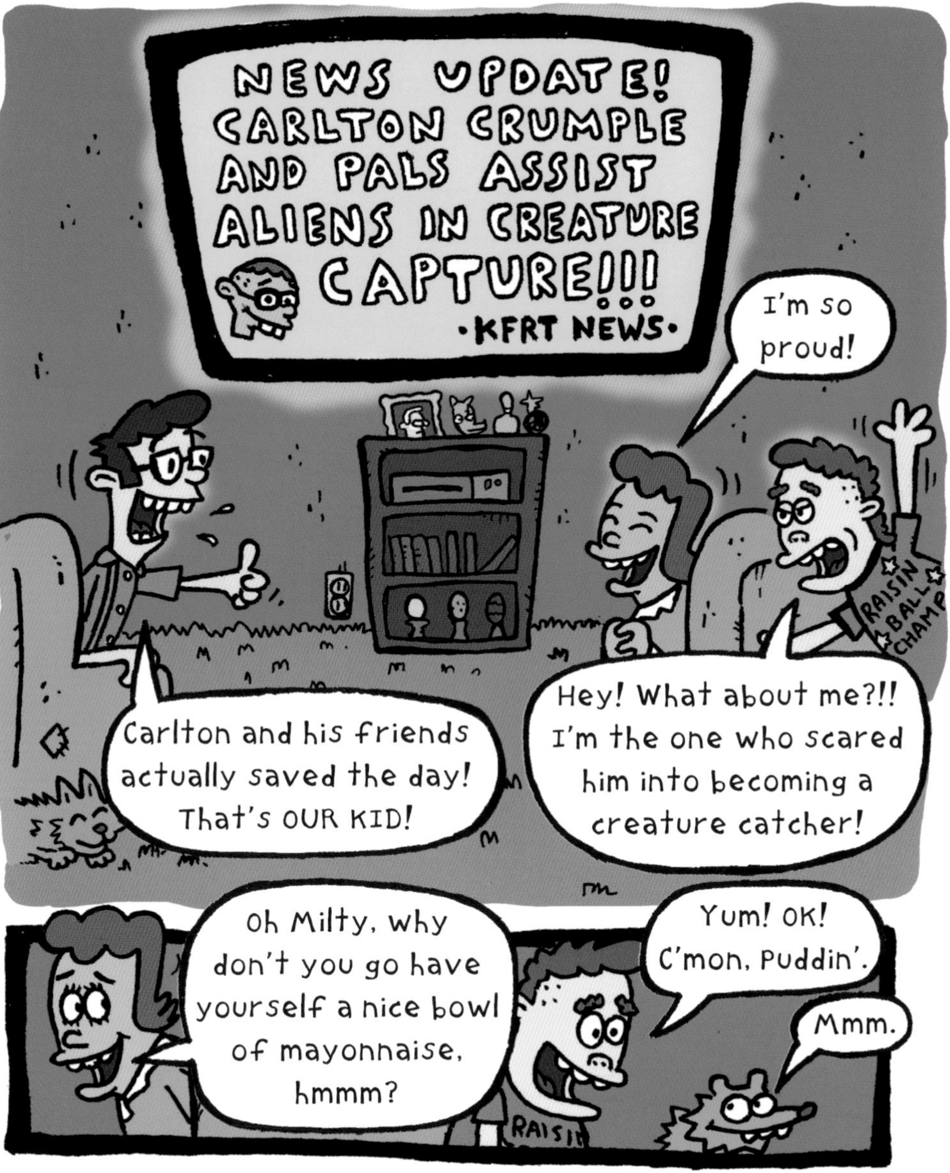
NEWS UPDATE! CARLTON CRUMPLE AND PALS ASSIST ALIENS IN CREATURE CAPTURE!!!
•KFRT NEWS•
I'm so proud!
Carlton and his friends actually saved the day! That's OUR KID!
Hey! What about me?!! I'm the one who scared him into becoming a creature catcher!
RAISIN BALL CHAMP
Oh Milty, why don't you go have yourself a nice bowl of mayonnaise, hmmm?
Yum! OK! C'mon, Puddin'.
Mmm.

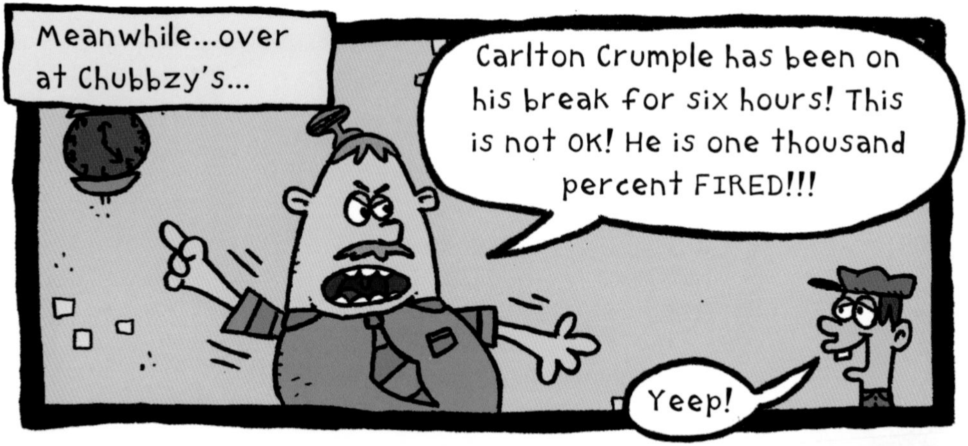
Meanwhile...over at Chubbzy's...
Carlton Crumple has been on his break for six hours! This is not OK! He is one thousand percent FIRED!!!
Yeep!

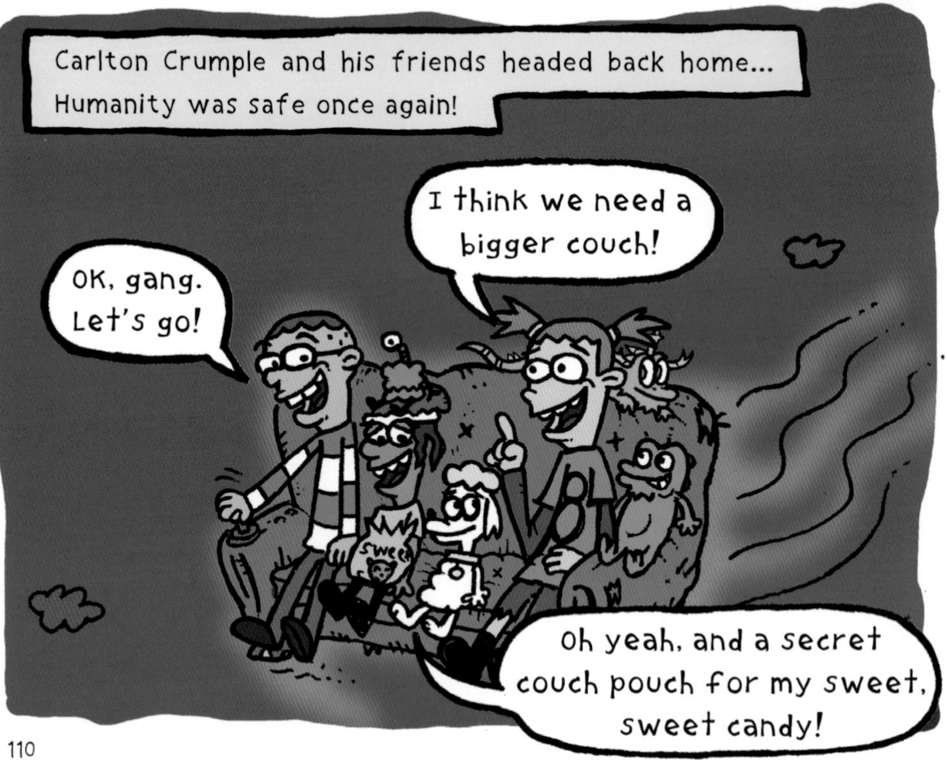
Carlton Crumple and his friends headed back home... Humanity was safe once again!
OK, gang. Let's go!
I think we need a bigger couch!
Oh yeah, and a secret couch pouch for my sweet, sweet candy!

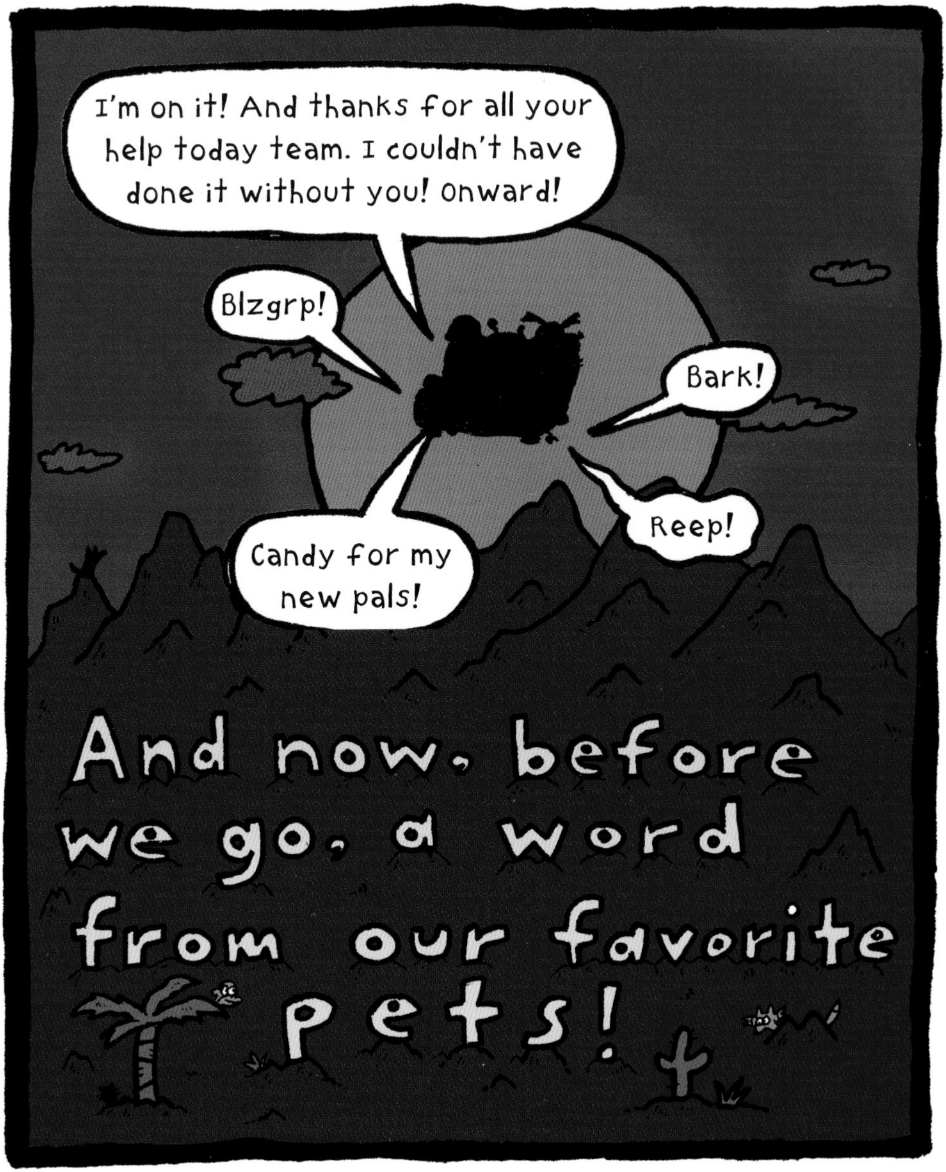
I'm on it! And thanks for all your help today team. I couldn't have done it without you! Onward!
Blzgrp!
Bark!
Reep!
Candy for my new pals!
And now, before we go, a word from our favorite pets!

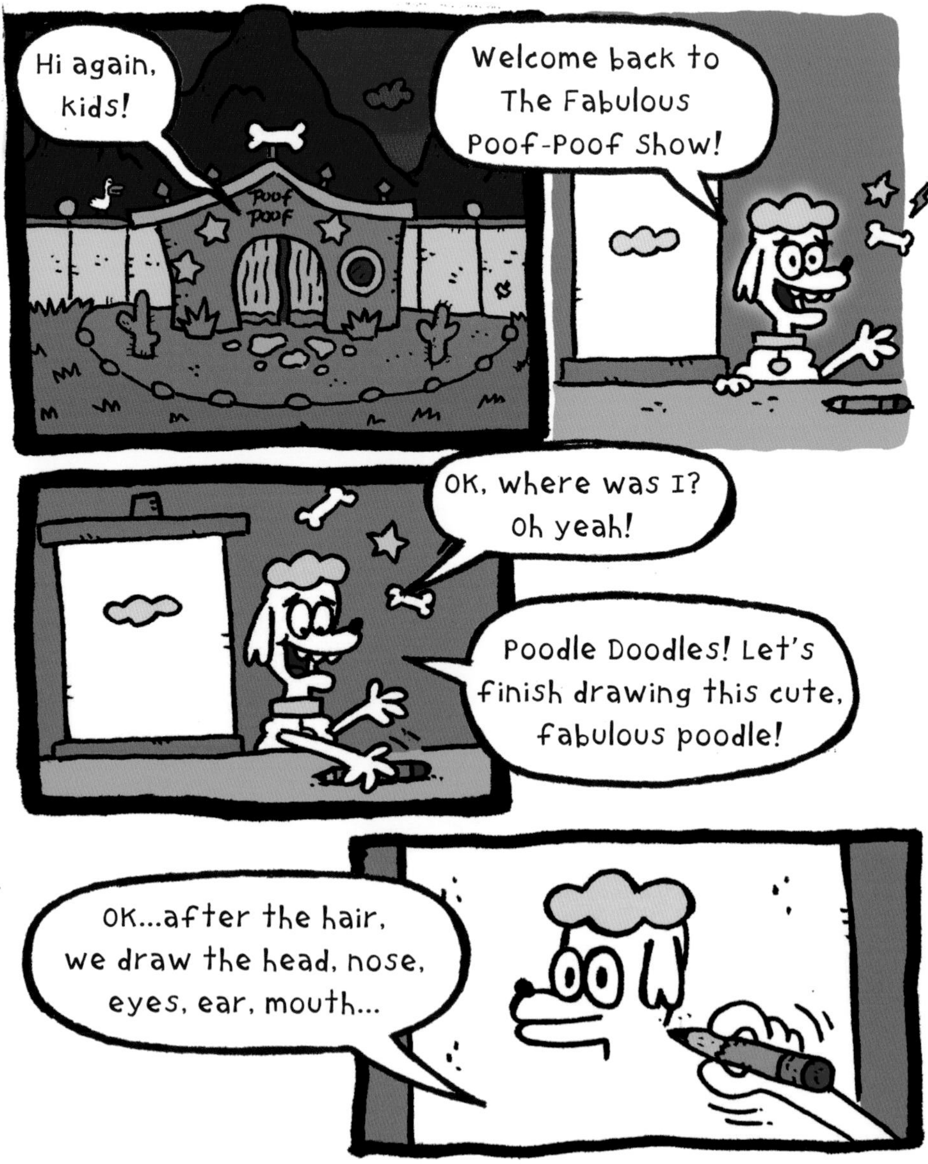
Hi again, kids!
Welcome back to The Fabulous Poof-Poof Show!
Poof Poof
OK, where was I? Oh yeah!
Poodle Doodles! Let's finish drawing this cute, fabulous poodle!
OK...after the hair, we draw the head, nose, eyes, ear, mouth...

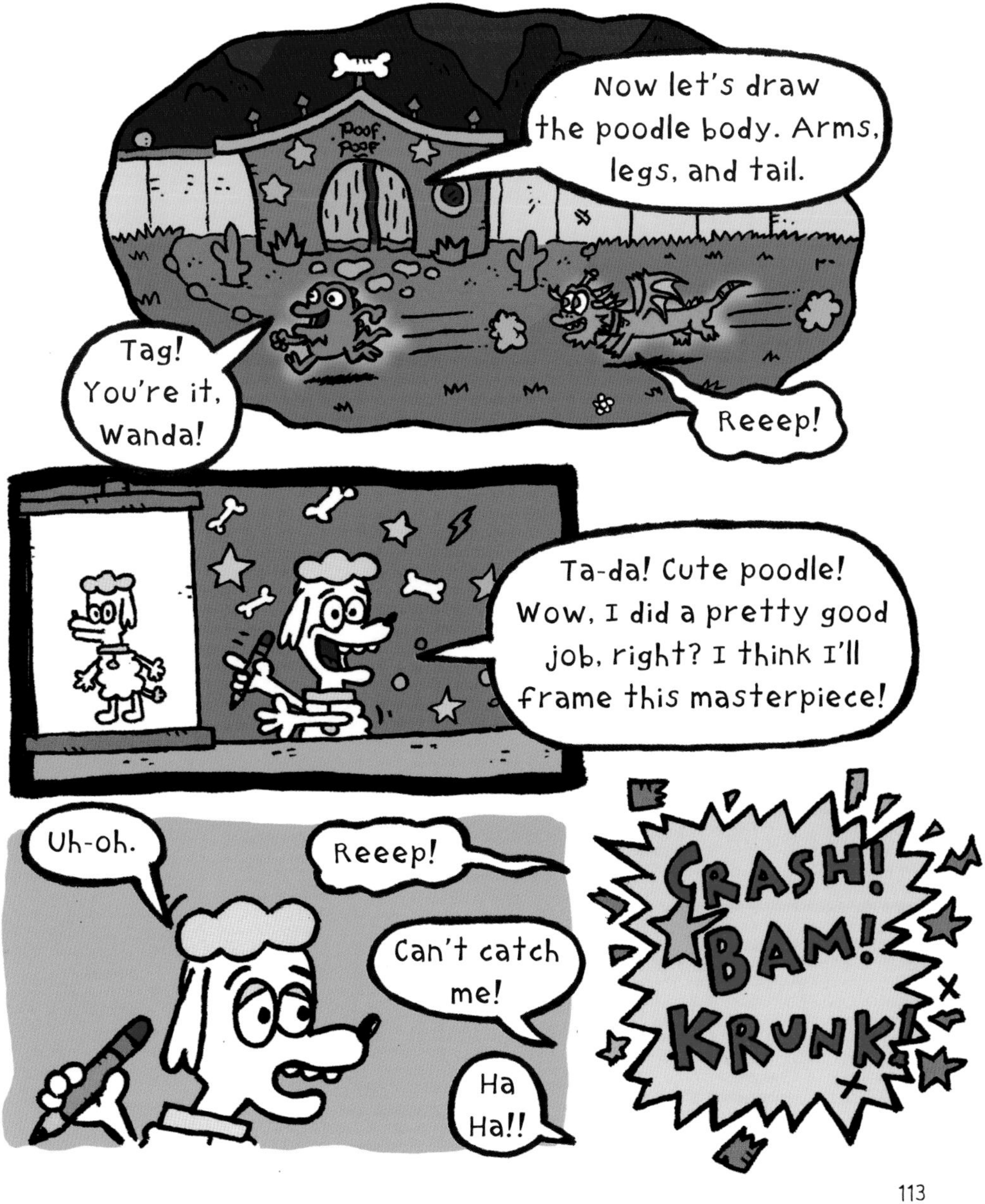
Now let's draw the poodle body. Arms, legs, and tail.
Tag! You're it, Wanda!
Reeep!
Ta-da! Cute poodle! Wow, I did a pretty good job, right? I think I'll frame this masterpiece!
Uh-oh.
Reeep!
Can't catch me!
Ha Ha!!
CRASH! BAM! KRUNK!

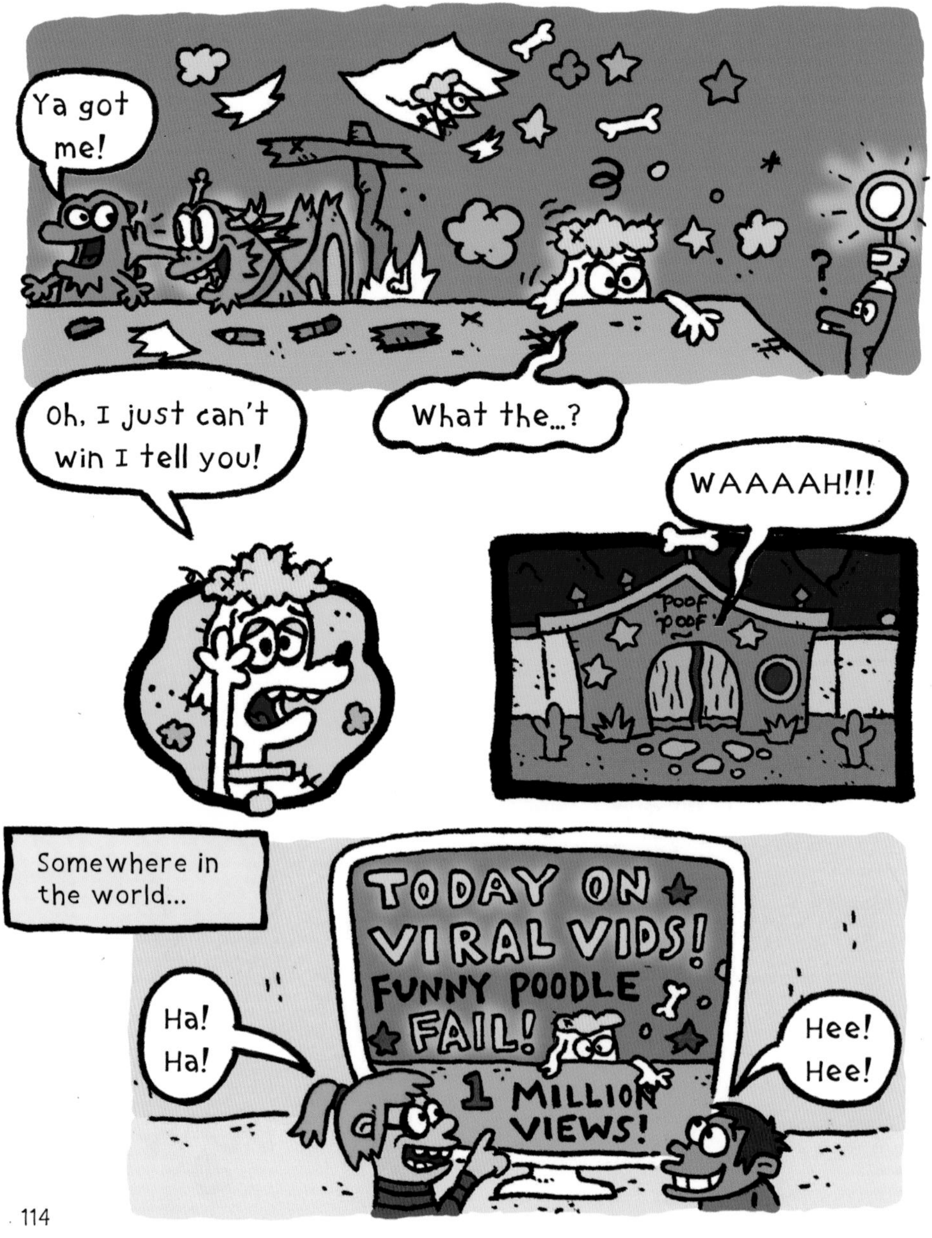
Ya got me!
Oh, I just can't win I tell you!
What the...?
WAAAAH!!!
poof poof
Somewhere in the world...
TODAY ON VIRAL VIDS!
FUNNY POODLE FAIL!
1 MILLION VIEWS!
Ha! Ha!
Hee! Hee!

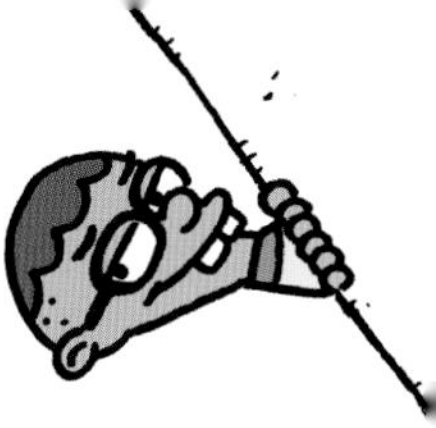

THE CREATURES THAT
CARLTON CRUMPLE HAS CAUGHT!

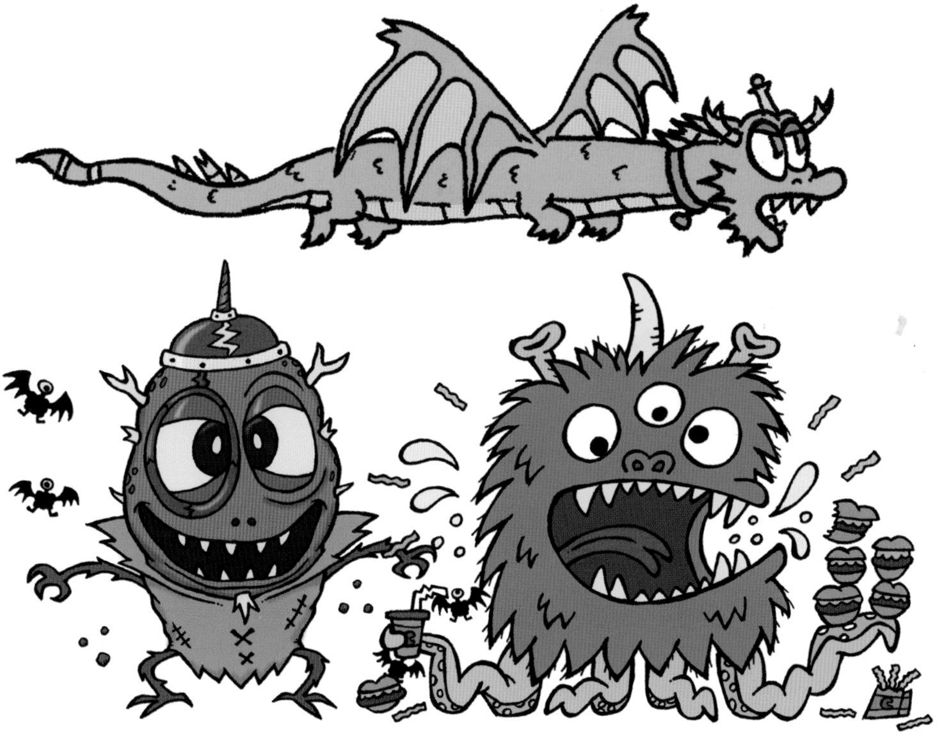

ACKNOWLEDGMENTS

Reptodactyl-size thanks to Team Reptoid for bringing this turtle ship in for a safe landing: cosmic captain Bethany Buck, color zapper Jimbo Matison, laser graphic designer Sammy Yuen, and astral art director Whitney Fine. Bright shiny shooting stars for my wife, Carol, for first draft copy edits and joining me for many work-at-home backyard lunches; my daughter Greta for expert advice on all things aerial and bringing me french fries; and my son Milo for tech support and afternoon studio visits. Clone fist bumps to my Trash Movie Club friends for many laughs and inspiring chats about tentacles, tarantulas, sea witches, and John Huston's jacket. Five-foot gummy worms for some of the artists who have inspired my comics and cartoons over the years: B. Kliban, Charles Schulz, Gary Panter, Sergio Aragones, Jay Ward, and George Lucas. Big Monster Mountain roars to all the creative kid reviewers at DOGO books and to all the young Creature Catchers out there who have read and enjoyed these books. Forever grateful to the marketing, publicity, and behind-the-scenes teams at Pixel+Ink, Holiday House, and Trustbridge Global Media for helping launch the Carlton Crumple Creature Catcher books out into the stratosphere. Onward!

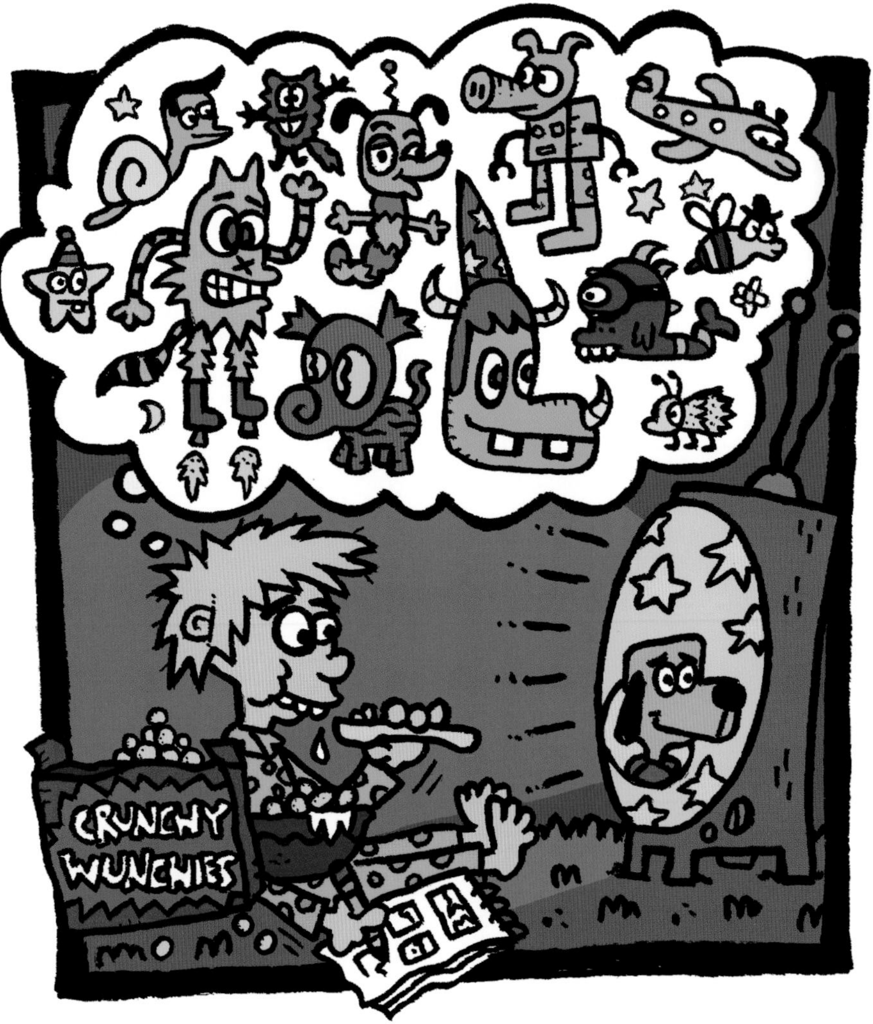
CRUNCHY
WUNCHIES

ABOUT THE AUTHOR

DAVID FREMONT grew up in Fremont, California—yep, a Fremont from Fremont! He loved watching *Underdog* cartoons, reading comics, and drawing with his brother. When David was eleven, his cousin Steve showed him a super-cool shark comic that he had drawn, inspiring David to start drawing his own comics. When David grew up, he moved across the bay to San Francisco, where he got a job painting cartoons at an animation studio. While at Colossal Pictures, he created projects for Cartoon Network and Disney. More recently, after moving to Los Angeles, he created a pilot for Nickelodeon and an online kids series for DreamWorksTV, called *Public Pool*. He currently lives in Woodland Hills with his family (and many furry pet creatures!), where he teaches cartooning classes to kids. This is his third book for children.

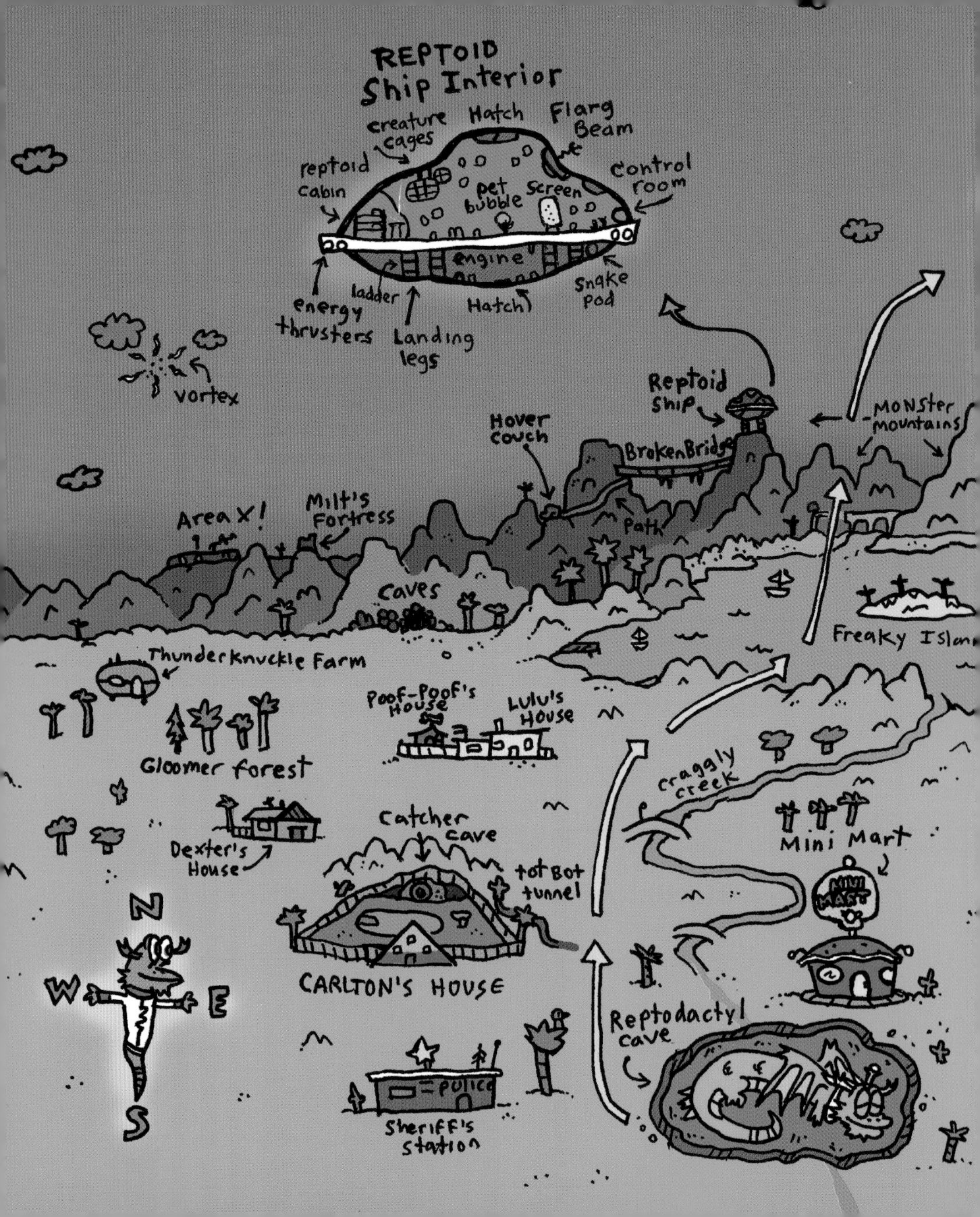
REPTOID
Ship Interior
creature cages
Hatch
Flarg Beam
reptoid cabin
pet bubble
Screen
control room
engine
energy thrusters
ladder
Landing legs
Hatch
Snake pod
vortex
Reptoid Ship
Hover couch
BrokenBridge
MONSter mountains
Area X!
Milt's Fortress
Path
Caves
Freaky Islan
Thunderknuckle Farm
Poof-Poof's House
Lulu's House
Gloomer forest
craggly creek
Dexter's House
Catcher cave
tot Bot tunnel
Mini Mart
MINI MART
N
W
E
S
CARLTON'S HOUSE
Reptodactyl cave
POLICE
Sheriff's station